THE CASELLA BROTHERS

THE CASELLA King

C.B. FREY

Cover Designer: Coffin Print Designs

Editing and Proofreading: My brother's editor

Interior Formatting & Design: Quirky Circe

Rating: R18+

Darkness is only feared when it isn't explored within.
To all the girls who like them tall, dark, and psycho.

Author Note

The Casella King is a stand-alone dark romance book part of an interconnected series. It does contain situations that could be triggering for some readers. It is intended to be for readers 18+.

Content warnings can be found on the author's website at
https://www.cbfreyauthor.com/

Alternatively, you can visit the author's Instagram at
https://www.instagram.com/c.b.freyauthor/

Playlist

Hail To the King ♔ AVENGED SEVENFOLD

Nightmare ♔ AVENGED SEVENFOLD

Monster ♔ SKILLET

Power Over Me ♔ DERMOTT KENNEDY

Sick Like Me ♔ IN THIS MOMENT

You Put a Spell on Me ♔ AUSTIN GIORGIO

Feel Invincible ♔ SKILLET

Come and Get It ♔ I PREVAIL

Kill the Noise ♔ PAPA ROACH

Darkside ♔ NEONI

PLEASE ♔ OMIDO, EX HABIT

Chills – Dark Version ♔ MICKEY VALEN, JOEY MYRON

Make Me Feel ♔ ELVIS DREW

Toxic ♔ OMIDO, RICK JANSEN

CHAPTER ONE
Aries

"I do," the groom says as the bride smiles from ear to ear. She stares into his eyes, like he's the best thing to ever happen to her, and a shiver rolls down my spine.

You'd think the day-to-day norm of watching people get married, saying their sappy vows and promises would make me somewhat fall in love with love over time, but no.

Sadly, that won't ever happen for me. Don't get me wrong. I absolutely love organising beautiful wedding events where the bride and groom end up ecstatic with my work and efforts, but there's just something about giving yourself completely to someone else that terrifies me.

I watch as the beautiful couple share their first kiss as man and wife, standing at the altar on a beautiful beach, the sunset creating a soft glow behind them. I feel my phone buzz in my pocket, and I don't dare move a muscle to see who it is because I already know. It could only be one person who texts me and calls me incessantly, until I answer or respond.

That would be the drunk, shitty excuse of a man father. I ignore it until it stops, watching as the guests congratulate the happy couple.

"Oh, you've done such a fantastic job with this

wedding, my dear, thank you so much for all of your efforts." The old lady beside me flashes her best smile as she looks up at me through her thick glasses.

I think she's the grandmother of the bride. Then there's that feeling again, a fleeting happiness in my chest, a zing, a moment where I can feel proud that all the time I spent planning, calling suppliers, and negotiating was completely worth it.

I get paid to do this job, but at the same time, I love what I do. I love seeing beautiful memories being made for those who wish to embark on this journey together. It should be a special time for the couple, and it makes me feel purposeful when I help them achieve that.

"Thank you for your kind words, I truly appreciate them," I tell the lovely old lady as I begin motioning to the guys to begin packing up the seats and the altar when the guests begin migrating over to the reception area behind us. My phone starts to buzz again, and I let out a sharp breath as I reach into my pocket to answer the call.

"I'm working." My voice is stern.

"Yeah, I know. Listen, can you bring back a box of beer on your way home?"

The audacity.

"No," I say as I walk away from the guys who've begun packing up.

"Why not? I did so much for you growing up, and you can't do this for me?"

Such a fucking narcissist.

"Because I will not help you poison yourself. Now stop calling me." I hang up before he has a chance to speak again and make my way to the reception area.

Everything looks like it's in its rightful place.

Perfect.

I wave to the manager on duty tonight and ensure everything is running on track as per the timeline I gave him, and he nods, assuring me that everything will go smoothly. Call me pessimistic, but I've planned and done enough weddings to know something almost *always* goes wrong.

I'm proved right when I am called to the ladies' room.

"No! I need to pee! Someone get this fucking dress off me!" I hear the bride yelling as I enter the room. I raise my hands and motion for her to breathe.

"Okay, let's all take a breath," I try to calm her. "What's the issue?"

"The issue is the zipper on my stupid dress is caught, and I can't get out of it!" There's pure panic in her voice and in her eyes.

I've done a lot of weddings, and this has never once happened to the bride, so even *I* am a little nervous as to how this will go. Her dress style won't exactly allow her to lift it, so we're going to have to figure out another way.

"This is what we're going to do. We're going to get you out of this dress so you can pee, then we're going to get you back in." I squeeze her hand as a sign of support as she turns around. I get a good look at the situation.

Okay, not bad, I can work with this.

The invisible zipper is indeed stuck between the fabric, so it's going to be difficult to get it off, however, not impossible. The dress buttons are already undone, so I grab a pen from my pocket and poke a small hole in the zipper. Luckily the bride's eyes are closed, probably wishing for all of this to be over. Slowly, I part the zipper and get her out of it. She didn't even glance my way, just went straight to the cubicle. After a moment, small sobs echo through the restroom.

"Lila, it's going to be okay." I knock on her cubicle door. "I promise you, no one will even know."

I give the dress to the bridesmaids and instruct them to comfort her whilst I figure out a solution to this mess. I think and think and think, but nothing comes to mind. Walking out the door, I see the staff walking around, getting the finishing touches done before the reception guests arrive. Then it comes to me like a lightbulb moment.

Safety pins.

I instruct one of the boys who had helped set up the altar on the beach to run to the van they brought all the material in to grab the heavy-duty safety pins they used.

As soon as they return, I rush into the ladies' room and tell Lila to come out. She does, and she slides the dress back on as the girls and I work to get the safety pins in place to make them invisible. I'm not a dressmaker, but I've seen this done before. This job kind of forces you to be a jack-of-all-trades.

"There." I place my hands on her shoulders as she looks at me through the mirror. "Lucky you chose to have a zipper *and* buttons." I smile at her, and she smiles back, wiping a small tear from her cheek.

"Thank you, Aries. You are a lifesaver," she says.

Folding my last pair of pants, I place them neatly on top of the rest inside my suitcase. The wedding location was an hour plane ride from London, but I'm lucky, I guess, that I get the opportunity to travel for work. Zipping up the suitcase, I gather the rest of my things and head to the airport.

The process is always the same, some business-y people pretending to be hotshots with their ten-thousand-dollar Rolex watches and latest tech gear, airport security always giving me a hard time about why I have two mobile phones, sanitising my hands until they feel like sandpaper, and finally landing back in my hometown—London.

Sighing, I take out my laptop as soon as I jump in my Uber on the ride back to Putney. I have a few quotes to send out to my potential clients, so I'd rather do that now than when I am back home. God knows what state my father will be in.

I can't even think of a good memory that I have of him anymore. It's just all consumed with him yelling, berating, and just being a complete dick to me and my sister. Although, I know Giselle still has a few fond memories of him. She tells me about them from time to time. I think she hopes that I don't end up completely hating him, but it has no effect on me. She's older, so she got to see him when he wasn't drunk all the time. I didn't. I'm not bitter about it. I just wish I could move out without feeling the crushing guilt override my entire body whenever I think about it.

Giselle just had a newborn with her husband, Arthur, and I would feel so guilty if I left them in the lurch with Dad right now. Closing my laptop, I place it back into its sleeve as we approach the house. It's small, nothing special, a typical house you could expect in Putney. Grabbing my things out from the boot, I thank the driver and stand in front of the house, taking deep breaths. My palms feel clammy, and I wonder if everyone feels like this when they are about to step into their home.

No.

The answer to that is definitely a no.

Rolling my suitcase over to the front, I push the key

into the door, and it clicks. Within seconds I hear my father's heavy footsteps coming down the stairs.

He opens the door and helps me bring my stuff into the small lounge room covered in burp cloths, nappies, and packets of baby wipes.

"Did you get me beer?" he asks without embarrassment. His hair is stuck to the side of his face, probably hasn't been washed in a week. He reeks of alcohol and looks like death personified.

"Hey Dad, nice to see you, too." I wave at him sarcastically as I set my things down on the lounge. "No, I told you I'm not aiding your alcoholism."

"I'm not an alcoholic!" he yells in frustration, his thick brows coming together in anger. He hasn't ever hit me, but he has hit my mother a few times, and for that I have always harboured nasty feelings towards him. It shouldn't matter what was said between two lovers, domestic abuse is never okay.

"And I don't give a shit." I walk into the adjoining kitchen and open the fridge, grabbing a juice box. "Tell your problems to someone who cares." Closing the fridge door, I turn to face him. "Or better yet, go get a damn job to support your own filthy habits."

He looks at me like I've grown three heads.

"How dare you speak to me like that?! I'm your father!" He stomps his foot like a toddler, and it's almost comical how much I don't give a fuck. I see Giselle pop her head through the kitchen doorway.

"Can you please keep it down? The baby is sleeping." She looks exhausted. Poor thing had to have a caesarean and now must take care of a baby by herself because they have no other choice. Arthur must work to pay the bills, so he wasn't lucky enough to take some time off to be with his wife and child in the precious first few weeks.

"Sorry, G." I grab my stuff and head to my bedroom, which thankfully is on the bottom level, whereas everyone else's is upstairs. At least that gives me some solitude in this hellhole. After throwing on some comfortable clothes, I grab my laptop and get in bed, not to sleep, but to work. These days work is an escape for me.

An escape from my father.

An escape from reality.

I think back on yesterday and how happy the couple looked together, watching each other so tenderly and lovingly as if nothing else in the world mattered to them. Sometimes I wish I had that someone for myself, then I remember my parents' marriage, and that feeling immediately vanishes.

I think about Leo, my ex-fiancé, and anger rumbles deep within my chest.

Coward.

I force the thoughts out of my brain as I focus on the checklist I have made for myself for the next event in a few days' time.

CHAPTER TWO

Ezra

Clenching my jaw, I watch as my father's casket is lowered into the dirt. A sea of people dressed in black surrounds his grave, mostly consisting of our family and other members of our world. Half the people are here out of respect and the other half out of obligation. I, on the other hand, can't think of anything else but the enormous weight now being put on my shoulders.

As the eldest son, it's my birthright.

Does that mean I want it?

I can't answer that yet.

How is a man supposed to mourn the death of his father *and* prepare for war?

No idea, I couldn't tell you.

Haven't had the chance to think about it yet. Not with all these people around me, suffocating me, and telling me I should marry as soon as I can, to secure the Casella line.

"Sorry for your loss, Mr Casella," a tall man in a black suit with shades tells me as he shakes my hand. I don't even know this man's name, yet I know he's been part of the Casella empire for years and would give his life for any one of us. "Your father was a strong man. I'm sorry it happened this way."

I nod my head in respect as the line of people give their condolences first to me, then to my mother, then to my younger brother, Nico.

After the service, Mother, Nico, and I sit in silence in the limousine as Henry drives us home to Chelsea. My mother is the first to speak, and what comes out of her mouth should shock me, but it doesn't.

"I have someone lined up for you." She places her hand on mine. "Don't fight me on this. You know we need to secure our bloodline."

I grit my teeth before I tell her to fuck off because I know she's right, but that doesn't mean I want to comply with the oldest tradition in the book.

Marrying someone I barely know to ensure the succession of our empire is archaic.

"Not now," I tell her and look to Nico who is staring at his palms in his lap. "We need to gather the boys." I feel the energy shift as he looks up at me, his brown eyes swirling with excitement. "I've got a plan."

"I've been waiting for you to say that all day, brother." A sinister smirk appears on his lips.

The house is filled with men dressed in black suits, some of them family, others not. Those who are standing turn to face me, and those who are sitting stand and turn my direction as I enter the large dining room with Nico by my side.

"Today, we buried my father."

Their heads begin to bow as I speak.

"I've known some of you in this room since I was a little boy. A boy who followed his father anywhere he went.

Some of you I haven't known as long, but I have no doubt you would give your life for a Casella." I notice one of them discreetly wipe a tear and shift his weight onto their other leg. "My father was a smart man, a strong man. He would want to be avenged."

Their eyes meet mine as I continue.

"This is why you're here. This is why you've been called on today." I watch as the fire in their eyes ignites at the promise of bloodshed.

"Listen, and listen carefully when I say this." I pull out my two guns from my holsters and lay them on the table. "Those motherfuckers will pay their debt in blood. Their sons will pay in interest, and we will take their homes down stone by stone if that's what it takes to see them squirm before we set their entire empire alight and watch it go down in flames in the name of my father." I watch as a couple of the men place their guns on the table beside mine.

"I will not stop until the Brayford family is on their knees before us." I breathe as one by one, the rest of the men in the room lay their guns on the table, until it's completely covered.

Nico places his hand on my shoulder as I watch the men in the room nod in acknowledgement at my speech, showing their unyielding support to the Casella family once again.

Showing their support to me.

"Ezra, may I have a word?" My mother enters the room, interrupting.

I sigh and exit the room with her and follow her into the large black marble kitchen.

"I'm in the middle of something right now, what is it?"

I ask as I watch her, the skin beneath her eyes dark and sagging.

"Listen to me before you speak again," she says, placing her palms on the kitchen bench between us. I nod and cross my arms. "Tomorrow there will be a wedding," she explains, my heart pounding in my chest, ready to yell all sorts of profanities at her because she wouldn't listen to me. "Calm down, this is not *your* wedding. Your cousin Fernando will be getting married, and there will be a woman at the event who I want you to meet—your betrothed."

I'm grateful for her, I am, but I truly despise this absurd tradition of an arranged marriage. I appreciate the way she is trying to skirt around the fact by having me meet her beforehand, but it changes nothing.

I consider my next words carefully, out of respect to my mother.

"If I meet her, will you stop constantly talking about it?" My voice is harsher than I mean it to be.

"As long as you accept this is something you must do for our family, yes," she says.

"Fine." My tone sharp. I return to the other room.

They all stand once again to face me.

"What's the plan, boss?" Henry asks, and I feel a sinister smile creep across my face as I imagine all the ways I have planned to make them suffer.

"Someone get me my laptop," I say as I watch the youngest member of the group race out of the room, returning with it in his hands. Grabbing it, I open it, turning it to face them. Their faces resemble shock and disbelief as they watch the screen.

"How?" Henry asks as he struggles to get his jaw off the floor.

"My father," I say as I shut the laptop, handing it back to the young man.

"He set up bugs in their offices?" he asks, still in disbelief, and I nod. "How?"

"Dominic approached someone on the inside of the Brayford family and convinced them to turn on them. How he did this, I don't know, but he did, and I say this is to our advantage." I point to the laptop.

With an insight like this, we will know their every move, their every thought, and their every secret. My father's only goal was to push them into the ground so deep, that they'd be forced to eat their own shit to survive.

That's exactly what I'm going to do.

"First, we hit them where it does the least amount of damage—their bars." I point to the tall guy in the corner of the room. "You're in charge of this, so don't fuck it up."

He nods.

"I want all their money. I know they hide it in the back where the large safes are. Rip it out of the walls if you must."

"Done." His husky voice fills the room.

"Then, we move to their clubs." I nod to the bulky guy next to Henry. "Gather some boys and take them down. I want to see the buildings burnt to the fucking ground," I command.

"Boss, what about their families?" Henry asks.

"I'm so glad you asked, Henry." I smirk as I grab my guns, placing them in their holsters. "Their sins are mine to judge."

The material of the dress shirt rubs my neck as I put my blue blazer on. I take a deep breath to prepare myself to meet the woman who will share my bed.

The woman who will take my surname and secure the Casella line.

The only reason I'm doing this is to keep my mother happy. I know she mourns my father a lot more than Nico or I, so I don't want to upset her further. The only reason I'm entertaining this is out of respect. Otherwise, there isn't a chance in hell you could make me do something I didn't want to.

We approach the church, and Henry parks the Bentley in the designated guest spot. Mother quickly exits the car, and I follow, holding my arm out for her to take. As soon as we enter the church, all eyes fall on us. Half the men stand, bowing their heads in respect as we walk to the front of the pews and take a seat.

The church is old but freshly renovated and whoever planned this ceremony has expensive taste. Flowers adorn the sides of the pews and the archway that runs from the large entry doors of the church to the front. Even amongst all these people, knowing that just yesterday we buried the Casella King, I feel absolutely nothing. To others it might be bizarre, or heartless, but this is me and always has been for a very long time.

My mother points out a blonde in the crowd of people, telling me she is to be my future bride, and all I can do is grit my teeth at the sight of her. There's no fucking way I'm marrying her. I wouldn't even give her the opportunity to be on her knees for me. It's not that she isn't attractive, because she is, but the idea and notion of being forced into something will never be okay with me, and I refuse to abide by *tradition*.

I feel my phone buzz in my pocket, and I excuse myself to walk out of the church into the garden area when I catch sight of a short-haired brunette running frantically through the rose garden. My brows pull in as I watch her dress catch between the metal of the arch frame, and she cusses so loudly, it echoes throughout the garden.

CHAPTER THREE
Aries

My heart beats faster with each lunge I take toward the church. I was supposed to be here thirty minutes ago. Fumbling with the folders in one hand and my phone in the other, I swirl around the bend into the large archway that starts in the garden and ends at the church, when I am pulled back by a strong tug on my dress.

No, no, no!

Great. Of course my dress would get caught on the metal frame of the arch when I am already late. Dropping my things on the ground, I tug on the hem of my dress that's latched and intertwined with the wire. I tug and tug, but it's no use.

I feel sweat beads pooling at my lower back under the hot sun, as I work to untangle myself without ripping my entire dress.

"Fucking hell!" I yell, and I'm startled by a husky voice behind me.

"Do you need some help?" His voice oozes masculinity as he walks around me, coming into my vision, and I almost stop breathing.

He towers over me, his buff frame perfectly outlined in his form-fitting suit. Dark brown eyes stare down at me, sucking me in like a hypnotic tunnel. The raw, masculine beauty he possesses floors me, and I forget even the simplest of words.

Hi, would be good.

"Do you mind?" he asks as he points to my dress stuck on the wire.

Now would be a good time to speak, Aries.

I let go of my dress and watch as his strong hands work to free me. My eyes are pinned to the intricate artwork tattooed on his hands, and in one swift move, he tears the hem of my dress, the sound of material ripping filling my ears. Gasping, I look down, and to my horror, my dress is now five inches shorter. Short enough for people to mistake me for a working girl.

"Oh my god." My hands move to cover my thighs as his eyes skate down to my bare legs. I feel a flutter inside my chest as he shamelessly devours me with his eyes.

"I think it looks a lot better." He smirks.

I could die right now.

"Better?" I give him a sarcastic smile. "I look like a hooker."

His wide grin covers his devilishly handsome face, and I hate how good he looks.

I scoff as I begin to pick up my things off the grass.

"You're welcome," he says as if he helped me.

"For what?" I turn to face him. "I could have done the same thing. The aim was *not* to rip the dress."

"I'll buy you a new one," he offers as he picks up one of my folders and hands it to me.

"No, thank you. I don't need anything from you." I turn to walk away, the muscle in my chest thumping harder than ever, threatening to escape like the traitorous bitch she is.

"Will you at least tell me your name?" he asks as I roll my eyes.

I hesitate for a moment, unsure if I want to.

"Aries," I say, without turning to face him, focused solely on getting into that church, and doing my job.

Once I walk through the large doors, I bring out my checklist and ensure everything is completed. My assistant, Rachel, offers to grab me some water as I check off my list. Everything seems to be in order, the flowers are here and set up, the candles are burning bright, the groom is here... that's always a good sign...and the mother and father of the bride are here.

Perfect.

Rachel comes walk-running with a bottle of water in her hand, and I am so thankful for her. From the heat to the stupidly good-looking man who ripped my dress, water is very much welcome right now. I place the bottle to my lips and take a few gulps, trying to regain my composure. I've never been late to anything in my life, but thanks to London traffic and my drunk father losing the keys to my beat-up car, I guess there's a first for everything.

"Should I ask?" Rachel eyes the hem of my dress, and I shake my head.

"Nope. Please, do not." I sigh, taking a seat in the pew whilst Rachel steps away to ensure the bride is not having second thoughts.

I've seen my share of those weddings too.

Taking out my phone, I flick through my calendar and make notes on what I have on next. Luckily, the next wedding isn't for a couple weeks away, so I might get some time to myself, although I'm not quite sure how much I want to be at home.

"For the dress." My eyes land on a solid gold credit

19

card in front of my face. I know exactly who it is by the deepness in his voice.

"I told you, I don't want your money." I return my attention to my phone, and I feel him slip into the pew beside me, his spicy, clean scent gliding into my nose. Although I don't want to, I wonder why he's interested in me.

God, he smells good.

Expensive.

"At least let me make it up to you." His strong features dominate my vision, and like a car crash, I can't look away. "Aries." His voice raspy, I can almost feel the vibrations through the small distance between us.

"I'm busy." I wave my phone, but he remains unfazed.

"And I'm stubborn." He smirks.

"I don't even know your name." I sigh, done with this conversation.

"We can change that." He reaches into his pocket and gives me his phone. "Give me your number and a date," he says, with that same smile still on his delicious lips. I stare into his beautiful, dark chocolate swirls, which I now realise is a mistake. The men I usually meet are either living with their parents or have absolutely no goals in life.

"If I do, will you leave me alone?" I ask.

"We're just getting started, sweetheart." His voice is like a trance, pulling me in, and I realise he isn't going to relent.

I kind of like that.

I grab the phone out of his hand and enter my name and number.

"There, now will you please vacate this seat for my assistant?" I raise my eyebrows to say '*now*'. He ignores me and begins dialling, bringing the phone to his ear, whilst his eyes remain on the phone in my hand.

My phone begins to ring, and he hangs up.

"You can save that number under Ezra." He winks as he stands and walks over to the front pew, taking a seat next to an older woman. My eyes are still on him, on his large, muscular frame underneath that classy suit.

My mouth suddenly feels dry.

"What the hell was that?" Rachel slides into the pew and turns her body to face me.

"What?" I return my focus to the calendar on my phone.

"You do realise who that man is, right?" She raises her eyebrows as I take another look at him. Multiple people have now walked up to him to shake his hand, some have even bowed.

"No? Should I?" I rack my brain for a celebrity name but come up short.

"That's Ezra Casella." She looks at me, waiting for me to react. "You know, crime boss, mafia, killer, son of Dominic Casella...now currently known as the *Casella King?*" She whispers the last words, and my heart starts back up again.

Music filters through the church as the priest begins to do his bit. I'm not religious, so I never really pay attention to this part. Usually, I just use this time to plan my next event or make some phone calls to suppliers, but now I can't stop thinking about Ezra and why his sudden interest in *me*.

A short whilst later, it's the bride's turn to enter the church. The guests all rise and face the entry whilst I watch the groom. I can almost tell when, or if, a marriage will end by the groom's reaction to seeing the bride for the first time. Usually, it's the ones who cry who are willing to work through any issues that arise because of their love for their partner.

It's the ones who hardly react that you should be worried about.

Lucky for the bride, the groom begins to shed tears as she walks down the aisle in her beautiful white lace dress.

My eyes skate down to where Ezra is standing, his eyes glued not on the bride like everyone else, but on me.

The reception is like any other Italian wedding, over the top and obnoxious.

Not to say that's a bad thing. That's just what they like, which is completely fine with me because I make more commission on these weddings, and the great part is, they are always willing to pay.

I walk over to the bar to grab myself a drink, feeling the day and the night catching up with me. I think I might need this two-week break more than I originally thought.

Ordering a Jack and Coke, I take a seat at the bar and revel in the one second of alone time I have before I see someone creep in beside me.

"Is this seat taken?" he asks, but he doesn't wait for me to answer as he sits.

"It's polite to wait for a yes or no," I say without taking my eyes off my drink because I already know who it is sitting beside me.

"Sweetheart, I'm anything but polite." His voice, like honey, sweetens the bitterness inside me, but I'll never let him see that.

"I'm not your sweetheart." I turn to look at him, and his eyes immediately drop to my lips.

"Not yet." He brings his glass to his lips, and my eyes linger too long for my liking. Ripping my eyes away, I watch the bartender shaking drinks. "About that date."

"There is no date," I say, not believing a word that comes out of my mouth right now. Not trusting my body to hide my attraction towards him.

"Why not?" he asks.

"Because I'm not dating right now," I confess, my heartbeat picking up speed at his closeness.

"That's a shame. I could show you a great time."

"I'm sure you can, but I'm not interested."

"You should just give in now whilst you have the chance, before I truly turn on the charm." He smirks as I feel my lips betray me and curve into a smile. I hate that he can charm me.

Noticing my smile, he chuckles.

"Fine. No date. Just an 'I'm sorry I ripped your dress' dinner?" He looks at me expectantly, waiting for an answer, and I debate shooting him down again, but I'm interested. His eyes drop to the hemline of my dress, and heat flushes my cheeks. I've only ever been with one man. He was my first for everything. I've never again allowed myself to let my guard down and trust someone to not break my heart. As I look at Ezra, the ice around the empty cavity in my chest begins to melt, and I have no idea how he's doing this. Is it the charisma, is it the form-fitting suit, or is it the fact that no matter how many times I say no, he just will not relent?

"I'm free tomorrow night," I say, taking another sip of my drink, my heart thumping loudly beneath my chest.

"I'll pick you up at eight," he says as he motions to the

bartender to come over to us. "She doesn't pay for anything, got it?" He nods in what seems like fast-forward speed.

He leans into my ear, sending a shiver through my spine. "I'll see you tomorrow, sweetheart." His husky voice vibrates through me.

The rest of the night goes by in a blur. Anytime I looked over to where Ezra was, I saw him surrounded by big, scary-looking men, almost like they were planning something or talking about something that came with heavy consequences if they got the answer wrong. As soon as the reception is wrapped up, I gather my things and begin heading to my car, ready to shower and get in bed as soon as I get home. Opening my car boot, I throw all my things inside, and it isn't until I walk around to the driver's side that I notice both tyres are flat.

You've got to be kidding me.

"Need a ride?" a familiar husky voice asks, and my head whips around behind me as I stare up into Ezra's eyes, almost as dark as the night itself.

Did he pop my tyres?

"It's fine. I can just call roadside assistance." I grab my phone from my clutch bag.

"It's pretty late. Generally they won't arrive for another hour." He smirks, and I'm almost certain he has fucked with my tyres. "I promise nothing shady. Just want to drop you off at home."

I really shouldn't go with him. I should call roadside assistance and wait for them to come.

"You're lucky I'm exhausted and don't have a strong will to argue right now." I walk over to grab my things from the boot when his hand reaches out to stop me.

Electricity buzzes from my fingertips all the way to my ears at his touch, unbalancing me.

"Henry will grab your things." I watch as a large, bald man in a black suit, camouflaged by the night steps out from the darkness. "This way." He motions as my eyes follow, landing on a sleek black Rolls Royce Phantom limousine. I stop my jaw from dropping and scraping on the ground as I enter a world of luxury. Possibly a small portion of the luxury this man is used to. I try to not make it obvious I've never been in a custom limo before, so I take my seat and begin writing email responses to clients in my inbox.

"Put your phone away," he commands, as he slides in next to me.

"Why?" I smirk. "Does it bother you?" I almost want to glue my phone to my face in response to the annoyance on his.

"Because it's one in the morning, and you shouldn't be working right now." He looks at my phone, irritated that it's still in my hands.

"What if it makes me feel safe?" Henry has begun driving, taking us onto a freeway.

Ezra chuckles at my words, and a shiver rolls down the back of my arms.

"Sweetheart, if I wanted to hurt you, I wouldn't be escorting you home, in a limo, with a bodyguard." He flashes a panty-dropping smile, and slowly opens his blazer, revealing his double holster. My eyes go wide as they land on two gold pistols, tucked safely away inside the holsters.

Okay, now it definitely feels real.

"No one can hurt you, not whilst you're with me," he comments, like it's supposed to make me feel safer.

I don't know what to say so I just stare ahead, watching

Henry drive through the small partition, a million and one thoughts floating through my head.

His hand lands on mine, and I snatch it back.

"What's wrong, sweetheart? Are you scared?" He smirks, knowing I am.

"Just hesitant on being alone in a limo with a man with not one, but *two*, guns," I admit. "I mean, you understand that's not normal, right?" I try my best to keep my voice steady.

He licks his lips as he stares at mine.

"My world is anything but normal. You'll get used to it." He winks, his eyes skating to the hem of my dress again, then back to my eyes.

"I'm reconsidering my answer to your *non-date*," I say, which makes him slide closer to me, his spicy, sandalwood scent engulfing me in its embrace once again, making me twitch with the need to lean in and smell him.

"It's too late for that now." His face is just a few inches away from mine, my focus no longer on my phone, but on his beautiful shadowy irises, a swirl of chocolate embers surrounding them.

"I'll pick you up at eight. There's already a dress waiting for you in your bedroom."

My throat closes as his words, a slight hint of terror bubbling up inside me.

"H-how?" I fumble to get my words out. "W-what?"

"You will find a box with a brand-new dress in your bedroom on your bed," he says slowly, making sure I understand that he's speaking English. "Accept it as an apology for tearing this one." His fingers lightly brush the torn layer on my thigh as goose bumps raise underneath my skin.

"But how do you know where I live?" Then I realise I

never told him my address. Among the mayhem of popped tyres, tiredness, and this ridiculously attractive man, it had escaped my mind.

"Sweetheart, there is nothing I don't already know about you." A smirk plays at his lips as his eyes linger on my lips.

I'm lost for words, a little scared, and a little impressed.

We pull up in front of my house, as Henry turns the car off and exits to grab my things. Ezra waits for me outside with a hand extended for me to take. I step out of the limo without taking his hand as a sign of protest, but he makes it feel like there really is no chance of a retraction as he chuckles and puts his hands in the pockets of his dress slacks.

I grab my things from Henry and head for the door.

"Eight o'clock, I'll be waiting," he calls from behind me as I hastily slide the key in the door and bang it shut behind me, leaning against the frame with my heart threatening to shatter my ribcage.

What the fuck did I get myself into?

CHAPTER FOUR

Ezra

Mother was relentless at trying to get me to talk to whatever the fuck her name was at the church the other day, but the person who was occupying my thoughts was Aries. The second I met her, I knew I wanted to pitch her the idea of a fake marriage, to get my mother off my back, for now at least. She is smart, not bad to look at, and has a mind of her own.

Her best quality?

She has no ties to the mafia.

It's proving to be a challenge to woo her, though, that much I will admit. She's headstrong about not wanting to date and seems to have an aversion to males in general. There were about fifty men who were eating her up in her little torn dress at the reception, and she didn't want a bit of any of them. Not that I would have allowed it anyway. It's been years since I had this much interest in one woman. My nights are usually filled with meaningless sex with women who not only want me, but also want the title that comes with being with me. They never get it, and they never will. No woman is worth that amount of trouble. Except maybe Aries.

I feel my cock harden at the memory of her sitting in my limo with her torn dress, sliding up her thigh.

My new plan is foolproof.

Marry her, then divorce her in a few months' time, just to get my mother off my back for now. I'll do whatever it takes not to marry whatever the fuck her name is. It's not that she's unattractive. It's that she's batshit fucking boring and can't hold a conversation if her life depended on it. I liked that Aries had a mouth on her. I liked that she was fiery, and I want to know just how much heat she could handle.

"What did you think of Bianca?" my mother asks as we sit at the dinner table with Nico beside me, snickering as he eats his bowl of homemade gnocchi. I place my cutlery down and look my mother dead in the eyes.

"I'm not marrying her," I admit, my tone firm.

She sighs as she shakes her head. "You promised you would do this for our family."

"I'm not marrying someone who doesn't have a mind of their own. She has the personality of a paper plate." Nico almost chokes on his pasta at my remark, and I raise my eyebrows at him to stop.

"Love grows, son. You just need to put in some effort." She tries to change my mind, but it's no use. I's already made up.

"I will be marrying an outsider; her name is Aries," I confess, and they both stop what they're doing and turn to look at me, like I just announced something preposterous. Mother stands and yells every Italian profanity in the dictionary known to man.

"*Stupido! Idiota!*" She paces back and forth. "How can you do this, Ezra? Huh?" she yells as I stand, wiping my mouth with my napkin and throwing it on the table. "You spit on your father's grave if you do this!"

"It's done. We will be getting married in a week. Make the reservations." With that, I leave, the tension in the room rising, bubbling to the top as she continues to swear at my back, but I couldn't care less. I'm not about to do things the way my father did.

I have more important things to worry about now.

To convince my future bride to marry me.

I decided to take the Porsche today, given she's been sitting in the garage for a few weeks, and when I make it to Aries's home, I text her to let her know I'm outside.

Ten minutes pass.

Then another ten.

There is no response from her, then I realise she isn't home. Annoyance and anger sizzle in my gut as I call our on-call inspector and tell him to track her down. I'm not used to being turned down or stood up, so when it happens, of which this is the first, it makes me feel *murderous*. I can't afford to show her my true self yet. She's too much of a flight risk already. I need to convince her in other ways.

A few moments later, I see my phone light up with a location on Aries, and I floor it to her location with every intention of making it known who she's dealing with. There is absolutely no chance she's getting away from me. I'll fucking make sure of it.

As soon as I enter the bar, everyone's eyes are on me, except hers. She's too busy staring into her drink to notice. I nod at the bartender, and the music stops, the lights come on, and the entire place is empty within seconds. She looks to me and stands, her silky satin dress falling past her knees, the rest of the material resting between her breasts. She's lucky she's fucking sexy, otherwise I wouldn't be so nice about this. She's not ready to see who I truly am, not yet.

"There you are, sweetheart; I've been looking for you." I walk over to the bar, lean over it, and grab myself a bottle of whiskey and a glass. I begin pouring myself a shot, and I feel her eyes watching me. I don't usually drink, but tonight I need it. The pressure of taking on my father's role, combined with the pressure of needing to secure our line, I feel like I'm being chewed up from within, and that's not normal for me.

"How did you find me?" Her voice is almost a whisper.

"You really think I don't get what I want?" I take a sip and watch the fear in her eyes multiply as she begins adding things up, sizing me up, and finally getting the point. "Take a seat." I motion to the barstool with my glass as I sit beside her.

"What do you want? I tried to say no, but you don't take no for an answer." She takes a sip of her cocktail and watches me.

"That's right, sweetheart, I don't. You're learning."

My eyes skate over her chest, the material of her dress clinging to her skin. Her chest rises and falls, her breasts following suit. I don't bother with hiding my obvious staring because it's no secret I'm so fucking attracted to her.

"I want you to go on a date with me, then I want you to marry me." I watch her face go from scared to amused within a second before her laughter bellows through the empty bar.

My face is set in stone.

She regains her composure and looks back at me, her laughter fizzling out.

"Wait, you're joking, right?" She smiles.

"Do I look like a man who jokes?" My tone is sharp. I'm about ready to fling her over my shoulder and take her home with me. I'm getting bored of doing this the nice way. "I think this can be mutually beneficial." I expect her to protest, but to my surprise, she listens. "I know you're struggling with finances, and I know you live with your sister in a small place. Would you not want to have some space of your own?"

She looks down at her palms.

"We will only be married for a few months, then we can file for divorce and go our separate ways. It wouldn't have to mean more, or less."

The way she plays with her lip between her teeth does something to me, and I feel my cock harden beneath my pants. I start planning what angle of attack I want to take next, in case she shoots me down again.

"What do *you* get out of it?" she asks.

"It's simple. I get my family off my back for a few months whilst I deal with some…*issues.*"

She looks down at her drink as she considers my offer, and I can practically see her brain working through her furrowed brows.

"Do you know who I am?" I have to ask, because I need to know how much she knows about me and my family.

She looks to me and nods.

"My assistant mentioned you're part of a crime organisation," she whispers the words as she looks around, and it's cute that she doesn't know I own almost every part of the city.

"My name is Ezra Casella, and I run the Casella empire."

Her eyes lock on mine, a mix of intrigue and hesitation swirling around in them.

"You don't have to answer right now, sleep on it, but I still want that date." I lean in to kiss her on the cheek, and as I do, I'm overcome by her scent. I close my eyes and breathe her in, brushing my lips on her supple skin. A rosy flush adorns her cheeks as she averts her eyes from mine, and all I can think about is how good she would look bent over this bar.

"I was enjoying my night before you showed up." She smirks, swirling her drink in her glass. A smile tugs on the corner of my lips as I motion with my hand to the bartender, and a few moments later, the bar is full again, the music on, lights dimmed. She orders two more drinks from the bartender and skulls them both.

"How many of those have you had?" I watch as she covers her mouth with the back of her hand, swallowing the last bit of drink.

"I don't remember, but I think I need another one to tolerate a date with you." She motions the bartender for another, his eyes skate to me, and I nod my head slightly, letting him know it's okay to pour her another.

"Did you just ask him for permission to pour my drink?" she accuses the bartender, his eyes going wide. "I'm a *paying* customer...pour me the damn drink, or I'll do it myself."

"It's fine, Justin. Go take your break," I say, and he promptly leaves the bar as she faces me. "I own this bar, sweetheart, if that much wasn't clear. That means I own everyone in here." I smirk as she crosses her arms across her chest, pushing her breasts out, making my cock run out of room underneath my pants.

"Everyone but me," she says matter-of-factly. It's cute that she thinks she stands a chance against me, against the power I hold over this city, but what I'm starting to wonder now is how much power she could potentially hold over me.

"For now." I swallow down the rest of my drink and place the empty glass down on the bar. "How about this?" She looks at me with intrigue. "I'll pay you fifty grand to pretend to be my fiancée for the next seven days, and if you still think this isn't going to work, I'll forget about the whole thing." Her eyes narrow at my offer, and what comes out of her mouth next makes me want to force my cock so far into her throat that she chokes.

"You know there are hookers for that, and I very much doubt you'd have to spend fifty grand to get what you want from them." She smiles as I scratch my stubble.

She's really fucking testing me right now.

Testing my will to be nice about this, to *allow* her to argue with me.

"Aries, I'm going to say this once, and only once. I want *you*, and no one else will do."

She stops, looks me dead in the eyes, and finally after all my efforts, she relaxes.

"Fine," she relents, and my lips curve into an evil grin.

"Fine to which part exactly?" I want to hear her say it. I want to hear it from her cherry-red lips. The lips that I will soon have around my throbbing cock.

"To the date and the fake fiancée thing."

Maybe I should have offered her the money sooner. It may have saved me from all this pursuing. I wasn't used to this, the whole process of wooing a woman to get her to do what I want. They usually just fall into my lap, or onto my cock. Nevertheless, my plan is now in motion, and the sooner I'm done with this bullshit, the sooner I can avenge my father's death because the more time I spend trying to win Aries over, the more time the Brayfords have to realise they have a mole amongst them.

CHAPTER FIVE
Aries

It's okay. It's fine. It's just dinner.

I open the box I never had the guts to open when I got home from the reception. Slowly, I pick up the beautiful, silky, red satin dress and hold it up, taking in its exquisite luxury. I've never been able to touch something of this calibre of luxury before, let alone put it on my body. Part of me hesitates to, in fear of ruining it. I'd considered the pros and cons to Ezra's offer, and I had to be real with myself. Sure, I had my own life and lived it my way, but I did not want to stay in the same house with my sister and father anymore, and this way, if I could get that money, I could send some to Giselle to help her with the baby. Maybe even get her a regular cleaner, so she doesn't have to worry about doing everything herself. I didn't know him, that was a fact. Ezra seems like many things, but the way he was relentless with pursuing me proved to me in my sick head that maybe he doesn't want to force me into this, like he wants me to have a choice.

Maybe this *could* be beneficial for us both.

I slip the dress on over my G-string and bare breasts. Turning around in front of the mirror, I smile at the way the thin straps come down to meet the rest of the dress, just above my ass.

It's a killer dress, that's certain.

I had done my makeup and hair prior to putting the dress on so all that's left to do now is grab my clutch and wait for Ezra. I feel my breathing pick up as I think about the night ahead, wondering what was going to happen, where he is going to take me. After he dropped me home from the bar, he promised we would work out finer details on our date, so I'm wondering if there would be a full contract, or would it just be spoken?

I sigh, shaking my arms, attempting to rid myself of pre-date jitters. I know this wasn't a real date, but whenever I knew I was going to go on one, my body would always react this way. Sweating, heart thumping, fingernails tingling, cottonmouth, and jelly legs.

Oh god.

My phone buzzes, letting me know he's outside. Walking out the door, I say bye to Giselle, who has Ryan suckling her boob as she watches telly. She waves, with a "where the fuck are you going looking like that" expression on her face.

No time to explain, sis. I have a mafia king waiting.

"This way, Miss Alterio."

Henry opens the small gate for me, as I make my way to the shiny Porsche with Ezra leaning beside it. He looks phenomenal as always, dark pants and a black button-up, the sleeves rolled up his forearms, showcasing his ink, and a few buttons undone, revealing his olive-toned skin and hard chest. He holds out his hand, waiting for me to accept. Slowly I slide my hand into his as he opens the passenger door for me. Slipping in as gracefully as possible, I gather the bottom of my dress to ensure it doesn't get caught in the door as he closes it, walking around the front of the car. There is a small glimmer of something shiny that catches my eye as he walks over to the driver's side. He wears a large ring on a chain around his neck that looks too bulky for that to be its rightful place. He slips in beside me and starts the car, the engine roaring to life beneath us.

"Henry's not coming?" I look to the back, but there are only two seats, mine and Ezra's.

"He'll follow in a separate car." He grabs my hand, electricity coursing through my skin up to my head, making me dizzy. Slowly, he presses his lips on my knuckles. "You look sensational." His husky voice fills my ears, making them burn, the heat travelling from my cheeks to his gaze on my chest.

Oh god, please help me get through this without making a stupid mistake.

I struggle to pick my jaw up off the floor as we walk hand in hand down the dock towards a gorgeous white yacht, *Fedele* painted in red on the back. He holds my hand as I climb the stairs, gathering my balance in my stiletto heels. Tilting my head up, I take in the beautiful twinkly lights of the upstairs decks, the gold trim railings glimmering in the night. Goose bumps begin rising on my skin as his arm slides around my lower back, guiding me through the yacht.

"This way." His husky voice emanates through the air, so close to me. Henry follows us from a distance as I'm led to the table covered with linen with two chairs tucked under it.

"So, this is a date *date*?" I ask as he pulls my chair out, waiting for me to take a seat.

"This is an 'I'm sorry I ripped your dress' dinner." He

smiles, and it takes everything in me not to smile back. I couldn't care less that he ripped the dress, but I can't help but feel good being shown this much interest, even though there's a different agenda to it. I take a seat, as does he, watching me as I reach for the water jug in the middle of the table.

His hand stops me.

He snaps his fingers, and a man emerges from inside the yacht, wearing a white apron and a chef's hat, beside him is a younger-looking man, dressed in what seems like a waiter's uniform. He hurries to the table and begins pouring water into both our glasses.

"Mr Casella." The chef nods to Ezra. "Tonight we have *fiori di zucchina* for the starter, *Fettuccine al Pomodoro* for the main, and *cannoli alla ricotta* for dessert." Ezra nods as the chef walks back into what I assume houses a kitchen, and the young waiter steps back, giving us some space. I understood only one thing from what the chef said, and that was fettuccine. I know that's pasta, and pasta is great in my books.

"When you're with me, you don't lift a finger, understand, sweetheart?" he says, his voice stern.

"I'm perfectly capable of pouring myself a drink, though. Is it really necessary?" I look to the waiter, and his eyes haven't moved from staring straight ahead. I feel the engine roar to life under me as we slowly begin floating out into the river.

"If you are to be my wife, yes." He smirks.

His wife.

Never once had anyone called me that before, and it feels nice, wholesome, but I have a nagging feeling that he doesn't mean it this way at all. His tone veils possessiveness, and although that should have frightened me, it doesn't.

Deep down, I have yearned for someone to want me, want me enough to be possessive over me, to want me for themselves, enough to destroy anything and anyone who would stand in our way, and I thought I had it with my ex. I gave him all of me, but all that ever got me was a broken heart. A year later, the trauma he caused is still there, resting on the surface, constantly waiting to sabotage my life.

"Well, I agreed to be your fake fiancée first. I haven't decided if I will be accepting the marriage offer just yet."

I take a sip of my water and wait for his response when I hear my phone buzz in my clutch. Taking it out, I look at the screen, and reality comes busting through thick iron doors. I silence the call and turn my phone off, an irritable feeling now swirling in my head and in my stomach.

"Sorry, that was my father." I look down at my hands as I rub them on top of my thighs. When I look up, he's studying me.

"Does he hit you?" His question floors me, his face as hard as stone, his jaw pulsing as he clenches his teeth together.

"What?! No! It's not like that, he's just..." I pause, trying to search my brain for the right word, but really, there is only one word that describes him perfectly. "A drunk."

"Has he *ever* hit you?" His jaw seems to relax a little, his eyes boring into mine.

"Not me." I look away because it shames me to say it even though it shouldn't, because it wasn't me who was hitting her. "My mother."

He nods slowly as he stares at his plate, and I have no idea what's going through his mind right now, which frustrates me. I don't understand why he would ask such a question without knowing anything about me.

"What?" I ask.

"You shouldn't be living with him." He looks to me again, the embers in his eyes flaming brighter than before.

"I can't leave my sister with him. She has a newborn and is struggling with her husband going back to work," I confess.

"Is that why you're hesitating to accept my offer?" A light twinkles in his eyes. "Because if that's the case, consider it taken care of."

Before I can protest, he waves Henry over and whispers something in his ear. Henry nods and walks away, dialling a number on his phone.

"Ezra, you can't make every bad thing in my life just magically disappear and expect I will accept your offer." I roll my eyes.

"Watch me." He smirks, and the confidence this man exudes melts the feminist in me. "I like the way you say my name. You should say it more often." His tongue darts out to lick his lips, his eyes wandering south of my chin. "In fact, I expect it."

"What did you tell Henry?" I ask, expecting him to hide it from me, but he doesn't.

"I told him to buy your sister a house and organise a moving truck. Tomorrow." He smiles as if he's proud of himself.

The waiter walks into the kitchen, emerging a few seconds later with our appetisers.

"I also arranged a nanny for her. I hear postpartum is not easy." He lifts his glass to his lips to take a sip, and I lose my words. All of them, gone, fallen out of my head.

"I-I don't know what to say."

I stand up, my heart beating through my chest, my hands shaking. My breathing shallow, I stumble to the side of the yacht, Ezra closely on my heels, steadying me by my elbow. My hand clutches my forehead as I take in the information he's just relayed to me. Something I thought I couldn't do for my sister was just taken care of in a matter of minutes. Her entire life would change drastically for the better because of this, but it is probably so insignificant to him.

"Are you okay?" His voice is laced with worry as he ducks his head, looking at me, checking me over. I feel tears sting behind my eyes as I look up at him, his brows furrow, unsure of what's happening.

I feel a mix of emotions flow through me as I wrap my arms around his neck, his arms immediately tightening around my waist, pulling me in further, our bodies pressed against each other. I don't know this man, but his actions, veiled or not, give me a sense of relief.

"Thank you." My voice comes out in barely a whisper as I fight to hold back the tears. I feel his face move into my neck, his breath tickling my skin. I now realise I am in the arms of the Casella King.

"You're welcome, sweetheart," he says as we slowly break apart, and he guides me back to the table.

"I'm sorry, I didn't mean to get all emotional—it's just, what you did in a matter of moments, I couldn't even dream of achieving in years." I wipe a tear away from my cheek with the back of my hand. "It's a big deal." I know he didn't do it for me. I know he did it to convince me to accept this deal.

"If you do this for me, I can promise you won't ever have to worry about your financial situation ever again," he says, looking straight into my eyes.

You'd be mad to turn down someone like Ezra Casella. Some would fear what he would do to you if you did, but right now, I feel like I need to repay him.

"I'll do it." I nod. "I'll be your fake wife," I say, his eyes smiling with victory.

"Perfect." He gestures to the food on our plates. "*Mangiare.*"

We devour our entrées, and to my expectation, it was sensational, almost like a five-star restaurant, but on a yacht.

"There's somewhere else we will be heading tonight." His husky voice disrupts my thoughts, my attention snapping back to him. It seems like he hesitates for a moment before he speaks. "I own a club in Shoreditch, and we need to be seen there together, tonight."

My eyes go wide, not expecting for this whole fake thing to start so soon.

"T-tonight? But I thought..." I stop because what did I think? I agreed to the deal. "Never mind. Okay, sure."

"You'll need to be pretty good at faking to be my fiancée for this to work. Are you certain you can do this?" He raises his eyebrows, doubting me, and the truth is I'm doubting myself right now.

"Yes, I'm sure. I can be convincing," I say in my best non-shaky voice as the waiter brings over our dessert. The light-brown embers in his eyes swirl as he takes a bite of his cannoli. Lifting mine to my mouth, I take a bite, and my eyes roll back involuntarily. Damn this is sensational.

"You'll be okay with me touching you?" he asks as he takes another bite.

I try not to choke on my food.

"Kissing you?"

I take a sip of water to wash down the flakes left in my throat.

Would I?

Be okay with him touching me?

Kissing me?

How far will I be willing to go?

"Yes." I keep my answer short because I'm still trying to process everything that's happened tonight. My brain is having trouble keeping up with all this crazy shit.

The music pounds through my ears and thumps through my chest as we walk hand in hand through the club. Ezra's fingers are laced with mine, pulling me through hundreds of sweaty bodies, all the way to the top VIP floor.

The floor is high up, with a clear view of the dance floor below and the main bar on the right. The VIP floor has a few people already in the corner of the booth on my left and at a smaller-sized bar on the right. Ezra pulls me into the love seat just beside the bar, onto his lap. I watch as Henry waits by the entry to the VIP floor, never taking his eyes off us. A bunch of women sitting at the booth across from us look our way, a sour look on their faces as they look me up and down.

What the hell is their problem?

I feel Ezra's hand move over my thigh, caressing, then squeezing as he leans into my ear, his hot breath raising goose bumps on my skin.

"This is where you show me you know what you're doing."

I feel the vibrations of his husky voice travel through me, louder than the music ever will be. I look at him over my shoulder as I lift my dress, showing the skin on my leg as I cross it over the other, and wrapping my arms around his neck, I lean into him. The side of my breast presses against him, and he looks to me as his hand reaches my exposed thigh, travelling further north, his eyes boring into my soul, watching my body respond to his touch. My breath shakes as I feel my heartbeat between my legs, throbbing, begging for attention. It's been so long since a man has touched me that I almost feel desperate for it. He takes my lips with his, and he's not gentle about it, his tongue demanding access into my mouth. I swirl my fingers through the base of his hair as my other hand travels inside his button-up shirt, our mouths moving together as one. I think I hear a moan, but I'm not sure if it came from me or him. I feel his hand squeeze my upper thigh once more, dangerously close to my ass. I try my best to catch my breath as his lips trail from my neck to my collarbone, sending a zap of electricity straight to my nipples, aching for his mouth. My body betrays my rational thoughts as his hand slips higher, clutching my ass, and I feel him beneath me, his hard cock poking into the side of my thigh, the sheer length, even beneath his clothes is enough to send my imagination running wild.

You don't know this man.

He's a killer.

He's involved with crime.

I squeeze my eyes shut to try and hear my own thoughts and to at least try to disassociate with my current reality.

But he's so fucking good at that.

His lips trace back up to my mouth, and when I open my eyes, I see his gaze directly on my breasts.

Fuck, fuck, fuck.

Think about anything else.
LITERALLY ANYTHING ELSE.

It's no use because all I can think about is his mouth over my nipples, sucking them, flicking them with his tongue.

I pull myself away from him.

"Excuse me, I—uh, I need to use the restroom," I manage to say through my ragged breathing, and he nods to Henry as I stand up, watching out of the corner of my eye as Ezra adjusts himself. Walking over to Henry, he directs me to the women's restroom. Entering, I bang my clutch on the counter, looking at myself in the mirror.

"You're in way over your head." I speak to myself softly, doubting my ability to keep this thing professional and not catch feelings or end up fucking this man. I take a few deep breaths in, trying not to focus on my throbbing clit, when the door opens, letting in the loud music, and there's laughter as a couple of women enter. They stop when they see me, and I try not to look at them, to ignore them. I open my clutch and reach for my lipstick.

"It shouldn't be you, you know."

I turn to the one who spoke, and I notice she's the one who was giving me dirties the whole time in the VIP room.

"Excuse me?" My voice comes out meaner than I wanted it to.

"You're not even in this world. You should run whilst you have the chance," she says as she walks into the cubicle and slams the door shut, leaving me staring at the other woman, now fixing her hair in the mirror.

"She's right. The Casella King is known to be unforgiving, relentless, and psychotic." Her words send a rush through me, when they should scare me. "She's just jealous she's not in your place, but if I were you"—she turns to me, looking me square in the eyes—"run, if you still have the chance."

I exit the restroom, suddenly feeling a little uneasy about the situation I have gotten myself into.

Maybe they're just jealous?

Or they could totally be right.

Henry guides me back over to where Ezra is sitting, now with what looks like a scotch in his hand. He waves me down, and I take my seat on his lap again.

"I got you a drink," he says, handing me a tall glass of which looks like a cocktail. I smile as I take it from him and set it down on the table. He doesn't look impressed, his eyebrows furrowed. "You're not going to drink it?"

I bite my bottom lip, unsure of how to tackle this. "Ezra, I don't really know anything about you."

He cocks his head to the side, thinking about what I just said, the creases in between his eyebrows deepening.

"You think I would drug you?" He sounds hurt, and I don't blame him.

"No, I just…" I pause, thinking about what I really want to say. "I think this whole thing would be more believable if we truly got to know each other, you know, in case someone asks me something, and I look like an idiot if I don't know the answer," I say, taking a breath, anticipating his answer, but I don't expect what comes out of his mouth next.

"Okay then, let's go away together. Just us," he says, his face returning to his usual serious look.

I laugh, a little too hard. "What? You can't be serious."

"I'm dead serious. It'll give us a chance to get to know each other quicker with no distractions." He lifts his glass to his lips as I watch the liquid dance into his mouth, his throat working to swallow.

Heat rises within me, forcing a rush to my cheeks. Thank God it's dark in here because I'm pretty sure my cheeks are as red as a fire truck.

"I'm not sure I can commit to that. I mean, what about my job?"

He shrugs, like it's the most unimportant thing in the world to him, and truthfully, it probably is. Why should he care about my job?

"What of it? You've agreed to be my wife, and if my wife doesn't want to work, she doesn't have to."

I watch his chest rise and fall, the exposed skin just begging for my lips.

Fuck.

"Do you want to work, Aries?" I feel his fingers brush my hair away from my face, such an intimate, romantic act for someone who has been called a psycho.

Did I?

I think I did—I mean, I've worked all my life, since it was legal. I never really had the choice not to. I thought about it, and a few days off wouldn't hurt, given that most of the things that needed to be done were admin anyway, my next wedding being in eight days.

"Where would we go?" I question, a smirk growing on his lips as his eyes fall to my lips.

"I know a place." He looks back to me, his hand moving higher up my leg, making my stomach swirl with anticipation, then my attention is drawn to a man making his way into the seat across from us, placing his glass on the table in front of him.

"Mr Casella." He nods before taking a seat.

Ezra doesn't remove his eyes from me, and I feel them burning into the side of my face. "What is it?"

"We have hit a few…hurdles." He clears his throat as Ezra's hand glides up my thigh.

Sensing that I should be putting on a show, I gaze back into his eyes and trail my fingers from his temple to his jaw. My legs press together on their own at the intensity of his gaze.

"Hurdles can wait until tomorrow," he says as his hand travels up to my hip, pressing into my skin possessively. "I'm busy."

I look back to the man sitting opposite us, trying to avert his gaze from our obvious public display when I look behind him and notice a few other men at the bar, their eyes fixed on Ezra. They're all dressed in suits, and I can't tell if they work for him or not.

Who was this show for?

CHAPTER SIX
Ezra

I find Nico sleeping on the lounge in my office in nothing but his black boxer briefs. Scotch bottles scattered over the floor, his socks strewn over the armchair.

I whip the door shut, the bang startling him, as he rolls off the lounge onto the floor.

"Fuck, man!" He covers his eyes, struggling to open them.

"It's nine in the morning. Get up, we have work to do." I take a seat behind my desk, opening my laptop. Nico picks up his clothes from the floor, his hair looking like a rat's nest. "What happened to you anyway? Why are you here?"

He yawns. "Brother, don't ask." He scratches the back of his head with a huge grin on his face. "This woman I met at the club wanted to kick on after it closed at four in the morning, and her friend wanted to join. I couldn't bring them back to my place because I lost the keys, so I had to come here," He smirks. "They were both Brazilian." He winks, raising an empty bottle of scotch at me.

"I hope you covered your dick." I watch as he gathers

the rest of his things. "You know there cannot be an illegitimate heir."

"Yes, yes, I wore protection." He doesn't even bother putting his clothes on as he heads to the door. "You're beginning to sound like our mother," he mutters as he walks out, slamming the door behind him.

Nico is the type of man to drown his feelings in the bottom of a bottle or seek a sense of feeling through substances.

He gets it from our father.

I get it, the appeal of being numb, not feeling, not thinking, but it doesn't get you anywhere. All it does is shorten your life, make you a bitter person, and fuck with your mind. For Nico, he seeks that numbness. Our father wasn't someone who took us on bike rides or showed us how to fish.

No.

Our father showed us how to fight, to use a gun...to kill. He showed us what it means to be ruthless, and in the process, stripped us of a normal childhood. His methods and lessons of resilience weren't the best, and Nico saw the brunt of Dominic's frustration because he was smaller than I was. Slower than I was. I, however, don't crave the numbness because I feel it when I'm sober. There is a pit of nothing inside me, begging to be filled. No matter how many souls I take, or how much blood I have on my hands, it doesn't even come close to touching the sides of the chasm within.

I shake the thoughts of my father out of my mind as I see my phone light up on the desk.

ARIES

Can you at least tell me where this place is
so I can bring appropriate clothing? – Aries

A smile tugs at the corner of my lips as I press reply.

Bring a light jacket, might get cold at night.

With that, I get to work. Part of my role includes finances. Yes, we hire external accountants that have been doing our finances for years, but with my father gone, I need to know I can trust these people, and they will not bring shame to the Casella name. I begin the tedious task of going through each transaction one by one, ensuring I don't miss any for the month. I feel my eyes strain as I near the end of the list, resting back into the chair. I think about Aries's bare leg underneath my palm, her wet tongue on mine, the way she was panting as I squeezed her thigh moving up to her ass.

It is no secret to anyone who took a glance at her, she is *very* attractive.

I am drawn to her, a lot more than I should be, given the possible complications it could cause. It wasn't a secret I wanted her, more than I would like to admit. I'm just glad I didn't have to resort to other means to get her to agree to being my wife for a few months. I would have if I had to, but I didn't want her to see that side of me yet.

It's going to be entertaining.

I hear a knock on the door.

"Come in," I say, leaving my palms on the desk, and I watch as Henry opens the door and steps in, closing it behind him.

"Boss, there's been a bit of trouble with the second

phase of the plan." He looks down at his feet, which makes me wonder how big of a fuck-up they could've managed.

What was so hard to understand about "burn all their motherfucking shit down?"

"Go on." My voice is stern as I speak.

"The boys managed to get to the first two clubs, but the Brayfords managed to capture a couple of them as ransom whilst they attempted the Brixton job."

Well, fuck.

The Brayfords have proved to be a lot smarter than they led on.

"Get in there, and get them out," I command without hesitation.

"But…"

I don't let him finish. "Those are our boys in there, Henry, I don't give a fuck what the consequence is, if they see our hand or whatever the fuck you're thinking. I want you to assemble a team and get them the fuck out of there."

Henry nods and without another word exits, closing the door behind him. I clench my teeth at the thought of being bested by the Brayfords again, and I wonder if going away with Aries right now is the right thing to do. I should be here, fighting with my men. Showing them I don't abandon them when things get rough, which they were about to.

It was either secure the Casella line with Aries for now, get my mother off my ass, or hear about that bitch, whatever the fuck her name was, and how much of a good cook she is or what a perfect wife she would make, for the next month. Not to mention, if the Brayfords manage a hit on both Nico and me, the Casella line dies with us, no more Empire, no more kingdom to rule.

Absolutely not.

I cannot let that happen. I need to handle this ASAP.

Grabbing my keys, I head to my mother's house. The large four-story home comes into view as I step out of my car, handing the keys to the young boy out front. As soon as I walk in, I'm met with my mother showering me with kisses, shoving food in my face, telling me I look skinny and to eat. Which is not true, I am the furthest thing from skinny. I work out twice a day, sometimes three times when I can fit it in, partly because I like to stay fit for my role as the king, and partly because that's the way I like to fight my demons, unlike Nico who drowns them in a bottle or recreational drugs.

"When's the last time you've eaten?" She hands me a plate of pasta and forces me to sit at the table.

"I won't say no to your homemade pasta, Mama." I spoon some pasta and instantly watch my childhood flash before my eyes at the taste of her bolognese. "Where's Nico?" I ask, because he hasn't been answering my calls since he left the office.

"He will be here shortly. He said he needed to take care of a couple of things first," she explains.

"Well, I'm sure you're aware of what's happened with the Brayfords." I wipe my mouth and stare up at her. "Mama, I need you to know that Nico and I will need to do the next bit together. I know you hesitate whenever this is necessary, but it needs to be done, to show our power, our place at the top of the food chain, and it most likely won't be the last."

The Brayford family have been our enemy since I can remember. It's always been blood for blood between our families, and generations later, it remains unchanged. What's ironic is our ancestors were once allies. Working together to rule London. Each taking a cut of the pie, but something changed.

Someone got greedy.

The Brayfords blame us, and we blame them.

The age-old blood feud.

She pauses a moment before nodding. "Be careful, *per favore*." The door to the dining room opens and in walks Nico, striding through the room and dropping into the seat next to me.

"Brother." He nods.

"Are you drunk?" I ask, looking at him dead in the eyes.

"No."

"Are you high?"

"No."

"Great, get your shit. We have work to do." I take out my handguns, placing them on the table, then checking one by one, bullet by bullet, counting who I'm going to murder.

Nico stays there next to me, watching as I place the guns back into my holster.

"If you're not serious about this, don't fucking come." My voice is harsher than I mean it to be, but I can't fuck this up.

This is on me now.

"No, I want to." He stands, straightening himself up.

"Good, because I need you, brother," I say as he looks to me, pausing, then nods, gritting his teeth.

The engine roars as we fly through the streets, without a moment to lose, the boys following us from behind in black vans.

I kick the doors open to the bar and walk in, aiming

my two gold handguns in the direction of two men on opposite sides of the room, Nico standing beside me.

"Send him out boys, no one has to get hurt here!" I yell, making sure everyone heard me.

A dark figure emerges from the back of the bar, walking around it, clapping his hands slowly. "Well done, Ezra. I didn't think you'd actually show up." His two gold front teeth come into view first, then the rest of his distorted, ugly face. "I thought you'd send your men to do your bidding, you know, like with the two other clubs. Too much of a fucking pussy to do it yourself."

I grit my teeth at his words, promising myself that I will make him eat each and every one of them. "Send out the boys, and I won't put a bullet in your skull."

"Such a generous offer from such a novice player." He chuckles, his scar stretching with his smile.

"Come now, Charlie, we both know you're outgunned and outmanned. Put your guns down, or there will be blood." My heart thumps faster at the promise of a fight, a bloodbath.

"You're just a fucking child. What do you know of blood?" He spits at his feet. "Tell me, Ezra Casella, have you even killed a man before?" he asks.

Plenty.

"This is your last chance." I squeeze my gun tighter, assessing the room around me, who I will be shooting first.

He thinks I'm bluffing, and he's about to learn the hard way that I *never* bluff.

Bullets fly in every direction, blood splattering on the walls and onto the floor, over my clothes and almost into my mouth.

"Cover me!" I yell to Nico as he nods, crouching behind a

wooden table on its side. I sprint across the room, dodging the bullets, making it to the bar. I grab the cowering son of a bitch by his collar and drag him out into the open with a gun to his head. "Put your fucking guns down, or he dies right now."

The room goes silent as the rest of them place their guns on the floor, kicking them away.

"You'll never hear me beg for my life." Charlie struggles to speak as I drag him into the middle of the room.

"I don't give a fuck."

I drop my guns on the floor, whirling him around to face me. I grab his face with both of my hands so hard, I can almost hear his skull cracking. His eyes fill with terror as he looks at me, and it's this part right here that I revel in. Soaking up the power, the control, I glide my thumbs into his eyes and press deeper as they sink into his sockets, blood pouring out of them, soaking my hands as his screams rip through the bar, his weak hands gripping onto my forearms as blood splatters onto my face. He falls to the floor, and I pick up both my guns. With bloodied hands, I raise them both between his eyes and pull the triggers. Brains, blood, and matter splatter onto my clothes as the rest of our guys shoot the rest of theirs. Nico and the boys manage to wrangle the two youngsters from the basement. Luckily, they didn't suffer much, probably some bruises and scratches, though nothing major.

As the boys pile into the van, Nico takes his seat next to me in my car, just as the clean-up crew arrives. "What's our next play?" he asks, lighting a cigarette.

"I have a line to secure, then we annihilate the rest of the Brayford bloodline." I grin as I snatch the cigarette from his mouth and throw it out of the car window. "No fucking smoking in my Porsche, you dick."

After a long, hot shower scrubbing brain matter out of my hair, I managed to convince my mother that my 'fiancée' wanted a little getaway with the excuse that she was experiencing some stress over the upcoming events. I wasn't expecting to be somewhat relieved I didn't have to deal with running an empire for a few days, but the truth is, I felt lighter already. I had sent Henry to pick up Aries and bring her to the tarmac, where our private jet awaits. I watch as she steps out of the car, her short, wavy hair waving in the slight wind, her sunglasses covering most of her face and her flowing sundress resting just in the middle of her thighs. She tries to help Henry with her bags as he shakes his head at her. I chuckle watching her try to adjust to letting go a little. She walks over to me, her dress blowing in the wind, and I can't fucking look away.

"I thought it was only meant to be a little getaway?" she asks, her hands on her hips as she reaches me. "What is that?" she asks, pointing to my private jet.

"What? I can't take my fiancée out of the country? Don't tell me you don't have a passport." That's one thing I hadn't considered.

"I do, but that's not the point," she argues. I could watch her argue with me all day, though I'd have a pretty sore cock, and a serious case of blue balls from the constant raging hard-on she gives me whenever she's near.

"Great, let's go."

I hold out my hand to her, which she takes. I watch as she takes one step at a time, climbing the stairs, holding her dress from behind. If her ass moving beneath the light fabric of her dress right in front of my eyes was enough to give me a semi-hard-on, I was in trouble.

"You still haven't told me where we are going. Technically, you're still a stranger, you know," she says as she takes her seat on the white leather seat across from me.

"Norway." I take out my phone and my two gold handguns, placing them on the table between us. Leaning back into my seat, I watch her, her eyes wide, mouth open.

"Norway? As in, like, the country, Norway?" she questions, her eyes never leaving mine.

"Unless you know a different Norway?" I chuckle as she slowly gathers her jaw off the floor. "I have a cabin on a lake in a small country town which I haven't been to in a whilst, so I thought it'd be the perfect location."

She doesn't say anything, instead, she's silent, looking out the window. A moment passes before either of us speak.

"Tell me about this man who left you at the altar," I question, and my brows furrow at her body's response. She goes stiff, her palms clenching the arms of her seat. The plane has begun ascending into the air as she watches the clouds whizz past from the window.

"There's really nothing to tell." She shrugs, looking down into her lap, her hands now keeping busy with the fabric of her dress between her fingers. "He promised me something and couldn't deliver."

"Surely there's more to it than that," I urge her to go on.

She takes a deep breath. "Why do you need to know anyway?" she questions, and I really don't need to know. I want to know. I want to know everything about this woman, what makes her mad, what makes her cry, what makes her scream my fucking name.

"You're going to be my wife. I need to know about your past." I lean forward, elbows resting on my knees with my hands clasped together.

Reluctantly, she speaks. "We were together since our third year of university. I was studying a bachelor of arts, and he was studying law." She bites her bottom lip. "I'm pretty sure somewhere along the line, he fell out of love with me and never said anything, he just let it go on because he was afraid to tell me." Her voice is a little shaky before she says the next part. "He…" She stops herself, looking out the window, letting out a breath. "He was my first. First kiss, first everything."

Did not expect that.

"Your first fuck?" I ask, and her eyes shoot up at mine, pausing a moment, then nodding.

Well, fuck.

We arrive at the cabin, the lush green trees surrounding the small house on the lake. The crisp blue water rushing downstream. Henry unpacks our things and brings them inside as she takes in the scenery.

"It's so gorgeous here." She smiles, looking out onto the lake. The sun is almost about to set, creating different shades of pinks, oranges, and yellows in the sky.

"Let's head inside—it's about to get colder out here." I wait for her as she walks over to me slowly, her eyes plastered to the ground, making sure she doesn't trip over the rocks embedded into the grass. She looks up at me when she reaches me, and without saying a word, her fingers brush a strand of hair from my eyebrows, the brown in her eyes contrasting the greens in the forest surrounding us.

"I can never repay you for what you did for my sister, Ezra." Her face falls as she speaks, and I capture her dainty wrist in my hand, careful not to break her tiny bones.

"I never asked you to," I say, and I watch her gaze fall to my lips, every fibre of my being wants to devour her right here and now, but I hold back. As tempting as she may be, I can't have my head anywhere besides revenge, as much as I would love to bury it between her legs.

CHAPTER SEVEN
Aries

I stare at the large king-size bed right in the middle of the room, a plush white lounge on the left under the floor to ceiling windows, and a door that leads to the ensuite on the right. Exiting the bedroom, I walk over to Ezra sitting on the lounge across from the fireplace. There's no TV, no radio, absolutely no technology in this place, and not to mention, no reception. I guess he failed to mention that part, or did he just choose not to?

"We are most definitely *not* sharing a bed," I say in the most confident voice I can muster. He looks to me, a smirk growing on his lips.

"Great, you can sleep on either one of the lounges then." He grins, showing his stupidly perfect teeth.

"Excuse me?" I cross my arms, waiting for him to say he'll take the lounge, but I'm positive he's not going to back down without a fight.

"What? You're the one not wanting to share the bed, so you can sleep on the lounge. Seems fair to me." He shrugs, standing and walking to the bar cart in the corner of the lounge room.

Although it's a cabin, it's a lot larger than your regular cabin. A huge fireplace adorns the large wall across the lounge, animal heads hang above the fireplace, and I wonder if they're real. A large bookshelf takes over almost the entire wall on the opposite side of the room, filled with books from edge to edge.

I can't wait to get my hands on them.

Rolling my eyes, I head back into the bedroom and begin unpacking my suitcase, placing my clothes in the drawers beside the bed and in the cupboard across.

What in the world were we supposed to do with no technology?
I'm already bored.

It's times like these that I'm thankful I chose to bring my vibrator, because I need to pass the time somehow, and God knows how horny I'll get just watching Ezra be Ezra. I cannot give into temptation and let myself get swept up into this world, the luxury, and the power.

I *cannot* get sucked in.

It's nice to be away though, from family, the pressure of modern life. Living day in and day out, doing the exact same thing gets exhausting. I'm especially thankful to be away from my father. Just the thought of having a few days away from him is enough to turn my mood around.

Grabbing my little purple friend, I tuck it under my folded panties in the first drawer.

"What are you doing?" Ezra's voice comes from the doorway, and I turn, watching him lean on the doorframe, his biceps bulging from his black T-shirt.

"Unpacking."

I stand, walking over to the bathroom, with my toiletries in hand, Ezra on my tail. He watches me from the door as I place my bag on the marble counter, sneaking a look at him through the mirror.

"How adventurous are you?" he asks, crossing his arms.

I turn around, watching his eyes. "What?"

"I was thinking about having a Norwegian dinner—are you up for that?" He raises one eyebrow.

Right. Dinner.

"I don't mind. I don't think I've ever had a Norwegian dish."

"Great, Henry will grab it for us, meanwhile, we have" —he looks at his expensive watch—"about an hour before dinner."

"Is there anything to do in this cabin?" I question and immediately regret it.

"You could always do *your fiancé*." He smirks, and I roll my eyes, pushing past him, into the bedroom.

"Seriously, there's no TV, nothing, and you forgot to mention there's no reception. How will I work from here?" I cross my arms.

"You could always take a break, you know—take a walk, read a book, cook, fuck, there's plenty of things to do."

He knows exactly what he's doing.

"I need a drink. Maybe that'll get my mind off how mind-numbingly boring these next few days are going to be." I walk out to the bar cart and begin pouring myself a scotch. Throwing it back, I pour another one.

"Whoa, easy. That's a Macallan Lalique 50-Year-Old Single Malt Scotch Whiskey," he says, like I know what the fuck that means.

I turn around to him, raising my eyebrows, pouring another shot, without breaking eye contact. He grits his teeth, watching me.

Well, if there is nothing else to do, I guess I'll just have to entertain myself, and the look on his face right now is quite entertaining. I smile as I sip the third glass. It tastes like acid, but I'm not about to let up.

"Okay, how about we slow down on the alcohol before food." He walks closer to me, scooping my glass in his hand, taking it from me and placing it on the fireplace mantle. "Maybe we should start trying to get to know one another, you know, the whole reason as to why we are here?"

I take a seat on the lounge, the alcohol immediately going to my head. I forgot I hadn't really eaten much today. "Fine, I'll go first, how many siblings do you have?"

"One, younger brother, Nico, short for Nicholas." He leans forward, turning his body toward me slightly. "My turn, why haven't you fucked anyone since your ex?"

Jesus. Straight to the hard-hitting questions, like I expected anything else from him.

"Do you always have such a dirty mouth?"

"You don't know the half of it, sweetheart." He grins.

I look around, looking for something to save me from his question. "I don't know, I just"—I rub my hands on my thighs, feeling myself starting to sweat—"I just haven't."

"How did your father die?" The only reason I ask this one is because I should know, right? Just in case someone quizzes me?

"A bullet." He looks me dead in the eyes. "In the throat."

I look away from him, his gaze too strong. "My condolences."

He ignores my sympathy. "Do you ever give in to what you truly want?" I feel his eyes still on me. I look at him unsure of what he means.

"What?"

"When your heart wants something, do you immediately pursue it, or do you deny yourself?" he asks, and it takes me by surprise.

"Well, sometimes I do, and other times I don't." I stand up. "I feel like we're playing twenty questions, and it's weird." I walk over to where he placed my scotch glass and take another sip.

"How else will we get to know one another?" His eyebrows come together, watching me sip my drink.

"I don't know. Surely we can come up with another way that doesn't feel like an interrogation?"

He looks around the room in thought, then gets up and rummages through the console near the entry. I watch as he leans down, looking through the drawer, my eyes wandering south to the delicious curve of his toned ass. He turns to me, holding a deck of playing cards, smiling.

"Strip poker?" His teeth almost glimmer in the light as he grins, his hungry eyes waiting for my reply. Then there's a loud knock on the door. He doesn't even glance at it, just waiting for my response. Rolling my eyes, I open the door to find Henry, taller than the doorframe. He hands me the bag full of food and winks at me, and I swear I almost thought I saw a smile on his face as he turned around.

The smell of food makes my stomach rumble as I bring the bag over to the kitchen and begin unpacking and putting the food onto plates. I devour my food, placing the plate into the small drawer dishwasher, and picking up the rest of my drink, I begin to browse the books on the bookshelf. They all looked a little old, and tired, like they'd been read over and over. I didn't have much time to read, unfortunately, running a business and having the burden of a drunk father, taking precedence.

"Have you read an Agatha Christie novel?" he asks as he leans on the mantel of the fireplace. I shake my head as my fingers brush the spines of the novels lined up neatly.

"Her books are considered classics in the detective novel genre."

"How ironic, a mafia king, reading a detective novel." I try hard to hide my smile, but I fail. I throw the rest of the scotch back and feel it burn my throat as it makes its way down. Looking back at him, I notice he doesn't have a drink in his hand. "Do you want a drink?" I ask as I walk over to the bar cart and pour myself one. The food probably didn't help sober me up at all. I feel a strong buzz in my head as I walk over to him, holding the glass out.

"I prefer not to be inebriated." He looks down into my eyes then to my glass, his scent alone is enough to intoxicate me, and although I don't mean to, I inhale his scent, closing my eyes.

"Mmm."

"Are you feeling okay?" He grabs a hold of my arms, my eyes springing open at his closeness, my breasts almost touching his body. I feel my nipples harden under my bra as I grab onto his forearm to steady myself.

"I'm fine." I laugh a nervous laugh. "I don't even know how to play poker."

"What?" He laughs too.

"You know, when you suggested we play strip poker to get to know each other, I don't even know how to play." I sink back into the lounge, feeling the buzz become a little stronger.

"We don't need to play games to fuck, if that's what you really want." He smirks.

I swallow, unable to find the words in my current state. I desperately want his hands on me again, maybe even his mouth too.

Stop it.

"I don't play games," I say and sit up straight, hoping

my body language would give me back some sort of control, but it doesn't.

He leans into me, his lips close enough to touch mine, and I feel every bit of power slip from under me. "You're playing a very dangerous one right now." He rasps, and the octave of his voice has me melting in a puddle.

"I'm not."

"Sitting here, in that short dress, cheeks flushed, looking at me with those beautiful eyes beneath those lashes, begging me to fuck you, is conceivably a dangerous game," he states.

I stand up, heat flushing to my chest as I walk over to the other side of the room. I'm not used to being in the presence of someone like Ezra. His aura is all-consuming, sucking the oxygen from your lungs as soon as he enters a room. He stands and walks over to me, closing me in again, but I love it. I inhale his scent, the spicy sandalwood burning my nose as his fingers trail a line from my jaw down to the middle of my breast. My mouth goes dry, and I lose my words. I feel myself clench my thighs as I feel a warmth pooling between them. I hold myself back with everything I have in me to reach out and run my fingers down his perfectly sculpted chest.

"Why can't you admit you find me attractive?" he asks, looking down into my eyes.

I lick my lips. "Because we shouldn't sleep together..."

His fingers trail down to my navel on top of the material of my dress, and I can feel the heat radiating off them.

"Why not?"

"Because we shouldn't."

"Are you going to give me a reason?" he rasps in that

voice again, and it takes everything in me not to drop to my knees before him.

"I—" My eyes fall to his lips as his hands snake behind me, finding the zipper on my dress and slowly tugging it down. He's giving me ample time to decide if this is what I want, and I just stay quiet, not because I don't want this, but because I'm scared of wanting it.

He barely touches the shoulders of the dress, and the material pools at my feet, his eyes immediately burning with desire, or hunger, as they skate to my black, lacy bra, then to my itty-bitty black G-string. I almost stop breathing as he licks his lips, his throat working to swallow. Time almost stands still as I look from his eyes to his lips and back again, my blood running hot, my breathing growing quicker by the second at his closeness. I watch his chest rise and fall, noticing a tattoo peaking out of his singlet on his right pec.

His hand comes up to my face, my chest heaving at his electric touch, as he gently tucks a stray hair behind my ear. I feel tingles on the trail his fingers left and can hardly contain myself, all I want to do is reach out, wrap my arms around him and kiss him like I'm running out of time, like he's not the most dangerous man I've ever met.

He beats me to it, wrapping one arm around me, pulling me into him, his lips crushing mine with pure lust. Both his hands trail down to my ass, as a groan rumbles in his throat. The sexy vibrations in his voice stir something in me, and my arms wrap around his neck as his tongue forces its way inside my mouth, tasting me, devouring every inch of my mouth. I trail my hands from his strong shoulders, down to his biceps.

The more my hands roam, the hotter it gets in here.

"I've been dying to kiss you since that first kiss at the

club," he whispers into my ear, his hot breath tickling my neck. My nipples harden as he grinds his erection into my belly, and I fight the strong urge to put my hand down his pants to feel him. I create some distance between us, fanning my face with my hand.

"Maybe we should stop." I fan my hand harder as I feel my face redden under his stare. "Is it hot in here?"

"It's about to be." He smirks as he removes his pants, revealing the outline of his huge erection under his dark-blue boxer briefs. My mouth goes dry at the sight, and I can't peel my eyes away.

CHAPTER EIGHT
Ezra

"We really shouldn't." Her mouth moves, but all I see is her beautiful, plump breasts covered by her skimpy bra, just begging for my mouth around them. I forget about the revenge, the complication, because right now, all I can think about is burying myself deep inside her.

"Why not?" I move closer to her as she licks her lips. "I can make you feel like you've never felt before. I can give you something you've denied yourself for so long."

She squeezes her eyes shut and opens them again. "No, we should just keep this professional." She grabs her dress from the floor, bringing it to cover her body and sprints into the bedroom, slamming the door shut behind her. My cock strains against the material of my boxer briefs as I tip my head back and groan at the memory of her in her underwear.

How does she affect me this way? How can the mere thought of her naked have me ready to drop to my knees and beg for her to wrap her legs around my face?

I'm fucked.

I gave Aries some space last night after the intense moment we shared. I waited until she fell asleep, not to be a gentleman, but so I could get my mind off being inside her. If I had climbed into the bed with her right there and then, I know I wouldn't have been able to control my want for her. I need to ensure she agrees to my proposal, so I can't fuck this up, no matter how much I want her.

This morning's jog felt a lot more peaceful than usual, probably since I didn't have my entire family down my throat about the empire and securing the fucking bloodline, but the worry of the rest of it did creep in. The burden of taking on the family empire built on the blood of countless men before me. I shake off the thoughts as I wipe my forehead with the bottom of my shirt. I left Aries at the cabin, not wanting to wake her since she seemed comfortable in bed. It took everything in me not to pull myself off last night, my dick was throbbing, and my balls felt like fucking bowling balls.

One reason I love this place is that there's no one here —it's completely empty, just grass, air, and water. Such a perfect place to clear my head. I take a seat on the grass, watching the river flow by and wonder if Aries is awake yet. Pulling out my phone, I open the security app I have of all the cameras around the cabin. I click on the bedroom camera that faces the bed, and my heart picks up speed as I watch Aries slowly peel off the covers and walk out to the lounge room. She calls out my name and waits, then walks back into the bedroom, looking around. She waits a little longer, staring at the bedside table. She pulls out something small and gets back onto the bed. My dick jumps to attention at what I see next. She slowly pries her underwear down, reaching between her legs, and lets out a soft moan.

Is she fucking pleasuring herself?

On my fucking bed?

I can't peel my eyes away from my phone as I watch her, one hand on her breast and the other between her legs.

Looking around to make sure I'm alone, I slide my hand into my pants, pulling out my cock and wrapping my hand around it as I watch my fiancée pleasure herself. Her moans begin to get throatier as she bucks her hips, my hand pumps up and down my cock at the sight of her, my chest heaving. I haven't pulled myself off in a long time, I've never needed to, but fuck, watching Aries give herself pleasure, *on my bed*, is enough to make me explode. She pulls her top up, exposing her bare breasts, and the sight alone is enough to make me finish, with a few last pumps, I groan as I cum all over my stomach. I watch as she continues to pleasure herself, getting lost in the moment, closing her eyes, she whispers something, then she almost yells it.

"Ezra!" she screams as her body shakes, her moans filtering from my speakers. I watch as she comes down from her high, her breathing returning to normal, she places her little purple friend back into the nightstand. There is no chance of hiding the grin on my face right now. I just watched my fiancée pleasure herself, on my bed, and scream out *my* name when she came. What more proof did I need that she was into me?

After cleaning myself off, I jog back to the cabin. Walking into the lounge room, I notice Aries has showered and is wearing a pair of yoga pants and a tank. She's sat on the lounge with a book in her hand, and from what I can tell, standing from here, it's an Agatha Christie book.

"Did you sleep well?" I question with a smirk.

She looks over to me and smiles, a rosy colour to her cheeks. "I did, thank you for asking." I nod and walk over to the bedroom door, the bed has been made, and clothes put away.

"How was your morning?"

"Fine." She shrugs. "I could use some food, though. Do we have anything to eat?"

I bet—that orgasm sure looked appetite inducing.

"There are some eggs in the fridge, help yourself." I take off my singlet and feel her eyes on me. "I'm taking a shower." I walk into the bedroom that's been completely seized by her floral scent, I take a deep breath in, and try my best not to jerk off *again* to the image of her on my bed. My dick is rock fucking hard as I stand under the water, thinking about all the ways I want to make her scream my name.

"Eggs are ready!" she yells into the bedroom. I dry myself off and wrap the towel around my waist.

I feel her eyes on my chest as I walk out into the kitchen/lounge. Grabbing a strawberry, I pop it into my mouth, her gaze still on me.

"I forgot to mention, for security reasons, there are cameras all around the cabin." I watch as her eyes go wide, snapping to mine.

"What? Like, outside?" she questions.

"Yes." I watch her shoulders relax, then deliver the punch. "And inside." She takes a sharp breath in, covering her mouth with one hand. "Is there something wrong?" I smirk, watching her come to the realisation, the penny finally dropping.

"Did you…" she scoffs. "No, there's no way." She walks into the bedroom, I hear shuffling and then she comes out, pointing to the ceiling. "You have a fucking camera in the bedroom?!"

I grin, leaning on the kitchen bench, watching her as I put another strawberry in my mouth. "I must say, I didn't expect to see what I saw this morning." I chuckle at the memory, feeling my blood slowly draining from my brain.

"You watched!?" Her tone horrified that I'd do such a thing.

"Of course I watched." I move closer to her, our bodies now a mere inch apart. "I watched as you slid your hand under those black, lacy panties." I trail a finger from her collarbone to the middle of her breasts. "I watched as you grasped your breast, closing your eyes." I trail my finger farther down to her navel. "I watched you scream my name as you came." Her chest heaves as she looks into my eyes, licking her lips. "Why won't you just admit it? You're attracted to me." I smirk.

She lets out a little whimper as I snake my arm around her waist, pulling her into me. "I know you want to know what my cock feels like deep inside you," I whisper into her ear, my nose trailing from her neck to her jaw as I push my erection into her. "We could make this engagement a lot more fun, if you'd let me show you how."

"Oh god," she whispers, letting her head drop back. I kiss her neck, my tongue swirling on her velvet skin.

"It's just you and I here, sweetheart. God doesn't associate himself with the devil." I smirk as I remove my towel, stepping back, her eyes finding my cock immediately.

She takes a deep breath in, then looks to me and back down at my cock. She licks her lips first, then bites her bottom lip.

"If you want a taste, it's all yours."

I give my cock a couple pumps, her eyes watching my hand move up and down. I notice her nipples harden beneath her thin tank top which hugs her perfect curves, making my cock strain the more I stare at her body. She moves closer to me, her hand coming up to my face.

"I'm going to regret this, aren't I?" she whispers, before her lips are on mine, not giving me a chance to respond.

I rip off her shirt, literally tearing it at the seams, exposing her beautiful perky breasts. I give them a small lick, giving her a taste of what's to come, but first, I want to know what that pretty, little mouth can do.

"Get on your knees, sweetheart," I rasp, her eyes lock onto mine as she drops to her knees. "Such a good girl."

I grasp her hair from the top of her head, she opens her mouth, and I pull her mouth down slowly onto my cock. My head tilts back at the warmth of her mouth closing over me. She moves on her own, tasting me, sucking me, licking me. I force my dick to the back of her throat, her hands landing on my hips, bracing herself, and I watch as tears begin pooling in her eyes. She gags a little, then I pull back a couple inches, watching her struggle to catch her breath, her pretty eyes wide, looking up at me, and I almost want to grab my phone to take a photo of her, on her knees for me.

So fucking sexy.

I force myself into the back of her throat again and back out, watching as her mascara runs down her sweet, innocent face as she struggles to breathe through my thrusts. She moves her hand onto the base of my cock and squeezes as her mouth works, sending a jolt straight to my balls.

"Fuck baby, just like that." Her mouth feels so fucking good, just as good as she looks, knees spread, eyes focused on me, with my fist in her hair. I pull out of her mouth and watch her saliva create a string, connecting her mouth with my cock. She pants, watching me from the floor. I pull her up by her elbows and walk her back to the lounge, gently pushing her back down onto it. Her hungry eyes watch me as I kneel before her, removing her yoga pants and panties together, tossing them aside. Grabbing her thighs with her knees bent, I spread her legs wide, giving me the perfect view of her pink pussy, and I'm so ready for my favourite meal of the day. My mouth salivates at the thought of tasting her. I lower my mouth closer to her pussy, teasing her with the warmth of my breath as I blow on her clit, then kiss her inner thighs.

She lets out a whimper. "Ezra, please." She pants, bucking her hips, begging.

"Please what?" I lick her inner thigh, getting closer and closer to her pussy. "Tell me what you want me to do to you."

She squeezes her breast in her palm, bucking her hips again. "I need you, between my legs."

Fuck, I love the sound of her begging.

I don't give her the time to think about it, as I place my mouth completely over her pussy, licking her, sucking her, tongue fucking her and watching as her chest heaves in tandem with my tongue. I thrust two fingers inside her, and her head falls back.

"Oh my god," she whispers, barely audible.

"I told you, sweetheart, he's not here," I say, between licking her and sucking her, my fingers curling slightly inside her as they pump in and out of her wet pussy.

Her breathless moans fill the room, and my other hand travels up her torso, plunging two of my fingers into her mouth as she sucks. My dick hardens at her compliance, as

I watch her writhe beneath my touch. There is nothing sexier than knowing how much you can please a woman, but Aries takes it one step further. I need to hear her say my name, and then she does.

"Ezra." She moans my name, her hand grasping my wrist and moving my hand from her mouth to her breast. My mouth continues to move over her as she bucks, riding my face, taking her own pleasure, like a beast that's been locked away for years without access to fresh meat. I can feel her hunger. I squeeze her breast, playing with her nipple, flicking it and rolling it between my fingers. I groan at the sight of her, her cheeks flushed, breathless, my name dripping from her mouth, and I just know I have her right where I want her.

I know she will not deny herself this pleasure again.

CHAPTER NINE
Aries

I watch as his eyes darken with pure lust, his fingers exiting me as he brings them up to his mouth, sucking them.

"Tastes like my new favourite meal." He smirks, standing, one of his hands coming down to grip his dick as he pulls himself, his eyes devouring me. My hand travels down between my thighs as if it has a mind of its own, feeling the need for release, the pressure building inside me as I work my fingers over my clit.

"Fuck," he groans as he steps closer to me, positioning himself at my entrance. "I've been nice up until now, sweetheart, but watching you pleasure yourself is reviving the animal in me." He gives me no warning, pushing himself deep inside me with a hard thrust. "An animal you will come to know, that has no remorse." He thrusts. "No empathy." He thrusts again.

My screams fill the space between us as I grab onto anything my hands can find, which happen to be his arms, my nails digging into his skin, creating craters. I feel his large cock inside me, filling me up entirely, making me squirm under him.

"I want you to feel every inch of me." He pulls out a couple inches and rams right back into me. "I want your pussy to ache for me when I'm not near." He repeats the action. "I want you to scream my name like you've been possessed." He whispers into my ear, sending my pussy aching with his words, aching for more. A moan slips from my lips as I feel his hips begin to move, slow at first, gradually building tempo, my breathing following in tandem.

My eyes roll back as I feel his thumb on my clit, massaging, rubbing, giving me everything I want and then some.

In this moment, I'm just particles, energy, whirling like a tornado beneath him, begging to be liberated. I close my eyes, feeling the pressure building.

"Eyes on me, baby." His husky voice echoes through my ears, just barely making sense through my clouded mind. He grasps my hair into his fist on the top of my head, pulling my head forward, my eyes now plastered onto his. "Good girl." His breathy moans turn me on even more than I could've imagined, my pussy feeling like a fucking slip and slide. "Do you want to come?" He rams into me, over and over, the force of his thrusts sending me deeper into the lounge, my scalp aching from the tugging, but feeling oh so damn good in conjunction to the pleasure pulsating between my legs.

I nod as best as I can, as his hand moves to my throat, squeezing. "Please," I whisper, begging for a release.

"Not yet, baby." He squeezes my neck harder, the muscles on his arm flexing, his abs hard as rocks, tensing as he continues to thrust himself deep inside me. "Fuck, your pussy feels so good, choking my cock," he breathes, releasing my throat, coming down to kiss me, his hot lips greedily tasting my mouth.

My arms come up to his shoulders, and with each

thrust, my nails dig deeper and deeper into his skin. I'm dying to come. Holding back my release is almost painful, and just when I think he will make this go on forever, he whispers into my ear, completely undoing me. "Come for me, sweetheart." His dick hardens like a rock inside me as he continues to thrust, my moans ripping through my throat with an intensity I've never felt before. He thrusts a couple more times, growling into my ear as he fills me up with his cum. We lay there for a moment, both of us trying to regain some train of thought. Panting, he takes his dick in his hand and gives it a couple of pumps, watching me still coming down from my ecstasy.

My mind reels with what we have just done. I'm never this reckless in my life, but something about Ezra brings out the rebel in me.

I lay across Ezra's chest, absentmindedly tracing my fingers along the lines of his tattoos as I watch the sunset over the river through our window.

"I'm not ready to go back," I sigh.

He sits up, and I follow, wrapping the sheet around my body.

"I have a job to do." He runs a hand over his face as he stares at the wall, silence falling between us.

After what seems like forever, he speaks. "I didn't want it…" he admits, which confuses me. I don't speak, waiting for him to elaborate. "…The title of the King."

There's more silence as I purse my lips, unsure of what to say.

"But as the eldest son, I had no choice when my father died." The muscles on his back flex as his arms rest behind him. "I hate living within boundaries. I learnt at a young age that I have none."

"No, you don't." I laugh, but his face doesn't change, and I realise he didn't mean it in the way I thought he did.

"I don't like to live my life by rules, Aries."

I nod, the air seeming thicker between us.

"I've bent the rules for as long as I can remember, and now I break them because I have mastered them." He looks over to me, his eyes dark, sending a shiver down my spine.

"Dominic wasn't a true king." A sinister smile creeping across his face. "And that's why he's buried six feet deep." He talks about his father without feeling as if he wasn't bound to him by blood.

"He was your father," I whisper, and he chuckles.

"Dominic was many things, but a father remains low on that list." His voice drips with disdain, mimicking my own feelings in my chest about my own father.

"I guess we have that in common." I rest my head on his shoulder and sigh.

He turns to face me, pulling me on top of his lap, and I straddle him. He cups my face in his hands, and it feels like he looks directly into my soul. "I will never let your father hurt you."

My heart tweaks inside my chest at the thought of Ezra's father hurting him. "Is that what Dominic did to you?" I ask, my voice low. "Did he hurt you?"

He closes his eyes and grits his teeth for a second, then presses his lips on mine. "It doesn't matter now, sweetheart," he speaks, his voice coating me in what feels like velvet.

"Because of him, I feel *nothing*," he whispers and a

sinking feeling creeps its way into my chest, but I ignore it. I place my hand on Ezra's chest, and he clasps it within his.

"Isn't it funny that those who we are closest to end up hurting us the most?" I whisper, and he cocks his head to the side. "I spent years growing up with a father who believed I was a waste of space." I sigh, remembering the exact moment he said this to me. "It was because I refused to give him my hard-earned money to spend on his insatiable habits. I was working in hospitality, a small café in town, and I had just received my weekly pay. It wasn't much, but it was something that I had earned. When I got home, my father asked me for half, said I owed him for living under his roof." Ezra's eyes darken as he listens to me. "Ever since my mother passed away, he was always looking for someone else to blame, someone else to torture." My words slip freely from my mouth as if Ezra was no stranger to me, and I feel at ease being able to explain to an outsider how my father made me feel. "For years, half my pay went to him, and sometimes he would take it all, telling me that I used too much water that week, or making up some bullshit about the electricity bill." My chest constricts as I remember living off a loaf of bread that entire week.

"No child should have a parent dependent on them to survive."

Ezra's words send a knife into my gut, and it all makes sense to me now. That's exactly what my father had done, depended on Giselle and me to survive. The constant emotional abuse and manipulation we suffered whilst living under his roof is not a normal part of childhood, and I always pushed it aside, ignored it because everyone kept telling me *"he's your father,"* as if that means something when the person who's supposed to support and protect you treats you worse than a parent ever should.

"Although he never hit me——"

"Stop belittling it. Emotional abuse is still abuse," he interjects.

I bite the skin on my bottom lip, considering his words.

"Tell me what else he did." He pulls me into him, his eyes never leaving mine.

I hesitate for a moment, not wanting to share more in fear of his judgement, but it feels good to tell him. Right here, in his arms is the safest I've felt in a really long time, and what could it hurt if I told him? We'd be divorced and never have to look at each other soon enough anyway. That's what he said after all.

I sigh, closing my eyes and remembering parts of my childhood I had tried so hard to forget. "He used to hit my mother a lot," I confess. "She would always hide my sister and I in the cupboard and give us our dolls when she knew he was going to come home from work because it was always the same." I pause. "He would come home, throw his bag on the chair and shout at my mother, asking her why the smallest things weren't done. Then, when she says she was tired, or looking after Giselle and I, he would hit her and tell her that it wasn't good enough, that she needed to do better because this was her role as a mother."

His nostrils flare as he listens.

"One night, I woke up to the sound of their screams echoing through the hall…" I shift in his lap, the memory overwhelming me. "I walked out of my bedroom, afraid because they were shouting and just wanted comfort from my mother. Then I saw her kneeling on the floor, clutching her jaw, blood splattered all over her blouse."

"How old were you?"

My lip wobbles as my heart breaks for the child in me. "Seven, I think."

He captures my lips with his. "Do not waste a single tear on inferior men like your father, sweetheart." His lips hover over mine, his arms wrapping around me. "We are all broken in our own way, and it's up to us to decide if it's worth staying broken or to mend those cracks and fortify them."

"When I met you at that wedding, I saw something in you that I see in myself…" His eyes graze down to my chest slowly and back up to meet my eyes. "I saw a woman who had been dealt a hand in life and played the cards to her will. It's time you realise the power that you have."

CHAPTER TEN

Ezra

Thunder cracks in the sky outside as I lay here awake, alone with my thoughts. After our talk, Aries drifted off to sleep in my arms, and I let her be because the truth is, I want her to remain in my arms. My mind floats back to London and what my men would be doing right now, running in shipments, searching for a way to make the Brayfords beg for our forgiveness. The problem with the mafia is once you're in, there is no out. There are no second chances, and there's definitely no freedom. You learn this at a young age as you grow into the family and uncover the secrets hidden within generations. I never considered wanting a way out because I know deep within me, it's who I am meant to be.

A feared leader.

I don't mind being that for our family, but what rubs me the wrong way is when someone blatantly disrespects our power. The same power we've held for years. Someone always wants a bigger piece of the pie, no matter what their share is already. The world we're a part of is filled with greed, and there isn't anything in the world that will change that. We take what we want when we want it.

I feel Aries stir within my arms as she murmurs something. It's always been this way for me, unable to sleep, plagued with the thoughts of the future. Right now, it's my father's revenge, but tomorrow or the next day, it'll be something different. There's never a moment when everything is just.

"Why?" Aries mumbles as she begins to sob, and it isn't until I look down that I notice she's still dreaming.

I shift beside her, turning to my side, tucking her hair behind her ears. "Sweetheart?"

She slowly opens her eyes as tears stream out of them, realising she was dreaming. I grit my teeth, wanting to know everything that's going through her mind, even her subconscious. I want to know her. I want to know what's making her feel this way, even in her sleep.

"Want to tell me what that was about?" I ask, hoping she will open up to me.

"It's not important," she whispers as she wipes away her tears.

I decide not to push her, even though I want to be the one dominating her dreams, instead of whatever is plaguing her.

She scoots closer to me, burying her head beneath my chin, into my neck, and I slide my arm over her waist, pulling her in closer. After what seems like endless hours have passed, I finally drift off to sleep.

CHAPTER ELEVEN
Aries

The ice in my glass clinks as I bring my cocktail glass to my mouth for a sip, my eyes never leaving Ezra for a minute as he sits directly in front of me. The rest of our stay in the cabin consisted of plenty of hot sex, shower sex, bed sex, wood sex, every single sex you can possibly imagine. It wasn't that the sex was bad with my ex. It's that it lacked something, something that I knew should be there but wasn't. The problem was that I was too afraid to speak up, to let him know that I wanted more, more excitement, more passion, just *more*. I was never one to believe sex like this could exist, let alone happen to me, but here I am, sitting across from the King, in his plane, heading back to his house, planning a fucking wedding all the whilst sleeping with him. My pussy aches, just like he promised. I feel the heat in my cheeks as I think about all the ways he had his way with me, and how I enjoyed every fucking moment of it.

No, stop it.

It's just sex.

Really hot, passionate, dirty, sex.

And that's all it's going to be.

I put my cocktail down, watching as he sits there, on his phone, wearing his black jeans, black button-up shirt, his chain peeking through the open V of his shirt. His eyes meet mine, catching me.

Shit.

He winks, returning to doing whatever he was doing on his phone.

God help me.

"So, how does this work again? We just show up to dinner, eat, and then what?" I ask, fiddling with the hem of my skirt.

His dark eyes look up to me, softening. "Let's get one thing straight, sweetheart. I don't give a *fuck* what anyone thinks about this marriage. It's fucking happening…and if anyone decides to cross me, I'll show them why I cover my face with the mask of the King." A sly grin forms on his face. "I'm not taking you to this dinner for them to approve because this marriage is happening whether they like it or not."

At least when we get back to the UK, I can get back to working, something that always remains constant in my life. No matter how great or shitty my life seems to be going, at least I'll always have work to fall back on, to distract me, and right now, I need the distraction from Ezra. The more I let myself get close to him, the more I feel myself changing. I feel myself starting to wonder some dangerous things, like, what would be so bad about wanting Ezra?

What would be so bad about being in his life permanently?

My rational side knows this, and yet, something within me is still curious, and I can't exactly blame myself for it because just look at this man. He's what any woman would dream of.

"Talk to me." His eyes graze my thighs as he watches me. "I need a distraction right now."

"Uh-okay." I try to think of something on the spot and say the first thing that comes to me. "I'm allergic to bees."

His eyebrows come together. "What?"

"Yeah, I got stung by a bee when I was in school, and my entire throat closed up within minutes of the sting."

He continues listening intently to my babbling.

"Luckily one of the teachers had an EpiPen with them on duty. Without her I most likely would not have survived."

He grunts, picking up his phone, quickly sending a message, and putting it back down.

"Why didn't you tell me this earlier?" He leans forward on his elbows. "What if you had been stung whilst we were at the cabin?" His jaw clenches.

"I—"

"Is there anything else I should know?" he questions, and I can't tell if he's angry with me.

"No."

He leans back into his chair, picking up his phone and returning to whatever he was doing.

What the fuck was that about?

Trying not to think too much into his reaction, I pick up my bag from the floor and pull out the book I took from the cabin. He quickly raises his eyes to look at me then to the book, and I swear I see his lip curl into a small smile before his face returns to serious again.

An hour passes, and I'm feeling a little bored as I stare out the window at the white clouds, wondering how I'm going to pull this off…how I'm going to keep this nagging feeling in my gut at bay.

I glance over at Ezra who is working away on his laptop, his Rolex glimmering in the light flowing through the windows. I'm not used to a life like this, a life of luxury. Giselle and I grew up surviving off crackers and noodles, and here I am in a private jet with leather seats.

I have no idea what I'm doing, and all I can hope is that I'm doing the right thing, for Giselle and my future. What I do know, though, is that was probably the best sex I've ever had. The way Ezra knew exactly what to do with my body and the way he praised me had me melting into a damn puddle.

I stand and make my way toward the back of the plane, coming across a door. I assume it's a bedroom, given it's completely private. Opening the door, I enter and close it behind me. Something catches my eye in the corner where the storage cupboard is, and I walk closer to it, opening the door.

My brows pull in as I examine the leather straps now in my hands, turning them over and trying to make sense of what it is. I place them back and pull out a wand of some sort, curious as to what it does. The handle rattles as Ezra walks in, and I quickly place the item back into the cupboard, closing the door and moving beside the bed. I watch as he enters the room, a smirk playing on his lips.

"Curious, are we?" he mocks.

"No, just bored," I say sarcastically.

"Hmm." He moves closer to me, his hand snaking around my waist. "I think I might have a cure for that." He reaches to the side and opens the cupboard. The room is relatively small, given it's a private jet, making everything easily accessible. He pulls out the leather bands I had in my hands earlier and holds them between us. "Do you know what these are?" he asks.

I shake my head, feeling silly.

"They're used for binding your arms to your thighs," he says, my eyes widening, finally understanding what the bands are used for. "I guess you've never tried it before, have you?"

"No." I swallow, excitement building within me at the thought of him binding me and fucking me up in the air. As if sensing my thoughts, he turns me around, my ass now pressing into his front, feeling his already hard cock pressing into me.

"Do you want to?" he whispers into my ear, causing my nipples to peak underneath my bra. "We have an hour until we land…we could do a lot in those sixty minutes." His voice vibrates through me as I bite my bottom lip.

I nod, wanting—no, needing—to feel him again. He tosses the cuffs onto the bed as he begins to remove my clothes. I'm down to my bra and panties whilst he's fully clothed. Slowly he walks me over to the bed, and instructs me to remove my bra, which I do, dropping it to the floor. His eyes move to my breasts as his brows pull in.

"You are truly so fucking beautiful," he whispers. "Take off your panties and get on the bed." I do as he says, now fully naked, laying on the bed. He grabs the cuffs from beside me and begins to fasten my upper arm with one end of the leather cuff and places the other on my thigh, pulling my thigh to my arm. He does the same to the other side, exposing my pussy to him completely as my knees bend, my legs cuffed to my arms.

He pulls out the wand I had in my hand earlier and holds it out to the side. "This may be too much for you, but I know for a fact you're going to enjoy it." He smirks as my chest heaves, so many thoughts bouncing through my mind. I lick my lips as he pulls me by my hips, towards the edge of the bed, my ass now almost hanging off. He runs his two fingers against my pussy, and I feel my body reacting to him.

"So wet already, sweetheart." He smirks, bringing his fingers to his mouth, and a low groan rumbles through his throat. "I can't wait to break you," he whispers, sending a lightning bolt of fear down my spine. "But right now, I want to show you how good I can make you feel."

He lowers the wand to my inner thigh, and I scream out as a shock zaps against my skin. He repeats the action on the other side, and I yelp as it makes contact with my skin. I feel my pussy pulse in tandem with my heart as heat rises inside my belly. The fact that he's still fully clothed and playing with me like a toy turns me on so much more than I ever thought it would. He lowers the wand to my pussy, and my eyes snap shut as a zap stings my clit. I cry out in pain and pleasure as he chuckles. My breathing picks up, my chest now heaving.

He unzips his pants and pulls out his cock, giving it a few strokes whilst watching me. "Oh fuck, I can't help myself." He pumps again, his cock growing in his hand. "Looking at you, bound on my bed, your pussy glistening with the arousal I pull from you makes me so fucking hard."

He moves on top of me, still fully clothed and straddles me with his thighs on either side of my face.

"Now open your mouth." I do as he says, and he grips the hair on the top of my head, pulling me down onto his cock. "Fuck…" he groans as the tip of his cock hits the back of my throat. I moan as I feel my arousal heighten at the sounds of his pleasure. His cock is not even halfway into my mouth, and it already feels too big, too much.

He pushes himself further, and I gag. He pulls out, giving me a second to breathe. "We will work on that, sweetheart." The way he calls me sweetheart and uses me like a toy does something to me that I will never understand. It makes me needier, hornier, and all I want is him.

"Ezra, please," I begin to beg, and I no longer know myself.

He chuckles, moving off me, and I watch as he slowly lowers himself to his knees beside the bed, his face between my legs.

"Open wide," he demands, and I obey, spreading my legs as much as they will go. "More." He pushes my thighs down further, and I cry out in pain. His hands land on my inner thighs, leaving a sting behind. "If you're going to have my mouth on you, you're going to need to work for it, sweetheart." I buck my hips at his words, my body begging him for release.

"Please," I whimper.

He lowers his mouth to my pussy as his tongue darts out, flicking my clit, teasing me. I moan and buck my hips again, trying to meet his mouth in desperation. His hands land down hard on my inner thighs again as I cry out.

"Don't fucking move," he warns, and I bite the inside of my lip as tears sting my eyes.

His mouth covers my pussy completely, and I almost pass out from the intense pleasure as he sucks hard on my clit. I whimper as his tongue dives into me, and back out, licking me from my entrance to my clit. I suck in a breath as I feel his two fingers enter me, his tongue flicking my clit.

He curls his fingers inside me and begins to fuck me with them. I close my eyes as euphoria builds within me, threatening to tip over at any moment as he hits all the right spots.

Bright lights dance in my vision as my moans rip through the air.

He slides his fingers out of me, and before I know it, I feel the tip of his cock at my entrance. "Breathe, sweetheart. I'm not done with you yet." He grips the hair on the top of my head, yanking my head up, and I watch as his cock slides into me. "I want you to watch every inch of me fill you up." He pushes inside me further, stretching me. "I want you to watch as I take my pleasure from you, and I want to watch you enjoy every fucking second of it." He thrusts deep into me as I cry out, his cock filling me up completely. I breathe through my mouth as my chest heaves, watching him fuck me.

"Look at you, taking me so fucking well." He begins to create a rhythm, moving against me and watching his cock move in and out of me. "Such a good fucking girl," he praises, and if I weren't bound, I would immediately drop to my knees for him. His voice alone is enough to spur arousal within me.

He thrusts into me harder, jolting my body further into the bed. "I want you so fucking bad." He releases my hair and grips behind my knees, pushing my knees further apart as he slams into me. "I want to fuck you until my name drips from your lips and my cum fills your tight little hole." He growls as he looks down to my pussy. "Fuck, sweetheart. I can't stop watching your pussy swallow my cock."

A breathy moan leaves my throat as he thrusts into me faster, and I pull on the cuffs, wanting to touch him. I love the way he feels inside me, taking me in the way he wants, unapologetically.

"Ezra, it feels so g-good…" I whimper.

"I love it when you say my name," he groans as he thrusts. "Now I want you to fucking scream it." He slams into me harder, his fingers digging into my skin as he holds me open. My nipples harden as he moves in and out of me, and my core clenches, my eyes rolling back into my head.

"Ezra!" A scream rips through my throat as I feel his cock harden inside me.

"Fuck!" He groans as he continues to thrust into me. "You drive me fucking crazy," he growls as he slams into me with force, and I feel his cock twitch inside me. He stands there, panting as he watches me, still bound and helpless lying on his bed. He slides out of me slowly, and I feel his cum dripping from my pussy.

Sex with Ezra is explosive and all-encompassing. There is no room left for anything else.

He slides two fingers inside me again and pulls them out, both our arousals coating his fingers. "Open your mouth, sweetheart," I slowly open my mouth, and he places his fingers inside. "Taste that?" he asks, a smile playing on his lips. "That's the taste of true power. Mine and yours, combined."

Sliding my arm through the dress, I look into the mirror and smooth the silky satin over my hips. Looping my earrings into my ears, I take a deep breath.

It doesn't matter if they like you or not.

This is a business transaction, and nothing more.

There's a knock on the bedroom door before it slides open, revealing a very handsome Ezra, dressed in a suit, and I get the feeling this is his usual look, compared to his casual and very laid-back look at the cabin. Once we returned, I ended up having to tell Giselle and my father that I was getting married. My father responded just as I thought he would, didn't really give a shit as long as he had his beer in his hand. Giselle, though, was a little more hesitant. Obviously because she hadn't even met the guy before, she was sceptical of the entire thing. It killed me having to lie to my sister, basically the only other person in my life who I truly trust and talk to, but if this was part of the deal, I had to take it.

Ezra walks into the bedroom, his beautiful brown eyes softening as he takes me in.

"Are you ready to go?" he asks, walking into the room.

"In a minute." I hesitate, biting my bottom lip.

"What's wrong, sweetheart?"

I take a deep breath and voice my concern. "What if they don't like me?"

A smile curves into his lips, and all I can think about are his hands on me, my skin starting to itch in the places he has touched,

"I can save you some time and tell you right now they won't." His arm slides around my waist, his hand resting on my lower back. "But I don't give a fuck." His other hand comes up to tuck a stray strand of hair behind my ear. "I wanted *you* because I knew they wouldn't approve."

"But why?" I ask, looking into his delicious shadowy eyes.

"Because I am not one to do what I am told, sweetheart, unless it's you begging for my cock." He rakes his lips over mine, never truly kissing me, just teasing me. "Better put on your best show tonight."

My chest squeezes at his words. That's all this was. A show.

Why would I expect anything else? That's what we agreed on, wasn't it?

It was a short drive from Ezra's place to his family's house, but nevertheless, I spent every moment of it thinking about how to do exactly that, put on the best show of my life, and it didn't help that I had close to no idea what I was about to walk into.

We pull into the drive, and Ezra helps me up the steps into the house. The house is magnificent—large, bright, and fancy. Fancier than any house I have stepped into, that's for sure. I watch as a tall figure emerges from the stairs on the right side of the entry, a similar jawline, slightly lighter hair than Ezra's, same dark eyes with full lips. I can see the similarity between them which leads me to think this is his younger brother, Nicholas.

"Welcome to the family, sis." He winks at me, grabbing my hand, he brings it up to his lips as his eyes stare at Ezra, a small smirk on his lips. "How much did he pay you?" He drops my hand and looks me up and down, as if he's trying to scan me for something I'm hiding.

"Don't be a dick, Nico." Ezra shoulders him as he walks through the door, pulling me alongside him. I watch as Nico laughs and bows sarcastically, motioning for me to go ahead. He walks close behind me. I can feel his breath on the back of my neck as he whispers.

"Good luck."

If I wasn't feeling nervous before this, I sure as fuck am now.

"Aries! Ah, you must be Aries!" I hear a woman say as

we emerge from the doorway into a large dining and kitchen area. She makes her way to me, her heels clicking and clacking on the floor. She's a little shorter than I am, but her dress probably costs more than my kidney, and the style she oozes is unmatched.

"Ciao, uh yes, I'm Aries." I smile my best showmanship smile I can muster as she pulls me in for a hug. "You must be Ezra's mama."

"Please, call me Andrea." She motions for us to take a seat at the table. Ezra pulls out my chair for me. As I sit, he takes a seat next to me. There's a loud crowd of people talking which emerges from outside, slowly getting louder as they near the door. I watch as five people walk into the dining room, arguing about something, but I have no idea what they're saying as they're all speaking Italian.

"*Prendete posto tutti!*" Andrea yells what I assume means sit down, as they all begin taking their seats around the large dinner table. Nico takes a seat on the other side of me, leaning in to whisper in my ear again.

"These are all of our cousins." He smiles. "Vincenzo, Leo, Matteo, Marco, and Carlo." He points them out, but I'm sure I will forget their names in about a minute. "They're all here to judge you and your *so-called engagement* to Ezra."

Fuck, what was his problem?

"So, Ezra, how's the hunt coming along?" One of them asks, more like a challenge than a question.

"Always lovely to see you, Matteo. How's the leg?" Ezra smirks as Matteo's face falls instantly. Must be some sort of inside joke because I don't get it.

Nico leans into my ear again. "Ezra shot Matteo for speaking out of turn, looks like he hasn't learnt his lesson." He chuckles.

Okay, I really need to take this up a notch, all these eyes are on me, and I need to make it known that Ezra is indeed my man, and we are in love. I snake my hand through his under the table, and he interlocks his fingers with mine, bringing my hand up to his lips, kissing my knuckles as his eyes never leave Matteo's.

"So, Aries, what do you do for work?" another one of them asks, but he cuts me off before I can answer. "But I guess it doesn't matter now, does it?" He smirks, thinking he's funny.

"Actually, yes it does, you see, that's how we met." I look at Ezra, leaning in to give him a peck on the lips. "My dress got stuck on some metal at your cousin's wedding." Ezra's hand leaves mine to rest on my thigh, lightly massaging it. "I didn't want to rip the dress, so I was trying my best to get out of the snag without doing so, then Ezra came and had absolutely no regard for the dress whatsoever." Matteo's smirk slowly disappears as I tell the story. "Then he rips it and asks for a thank you."

"I did help you." He smirks as he lays one on me, and if his whole family wasn't here right now, I would probably straddle him.

"You ripped my dress and made me look like a hooker." I smile as one of his cousin's whistles.

"Looked better if you ask me," he says as his mother takes a seat beside him, her eyes falling onto his hand on my thigh.

"Hell yeah, I bet it did." One of them says, and Ezra gives them the filthiest look I have ever seen on his face. His cousin's hands immediately come up. "I take it back, don't shoot me." He chuckles.

"Alright boys, that's enough. Aries will be part of our

lives now so let's not give her a hard time," she says, with the fakest smile I think I have ever seen.

The rest of the dinner feels like a fucking interrogation. How many siblings do you have? How much money do you make? What's your intentions for five years into the future? What did you eat last?

By the time the end of the night rolls around, I'm exhausted and just want to sleep. I'm sure enough that all our PDA made it quite evident we were engaged *for real.*

Although, I got the feeling Nico and Andrea didn't really agree with it, Nico was accepting regardless, and I kind of liked him—he seemed light-hearted compared to the rest of the family, who was always so fucking serious about everything. Nico joked and gave me some good insights into Ezra, like how when he's got a lot on his mind, it's best to leave him be.

"Do you think it worked?" I ask, watching his hand resting on the steering wheel, driving us back to his place.

"I don't give a fuck if it did or not." He looks to me, his eyes dark. "You're going to be my wife, and if anyone has a problem with that, there's an easy solution." He smiles, and the dark of the night makes it seem terrifying, eerily sinister, and psychotic.

I know Giselle doesn't agree, and she knows there's something shifty going on because who the fuck buys a house for someone just out of the blue, and then her sister announces she's marrying that said someone the week after?

Regardless of what she thinks, I need to make this work. I somewhat feel like I'm forced to do this because of what Ezra's done for my family, and part of me likes that about him—whether or not he did it so I would agree to his proposal, or just because he felt like it. Anyway, it doesn't matter, it's done now, and I need to play my part.

The good, doting mafia wife.

I stare at the wedding dress sprawled across the hotel bed, and the foulest of feelings sprawl in my belly.

My heart thumps beneath my chest, threatening to break through my paper-thin ribs. I watch the clock on the wall, hearing the seconds tick by as the antique clock continues to work, nothing fazing its movements. It's almost one p.m., and the ceremony is already delayed by half an hour because he's late. I look over to my sister Giselle, who's dressed in her blush pink bridesmaid dress, watching me.

"He'll be here," she promises, but I don't believe it for a second.

I feel my heart break slowly with each minute that passes, the slow realisation setting in that he is not coming. I rip the pins out of my hair, one by one, launching them across the room, tears stinging behind my eyes as I struggle to undo the zipper of my dress. Giselle stands, a worried look on her face.

"Okay, okay." She tries to grab my hands. "Let's calm down." She tries to control my rage, but it's too late. I feel it brimming, begging for release.

I let out a scream, a toe-curling, shiver inducing scream that fills the entire room, and I'm pretty sure all the guests heard it too. I wipe my lipstick off my lips with the back off my hand and grab my dress with both hands, so I won't trip, and I run.

I run out of the church and onto the road, with no destination in sight.

I feel the wind in my face and my hair, pushing my tears to the side of my face. My throat closes up again as I remember what I'm running from.

Embarrassment, heartbreak, disappointment, you name it, I feel it.

I drop to my knees, in my ball gown wedding dress, in the middle of some park, and cover my face with both hands, giving in to my tears. I feel myself breaking, and I don't know how to stop it.

I feel my heartbeat quicken, my knees feeling weak. I stumble over to the bathroom, bile surging up to my throat as I grab the toilet bowl and hurl the entire contents of my stomach into it.

I can't do this.

I feel myself start to sweat; my palms are beginning to feel clammy as I try to swallow down the urge to vomit again.

There's a knock at the door, and Giselle's voice filters through.

"Hey, I just came to see if you need help getting into your dress. Your fiancé was insisting on seeing you, but you know, it's bad luck to see the bride before the wedding."

I don't respond because my mind is too focused on fighting off this anxiety attack. A few moments pass before she knocks again.

"Aries, are you okay in there?" she asks and still no reply from me. I grasp the edge of the basin and force myself up from the floor. I hold on to the basin as if I'm breaking and crumbling all over again. I hear muffled voices from the door, one of them sounds familiar, but my head feels light until I can no longer make out my own reflection in the mirror in front of me.

CHAPTER TWELVE
Ezra

"No, wait you can't go in there, it's bad luck." Her sister tries to stop me, but like hell she will.

"I don't give a fuck about a stupid fucking tradition!" I yell as I take a few steps back from the door.

My foot crashes into the door, and it flies open, ricocheting into the wall behind it. I run into the room, looking around for Aries, but the room is empty. My heart sinks as my eyes catch a glimpse of a body gripping onto the basin in the bathroom.

"Aries?" I walk over to her, but she doesn't answer me. I reach for her, and she collapses into my arms, her body going limp.

"Someone fucking get the paramedics in here!" I yell as I push her hair that's stuck to her face, feeling her pulse weaken under my fingers on her throat. She mumbles something, fleeting in and out of consciousness. "It's okay. I've got you." I see streak marks in her makeup beside her eyes, created from her tears, and it ignites pure wrath and chaos within me.

Was she in here alone?

What was she upset about?

After a few moments, the paramedics hustle inside the room and check her pulse, they put her on some IVs and check her oxygen levels as she slowly opens her eyes, latching onto my arm.

"What happened?" Her voice is hoarse, her eyes looking at me, searching for an answer.

"Miss Alterio, it seems you've fainted." One of the paramedics speaks directly to her. "Everything looks okay. Your blood pressure is a little on the lower end, but other than that, all other checks were normal."

"Do you know why she may have fainted?" I ask.

"It could be a multitude of reasons, low blood pressure being one, but if you're under a lot of stress, Miss Alterio, that could be another reason."

She tries to sit up and looks down. "Oh my god," she whispers as a rosy tint flushes across her cheeks as she realises what she's wearing. I take off my jacket and wrap it around her. Not because I care if she's embarrassed, but I don't want those two pervy fucks looking at my wife.

Giselle passes a glass of water to Aries, and I nod to her to leave. Once everyone has left the room, I pick her up off the floor, into my arms.

"I don't think this is necessary." She looks at me with her beautiful doe eyes, and something inside me ignites at the closeness of her body. "I can walk. I'm okay." I don't listen to her as I walk to the bed and place her on it gently. I catch her eyes fleeting to her wedding dress on the other side of the bed and back at me.

Was she having second thoughts?

"Are you going to tell me, or am I going to force it out of you?" I grit my teeth as I sit beside her.

"Do you promise not to react?" she asks.

Fuck no.

"I promise." I lie, and she tells me every single detail of how he left her, how she felt, and what she did. My knuckles go white as my hands flex. I look away from her, already thinking about how to rid this parasite named Ray from this world. It's one thing to give someone a promise, but to renege is one of the quickest ways to show the world you're a fucking coward.

"You promised," she says as she watches me.

"You ask me not to react, then you tell me about the most traumatising time in your life. Did you truly think I wouldn't?" I look back to her as she cradles the cup of water in both hands.

"It was hard to tell you because it's still such a deep cut within me that hasn't quite healed, and now this," she motions to the white wedding dress on the bed. "It's a lot for me."

"Fine, don't wear the fucking dress," I say, and she raises her eyebrow. "I'm serious. I don't give a single fuck if you're wearing a wedding dress or not."

"What would I wear though?"

"Whatever the fuck you want." I smile, trying to ease her mind about the situation and praying like hell to a god I don't believe that she will not bail on me.

"Seriously?" she asks, questioning me.

"As long as you're standing up there, swearing before everyone that you belong to me, I give no fucks as to what's on your body," I admit, and it's the truth.

I watch the church fill with guests, the same church where I met Aries, and although I'd been here before, it looks different today. Today, it's filled with my men, dressed in black suits, and mafia women, wearing their finest outfits, and red roses adorning the church all around.

I don't believe in marriage. I never did.

For us, it's about securing the line, ensuring the Casella fortune doesn't fall into the hands of others, mainly our enemies. Formalities such as a wedding and a ceremony are just for show. No one in our family really wants to be married to who they're marrying. It's a marriage of necessity.

I'm putting that shit to rest today because like fuck am I going to marry a woman I didn't like on some level or feel attracted to. This thing with Aries, I have no idea what it is, but I feel like if I can't marry this woman, and if she's not mine, I don't want anyone else to have her. Even the thought of the possibility of someone else makes my skin crawl.

I stand here at the altar, as Nico points out all the women he's fucked in the guests, and I roll my eyes. This guy can never be serious for even one moment, but it's better to have him like this than drunk or high.

"Have you decided who your mistress will be, brother?" He snickers in my ear.

"Fuck off, Nico, not today." I shrug him off. "Be serious, for just a minute of your slutty life, please."

"Wow, a please from the King? She must be a good fuck if she's getting you to say shit like that." His grin widens, making me want to punch him in his perfect teeth.

The music starts as the guests stand, all of us turning to the large doors of the church, waiting for the bride to appear. My palms start to itch as I shift from one foot to another. It's an odd feeling, considering I don't usually react or feel anything anymore.

She appears, and I release a breath I didn't realise I was holding. I watch as she strides through the doors in a red silky dress, the one I bought for her as an apology for ripping hers. My mouth almost drops just like it did the first night I saw her in it. She's fucking breathtaking, and she doesn't know what she does to me. What no one else has ever been able to do for me.

There are a few gasps from the guests watching her walk down the aisle in a non-traditional wedding dress. Looks of disapproval crawl onto their faces, and it just makes me so much prouder of her.

She reaches me, her hands reaching for mine immediately. I give her a supportive wink as she watches me and takes a deep breath in, trying to steady her breath.

The priest begins to recite his words, and all I can think about is her red dress pooled around her waist, hair in disarray, my cock inside her, making her scream my name as I pound into her perfect cunt. I push those thoughts out of my head, realising my dick is now semi-hard.

Someone amongst the guests gasps as a loud bang echoes through the church, making Aries jump. My head snaps toward the large doors of the church to find a man dressed in a blue suit, walking down the aisle.

Does this motherfucker have a death wish?

He reaches the altar and stops, dropping to his knees, and Aries grips my arm so tightly that her nails dig into my skin through my tux.

"Aries, please, don't marry him." He looks straight up into her eyes, and although I admire his courage to come here and admit he fucked up, which I'm assuming he's about to, I can't walk past the blatant disrespect of walking into *my* wedding and talking to *my* wife.

Henry and Nico both point their guns at him as he looks from one to the other, his eyes going wide. I motion to them to lower their weapons because I'm intrigued to hear what he has to say, even if I'll be slicing his mouth off later.

"Well, go on, what did you come here to say? I think we'd all love to hear it." I slide my arm around Aries's waist and pull her into me, watching Ray come up with something to say because I doubt he would have written it down beforehand.

"Aries, I—" he begins, and stops, looking from me to her. "I'm sorry." A laugh erupts from my throat, a manic, psychotic laugh, and the entire church goes silent as Aries stiffens in my arms.

I step toward him and circle him like a shark would circle its prey.

"So, Ray, let me get this straight. You came here today, to apologise?" I ask.

"No, I came here to ask her not to marry you."

I nod, pretending to care about why the fuck he came here because he's not fucking leaving without something that's broken.

"You object to this union?" the priest asks, and Ray nods.

"You know, I wasn't particularly in the mood for blood today, and I especially didn't want to stain the shirt that I will be fucking my wife in later tonight, but I've got to ask, are you fucking stupid?" I ask as Aries runs down the steps and grips onto me.

"Ezra, don't," she pleads, but it's no use. My mind is already made up.

I watch as Ray swallows the last piece of courage he had left. Taking out my gun, I aim at his head, directly between his eyes, feeling my grip on my gun tighten in my hand.

His eyes squeeze shut, chest hammering in and out as he makes peace with his fate.

I pull the trigger, screams, gasps, and shrieks filling the

church as Ray grips his thigh in pain, wailing around on the floor, looking like a fish out of water.

I wanted to shoot him in the head, but having Aries's grip on me, I couldn't, something held me back, and I don't like it. I don't like the sort of control this woman is beginning to have over me.

"Let it be known whoever has an issue with this union, has an issue with me. Take this as a warning, that if you so much as *look* at my wife with disrespect, you will be met with the barrel of my gun, and the next time I pull the trigger, it will be directly into your skull." I talk to the entire church, with my last words aimed at Ray. "I don't give second chances often, so I suggest you take it."

I walk back up the stairs, pulling Aries with me. A few people begin to help Ray up, and I turn around to them, giving them a look they know not to fuck with.

"He can watch." A smirk plays on my lips as he continues to cry in pain. Aries looks to Ray, then to me, and I can't decipher what she may be thinking. I've either lost her trust completely by showing her exactly who I am, or she's captivated with the power that comes with being a Casella.

CHAPTER THIRTEEN
Aries

My hands tremble beside me as I watch Ray writhing in pain on the floor of the church, for everyone to see. I knew Ezra had power, but this just didn't cross my mind, and it should have. I should have known something like this would happen. Whilst I'm glad Ezra didn't kill Ray, I feel a little confused as to how I feel about Ezra shooting him. Realisation rushes over me that marrying Ezra would be like this, bloodshed almost every day of the week, and I think I forgot who I was marrying when we spent those wonderful days in his cabin, away from reality.

Could I handle it?

"And do you Miss Alterio take Ezra Casella to be your lawfully wedded husband, in sickness and in health, until death do you part?" The priest speaks to me, but all I can see are Ezra's dark eyes, peering into my soul, consuming me from within. His jaw ticks as he waits for me to answer, and I let go of a breath I've been holding.

"I do." I breathe, his facial muscles relaxing, a devilish twinkle in his eyes as he smirks.

"I now pronounce you husband and wife, you may kiss the bride." The priest moves out of the way as Ezra pulls me into him and, to give the last dramatic effect, kisses me like he's been starved of my lips. The church erupts in clapping and whistles, and you'd think someone wasn't just shot in the leg a moment ago, the entire thing forgotten.

Because now the King has a wife.

Me.

I feel the blood rush back to my toes as I remove both of my high heels and place them on the floor. The night went unexpectedly quick, lots of people congratulating us, giving us money, wishing us well. Most of them were quite nice, although some were a little snarky, but I didn't let that bother me, and I tried to enjoy my fake wedding as best I could.

I fell asleep as Henry drove us to Ezra's holiday house, and when I woke up, I had no idea how long I'd been asleep or how far away we were from London until Ezra mentioned we were just past Windsor. The house was a little older than the one he has in London, you could tell it looked a little tired, but my jaw instantly dropped when we walked up to the house, which was on a vast amount of land, that much I could tell even though it was dark.

I watch as Ezra uncuffs his shirt sleeves and begins unbuttoning his shirt.

"Were you going to shoot Ray?" I ask, feeling the slight tension between us.

"I *did* shoot him," he answers, now with his shirt off, the dim lighting of the room accentuating his buff frame, tall and hard in all the right places.

"You know what I mean."

His jaw tenses as he turns and walks toward me, standing in front of me, he places his finger under my chin and tilts my face up to meet his gaze. "I would have ended his life without batting an eye."

My breathing hitches at his touch, a wave of energy coursing through me. "Why didn't you?" I ask, and he turns away from me, walking over to the dresser, placing his Rolex on top.

"Aries, if there's one thing I know, it's that I'm not afraid to kill." He turns back to me, his eyes piercing into mine as he walks over and places his hand on my cheek. "I've had a lot of blood on these hands over the years, and I'm not afraid to have more." His eyes fall to my lips, and I can't help but bite down on my bottom lip, watching him standing there in front of me half naked. "But you've quickly gotten under my skin, sweetheart."

I swallow as I watch his eyes darken, my heart thumps beneath my chest as I begin to stand, closing the distance between us. My hands travel up from his abs to his chiselled pecs, tracing a finger over his tattoo.

"Does this hold significance?" I ask, looking up to him, his hands circle around me, holding me closer to his body.

"It's the Casella crest," he says as his lips trace my jaw, sending a flutter between my legs. The crest is a calligraphy letter C with two guns crossed like a skull and bones, blood dripping from the barrels. His hands move down to my ass, grabbing me through my dress. "Why are you still wearing this?" He starts pawing at my dress, groaning as his dick presses into my stomach.

"You don't like it?" My breathing accelerates as my hands roam his broad shoulders.

"I'd like it better pooled around your waist." His lips crash into mine, stealing the air in my lungs, not giving me a moment to contest. He pulls one spaghetti strap down my shoulder, and I pull back from him, holding him at a distance.

His eyes roam my face, in search of an answer as to why.

"Maybe we should stop," I breathe as I step to the side and pull the strap back over my shoulder. His eyebrows pull together.

"And why would we do that?" he asks as he walks towards me.

"Because we need to set some boundaries." My heart pounds at his scent now all over me. My body craves his touch, his closeness, but my mind tells me no, denying my body of the ecstasy that is easily within reach.

"Don't you think it's a little too late for that?" He smirks.

"I just think we need to set some boundaries for this to work." I look around the room for something, anything, that will take my gaze off him for even a moment. "For things not to go too far or get too heated."

I feel the heat of his body in front of me, and he pulls my chin up to face him, being anything but gentle. "Is that what you really want?"

My breathing is uneven, as I watch the desire burn in his eyes. "I think it would make it easier for both of us if we kept things strictly professional." My voice almost a whisper. "Like a business agreement."

"Are you telling me the things we did in the cabin were a mistake?"

"No, I—"

He cuts me off. "Your body craves my touch, sweetheart." His hand rakes through my hair, pulling my head back. "You tell yourself I'm the bad guy, the killer, the mafia king," he whispers into my ear, raising the hair on my neck. "But I bet your panties were soaked, watching me point my gun at your ex."

Fuck.

"Because the truth is, you also have darkness within you," he whispers, and I feel my body melt in slow motion as he licks from my collarbone up to my jaw. "You just haven't embraced it yet."

"That's fucked up," I whisper.

"Is it? Or are you too afraid to admit to yourself that you enjoyed it?" he asks, snaking a hand around my waist, grabbing the material of my dress.

"I didn't enjoy it." I try to convince myself more than anything because there was definitely a part of me that did enjoy watching Ray writhe with pain, the same pain he put me through when he abandoned me on what was supposed to be the happiest day of our lives.

"Your mouth says so, but your body says something else." His jaw tenses as he yanks the material from my body, the satin ripping at the seams, pooling on the floor around my legs, leaving me in just my red G-string.

My heart beats between my legs, aching for him to touch me, and before I can comprehend what I'm doing, my hands fly out to his belt buckle, like an animal, and I tear it off him. He crashes his lips into mine and pushes me into the wall, gripping me in all the right places. His hands roam to my breasts, then to my ass, his lips never once leaving mine. His hand snakes between my thighs, caressing my pussy over my panties, and it feels so fucking good to have him on me.

"I was right, wasn't I?" he asks, his hand now inside my panties, massaging my clit. A moan slips from my lips as he inserts two fingers inside me, my hands gripping onto his neck as the world slips out from under me.

"So fucking wet for me, sweetheart," he whispers, his fingers going in deeper.

I grind my hips on his hand, craving the friction. It feels too fucking good to stop now, all my words ring to empty threats now with his fingers inside me.

"It's our wedding night, baby." He licks my lips. "What kind of husband would I be if I didn't fuck you on our wedding night?"

I groan as I continue to grind on his hand, taking what I want and not looking back. He pulls my head back roughly, fisting my hair.

"I crave the way your body shakes, Aries." He breathes me in, his lips beneath my ear as he fucks me with his hand. "The way you pant when my fingers are inside you." His body presses into me, my nipples hardening at the touch. "The way you fuck." I squeeze my eyes shut as the wave of release takes over me, shuddering as I come on his fingers. "The way you taste," he whispers as he pulls his hand out of me, bringing it to his mouth and licking his two fingers that were just inside of me. My toes curl watching him as I imagine his tongue between my legs.

I know I should run.

Hell, I should have run a long time ago, but my legs don't work, and I can't keep lying to myself.

I don't *want* to run.

My heart disobeys my mind yet again as my nails dig into his skin, creating a red trail from his chest, down to his abs. I feel his muscles tense as he sucks in a breath through his teeth, grabbing my wrists with force.

"I want to hear you say it," he speaks, but my mind is still hazy from the orgasm.

"Hmm?" I manage, through hooded eyes.

His hand comes up and closes around my throat,

pushing me into the wall. "I want to hear you say it, sweetheart." He squeezes forcefully and my hands fly up to grip his wrist, the air slowly thinning in my windpipe, the haziness now well and truly gone, replaced by pure adrenaline. I try to speak, but nothing comes out as I claw at his wrist, and that's when I feel his other hand snake into my panties, and something I never thought possible happens next.

It starts to feel good.

He releases the force on my throat slightly, allowing me some air, but doesn't take his hand away. His eyes grow darker. "Use your words, baby." His fingers enter me, causing me to rise on my toes, the already sensitive area quickly beginning to send pulses through my body.

"I want you." My voice comes out in a whisper, barely audible as a smirk curls in the corner of his mouth, his eyes gleaming with a hint of victory.

"Beg," he says, and my eyes go wide.

His jaw tics as he watches me hesitate.

"Please." My mouth salivates as his fingers slide out of me, rubbing my arousal over my pussy, the muscles in my legs tensing as his hand flexes over my throat again.

"Beg harder," he rasps as my nails dig into his wrist, breaking his skin.

My mind flurries as I try to breathe, his hand like a vise around my throat. My vision begins to dim, and just when I think I see stars, he loosens his grip as I gasp for air.

I feel my arousal slide down my thigh, and embarrassment seeps into my gut, heat rising to my cheeks.

How can this turn me on so much?

The power.

The domination.

The submission.

Everything about this is masochistic, and yet, my body is enjoying it, even when my mind is playing catch up.

He watches me intently, as I look down, and his eyes follow.

He slides his hand over my pussy, feeling how drenched I am.

"Mmmm." He growls. "Is this turning you on, sweetheart?" He grabs my wrist and whirls me around, my ass now pressed firmly on his pants and the entire length of his body pressed into mine as my hands plant into the wall. "If I didn't know better, I'd say you like it when I'm rough." I feel him move away slightly then hear something fall to the floor, and when he presses against me again, I feel his bare skin on mine. I hear the sound of material ripping as he discards what's left of my panties straight onto the floor. He pushes his hard, thick cock against my pussy, my nipples hardening against the cold wall as his hand snakes around and massages my clit.

"Please." I don't know what I'm begging for, but I know I want it.

Bad.

"Please, Ezra." I begin panting.

"Have I told you how much I love it when you beg?" he whispers into my ear, his hot breath fanning my neck. "How much I love the way your cheeks redden whenever I make you come?"

I feel the tip of his cock right at my pussy, and I push myself back into him, wanting him inside me already. He chuckles and pulls both my wrists behind me, holding them in place with one hand, resting on my lower back, whilst the other fists my hair, pulling my neck backward with a jerk.

"Patience, baby. By the time you go to sleep tonight, I'll know every curve of your body, every line and scar on your skin." He nips at my ear. "And every inch inside your warm, wet cunt." He pushes his large cock inside me without warning, groaning as he reaches the hilt. I gasp at the feeling of fullness, his dick so deep inside me it almost hurts.

I never knew what I was missing sexually until Ezra came into my life, and I feel like it would be a continuous ride with him, a ride into the abyss, all senses heightened except our sight. I understand now why women love giving up control to their partners in the bedroom, the amount of pressure that is taken away once we give up power is freeing.

Ezra's deep groans fill my ears as he thrusts in and out of me, pushing my breasts deeper into the wall. I make the mistake of trying to pull my arms out of his hold, and his hand comes down hard on my ass as my scream echoes throughout the room.

"Move your arms again, and I will tie you to the bed." He growls in a breath as his body slams into me hard. I don't dare argue because now my arms are going slightly numb from the pressure.

A moan escapes my mouth as he leans forward, kissing the nape of my neck, thrusting his dick inside me to the hilt.

"From this day forth, this pussy is mine," he whispers, his breath fanning my skin. He releases my arms, and I slap my hands on the wall, bracing myself. His hand slides down my back as he fucks me into the wall, and I feel my arousal sliding further down my thigh.

I jump when I feel him slip his thumb inside my ass.

I've never had anything or anyone close to my ass, and

the feeling, although foreign, sends a different type of arousal through my body.

"One day, you will have more than my thumb in your ass." His words send a shiver down my spine as I feel his cock slide in and out of me. The pressure builds inside my belly, my clit begging for attention, and I can't help myself, I begin to snake a hand between my legs, my fingers placing pressure on my clit.

I feel him slide out of me in a flash. I groan at the emptiness, my pussy aching for his cock back inside me. I watch from over my shoulder as he drops to his knees, then his tongue meets my pussy which sends my body and mind reeling with the pleasure of his warm, wet mouth.

"Mmmm, so fucking delicious." His husky voice, the possessive placement of his hand on my ass and the sex in the air have me coming undone on his tongue as my orgasm rips through my body. I feel his tongue slide from my inner knee all the way up to my entrance, lapping up every single drop, and it is the hottest thing I have ever experienced. He chuckles, watching me sag a little on the wall, my breathing heavy like I've just swum across an entire ocean.

Turning around to face him, my eyes take him all in, his chest is glistening with sweat, arms and shoulders perfectly carved, his full lips glistening with my arousal, and his dark eyes filled with an equal amount of lust and power. I leap into his arms, and he catches me effortlessly as I wrap my arms and legs around him and walks us over to the lounge near the foot of the bed, sitting me down on his lap. His lips touch mine, softly, kissing me with tenderness, something I haven't seen from Ezra before, as his hands caress my arms.

My heart thumps beneath my chest in tandem with his,

stirring a whirlwind of feelings inside me as I stare into the blackness of his eyes. I lift myself and reach behind me, aligning his cock at the entrance of my pussy. My eyes focus on his as I slide down onto his cock, watching his eyes roll back ever so slightly, revealing a sliver of his dominance breaking, giving me great pleasure. Watching him lose control, over me, over my body, and watching what I do to him makes me want to keep going, just to see how much more I can take from him.

Push his dominance, his power, his control.

I sit on him all the way to the hilt as his hands grab my ass, his eyes falling to my mouth. I begin to grind my hips, the tip of his cock hitting all the right places inside me, creating a thunderstorm inside my belly, brewing slowly. I moan as I lean my head back, my hips now moving on their own, taking my own pleasure.

"Fuck, you're going to make me come," he grunts as I feel his hands grip my ass tighter, his mouth coming down on my breast.

I face him again, resting my hands on his chest as he rests his head on the couch, my face just above his, watching as his mouth creates the shape of an O, my hair falling around us. I grind my hips faster, our breathing accelerating together, as his eyebrows come together.

"Aries," he breathes, and it does something to me, the way he says my name. "Come for me." That's all it takes. I come undone, my pussy clenching around him as he grips me tighter, his groans filling the room as his cock jerks inside me.

CHAPTER FOURTEEN
Ezra

I t's close to dawn when I wake. I feel Aries's arm over my chest, her leg over mine, and her head nuzzled in the crook of my neck. Her hair smells like strawberries and coconut. Slowly peeling away from her hold, careful not to wake her, I pick up my phone, walk out into the freshly renovated modern kitchen, and dial Nico's number.

"Calling me on your honeymoon, just hours after getting married? Fuck, brother, you need to learn how to relax a little."

"Shut the fuck up, tell me what's happening with the intercept."

"Seriously…would you not rather be fucking your wife right now?" He chuckles.

"Nicholas."

"Alright, alright." He sighs. "We've found their shipment heading into London in a couple of days or so. We plan on intercepting it with a few men."

"We'll be back before then; I need to be there."

"It'll go to plan; you don't have to worry. Enjoy your honeymoon, brother."

"Do we have a lead on the accountant?"

"Not yet, but the men who will be delivering the

shipment will have some information, they're a couple of Leo's closest men."

"They fucking better." I clench my hand into a fist beside me. "I swear to everything that is holy, Nico, if they don't pledge their loyalty, I will have their fucking heads."

I hang up the phone and walk back into the bedroom. I've been preoccupied with this whole ruse of *securing the Casella line* that I've put revenge on the back burner, not being fully present with my men. I haven't been away from a war or a fight in a long time, and it feels good for some positive thoughts to occupy my mind for a whilst, however long it might have lasted. This is too important to fuck up. I need to be there with my men when we intercept the Brayford shipment. We need to have some sort of insight into their kingdom, and our way in is through this accountant that they have.

Leo is smart, but his men aren't very tight-lipped, and that's what I'm counting on. If I'm honest with myself, I *want* there to be bloodshed—it's almost like I crave it, like I miss it.

My eyes find Aries, her body sprawled across the bed, the blanket covering only her ass as she lies on her front. I watch as her back rises and falls in shallow breaths, deep in her slumber, and I feel something inside me change. I started this night off thinking I would keep her out of convenience and entertainment, but when I look at her, my heart picks up speed, my palms begin to sweat, and my dick reacts almost immediately.

She's never leaving me. I won't let that happen.
No matter how much she begs.

Slipping in beside her, she nuzzles into me, almost like it was second nature.

"I thought I could let you go, sweetheart, but you're

stuck with me," I whisper into her hair, and she murmurs nonsense. "Until each and every atom in my body dissipates into nothingness."

My arms are wrapped around Aries, carrying her over the threshold of the front door of my Chelsea home. Some traditions I'm not opposed to. As long as I get to have my hands all over my wife, I'll comply. She gasps as I place her on her feet, Henry bringing in the last of our luggage. My dick is almost raw from how much we fucked—basically on every surface of the house we honeymooned at, even outside in the garden, the sun beaming down on us. I loved watching her bare tits shimmer with sweat in the brightness as she came undone over and over again on my cock, the sight imprinted in my mind.

"Come with me. I want to show you something." I grab her hand as we begin walking up the stairs, and she stops halfway up.

"Ezra, when did you…" she begins to say as I turn around and see her place her fingers on our wedding photo. It's of us at the reception, our first dance.

"I'm glad you like it, but this, you will enjoy far more." I pull her up the stairs, swirling her around as I ask her to cover her eyes and guide her slowly into the back upstairs room, which I had completely renovated just for her whilst we were away.

"Okay, open."

She takes her hands off her eyes and is completely speechless at the sight of the room. This room used to be a storage space, but now, it's a light, bright office. A large desk in the middle of the room with the latest computer sitting on top. A lush rug underneath and a large bookcase running across the back wall. The room length window brings an abundance of light during the day, covered with sheer curtains.

"This is all for me?" she breathes, almost not believing me, walking farther into the room.

"All for you, baby," I say, crossing my arms, leaning into the doorframe.

She lightly sweeps the oak desk with two fingers. "I don't know what to say."

"You don't need to say anything." I watch her, watching me. "But I can think of other ways you can thank me." I smirk, thinking about all the things I'd like to do to her on that desk.

She rolls her eyes and walks to the large window, her hand running through the sheer curtain. "Ezra, it's honestly beautiful. Thank you." She turns her head to me, her eyes filled with something other than lust, but I can't quite place it.

"You're beautiful." I don't know why I say it, but she makes me want to tell her exactly what I feel, when I feel it.

"Stop it." Heat rises to her cheeks, turning them bright red, and my dick tents inside my jeans.

"Why?" I begin to walk toward her. "I mean it," I say as I wrap my arm around her lower waist and pull her in.

"Don't you have people to shoot?" She chuckles nervously, placing her hands on my chest, her eyes falling to my lips.

"You'd like that, wouldn't you? Me covered in blood, standing over you as you suck my cock?" She bites her bottom lip as I speak. "I bet if I slip my fingers inside your panties right now, they will be soaked with the thought of me thrusting my cock deep inside your throat." I don't get the chance to find out, because my phone interrupts, buzzing incessantly in my pocket. I groan as I pick it up and put it to my ear.

"This better fucking be good, or someone's going to lose a fucking arm for interrupting me." I watch Aries move closer to me, her lips planting small kisses on my neck, her strawberry scent enveloping me, searing its mark inside my nose.

"It's time—the shipment will be at the dock in a couple of hours. We are starting to prep," Nico explains.

"Fine. I'll be there in twenty minutes." I hang up the phone and shove it back in my pocket. "As much as I would love to bend you over this table and have my way with you, I have to be somewhere." I explain as my hands lower to her ass, giving it a tight squeeze, pushing my erection into her. She pouts her lips in annoyance, and I groan.

"Promise to make it up to me later?" she asks as her eyes twinkle with deviance.

"I'll do you one better." I bring my mouth to hers, hovering over it. "If I come home tonight, and you're in bed ready for me, I will let you have your way with *me*." A smile curves on her lips before I place mine on hers, my tongue parting her mouth, forcing entry.

The night is slightly cooler, the breeze blowing through my car windows as Nico and I sit, waiting. Our men have concealed themselves throughout the port, hiding behind various cargo.

"How was your honeymoon?" Nico asks, the usual sarcasm hanging in his voice.

"Fine." I watch the port, my eyes never leaving the

approaching ship. Usually, the shipments happen during the day, whilst all the port employees are on shift, but being the King, I have certain pull, and what King would I be if I didn't use it to my advantage?

"Just fine?" He chuckles. "Do you need me to tell you how to properly fuck a woman, brother?" He snorts as I flip him off.

"My wife is perfectly satisfied with the way I fuck her, Nico." I clench my jaw, my body becoming tense as I watch the ship docking, a few men pulling ropes and dropping anchors. "Now shut the fuck up. We're here to do a job, don't fuck it up."

"*Me* fuck it up? Brother, *you're* the one who's pussy-whipped." He checks his gun is loaded and leans into me. "Your wife isn't going anywhere tonight, so try to focus on getting our revenge." With that, he slips out of the car, leaving me with his words.

I hadn't stopped to realise that maybe I am, and maybe that wasn't such a bad thing. I'd fucking beg on my knees to have my face in her pussy at any given hour on any given day, and if that makes me whipped, I could not give a fuck.

Exiting the car, I pull out my two guns from my holster, one in each hand, and walk over to Nico, staring and watching as they unload the cargo.

"Ready, brother?" I ask, turning my head to face him.

"Till death." He smirks, striding into the den of our enemy. "GET ON THE FUCKING GROUND, YOU COCKSUCKERS!" he yells as he sprays a couple of bullets into the air, then aims for two of the men beside the cargo, shooting them straight in the head. I know people call me a psychopath, but Nico's wrath could scare even the most hardened men.

Our men come out of hiding and bullets fly through the entirety of the ship and cargo, automatic machine guns almost always get the job done quicker and easier, and the way I'm feeling right now, I just want to get this done, go home to my wife and sink my dick deep inside her wet cunt.

I watch as Nico captures one of them in a headlock, Nico's height towering over him, making him look small. "This is him; this is the guy we want."

I point my guns straight at his head, resting the barrels between his eyes as our men take care of the rest of them. The man struggles to breathe as Nico's arm places pressure on his throat.

"Now is the time to say something." My voice stern.

He splutters as Nico releases his hold just a fraction. "I don't know anything," he says, and I lower my gun to aim at his dick, maybe if he doesn't care about his brain, he might be shallow enough to care if his dick is mangled for the rest of his life.

"Try again."

His breathing quickens as he begins to struggle in Nico's hold, looking from my gun to me. Just like I guessed, the cockhead cares more about being a eunuch than death. "Okay, okay." He breathes, saliva and blood running down his chin. "His name is Neil. Neil Ferguson. He's the accountant, and your way into the Brayford's empire." He looks to me, pure fear rippling through his eyes. "Please don't shoot me in the dick." His voice wobbles as he speaks.

Nico releases his hold on him and moves to my side, and I pull the trigger, his screams echoing through the port, in the black night sky. I feel nothing as I watch him standing there, cupping his groin, and a twisted smile curls on my lips as I raise the gun in my left hand and shoot him between the eyes, his blood splattering over my face, my shirt, and arms from the proximity. Blood rushes through my veins like water in a rapid river, thrashing about. I'm in the mood to kill and I'm disappointed that all the killing has been done.

For tonight at least.

Walking into our bedroom, I open the double doors and peek in, seeing my beautiful wife sleeping on her front, her plump, bare ass shining in the moonlight seeping in through the window. I could get used to this sight, coming home every night to a naked Aries, waiting for me to fuck her brains out. I begin to remove my jacket when I notice her phone light up on the bedside table. I grab the phone in my hand, unlocking it, seeing a new message from an unknown number.

UNKNOWN

I know you didn't want to marry him, and I know you're still hung up over us. Come back to me, Aries. I promise I will treat you right this time.

I don't even bother reading the rest of the message as my ears thump with blood. This motherfucker has some fucking balls contacting my wife after I shot him in the leg just weeks ago. He must have a death wish. A wish I'd be happy to grant, but first, I'm going to have a little fun.

I remove my blood-soaked clothes before sliding into the bed beside Aries, the blood of another man's smeared on my face, chest, and hands, tainting the crisp white sheets. Brushing a strand of hair from her face, she stirs and slowly opens her eyes, still hooded with sleep. Sliding my hand down her naked body, her eyes almost bulge from her sockets as she gasps and jerks her body up, covering herself with the bedsheet.

"It's me, sweetheart." I chuckle as I watch her calm, her body beginning to relax again.

"Is that—"

"No, it's not my blood." I answer her question before she can ask it.

She begins to move closer to me, reaching out her hand, she places it on my chest, and her eyes twinkle in the dim lighting of our bedroom.

"How did you sleep?" I ask, my hands resting on her hips as she now straddles me.

"Thinking about the promise you made me before you left," she whispers as her hand moves up to run through my hair, my head moving back, watching her lips. My dick is throbbing in anticipation as her pussy hovers over me.

"I'm all yours, sweetheart," I say as her lips crash into mine, her hunger evident in the way her tongue writhes with mine. "Only you can have your way with me," I say through the kiss. "No one else." I hold the base of my cock, and with my other hand on her hip, I push her down, her warm pussy enveloping me as she moves herself down onto the length of me. I groan as her breasts now fill my vision, and I take one in my mouth, sucking and licking as she purrs, grinding on my dick, taking her pleasure.

"Tell me what you want, sweetheart," I whisper through sucking her pink nipple into my mouth. She sucks in a breath as her hands grip the back of my neck.

"Grab my ass," she says between breaths, and I comply. Giving my wife the pleasure she well deserves. "Ezra," she whispers as her hips grind over me. I lean into her neck, planting kisses, sucking, and biting until her breathing is uneven, her moans filling the room and sweat beads running between her breasts. "I need you," she says, her voice almost desperate.

"Tell me, tell me what you need," I groan.

"I want you to fuck me like you hate me." She stops moving and looks into my eyes, her eyes wild with lust.

A smirk curls on the corner of my lips. "Gladly." I flip her onto all fours on the bed and enter her from behind, not wasting any time. Grabbing her hair, I yank backward, her back now arched, breasts pushed out in front of her.

I begin to move in and out of her as I place my other hand over her throat.

"Oh, fuck," she breathes out as I slam into her, squeezing her neck tighter with each thrust.

"I love when my queen requests to be fucked like a dirty little slut," I whisper into her ear, feeling her pussy becoming wetter and wetter with every word.

I release my hold on her throat and reach for her phone on the bedside table, still fucking her, holding her hair. I press dial on the number I know to be Ray.

"Tell me, sweetheart, tell me how much you like to be fucked hard." I ram into her as she moans, making my dick harder than a fucking rock. I see the call connect as she speaks.

"Ezra, I love when you fuck me, I love when you're so deep inside me." She moans, her hand reaching between her legs. "Oh fuck, I'm going to come." She raises her voice, her moans filling the air.

"Come all over me, sweetheart. Show me how much you love my cock deep inside you." I growl as I grab her throat again, and she comes undone on my cock, her tits bouncing as I thrust once more, unloading deep inside her.

I see the call disconnect as he hangs up, and I admit, I did it purely to claim my territory.

She's mine.

Nothing can take her from me, and although I know for a fact he doesn't stand a chance, I wanted to show him just how much she screams for me, how she undoubtedly never used to scream for him. I place her phone back on the bedside table and pull her back into me. Laying down, I spoon her from behind.

"That was," she exhales, "amazing."

"You can thank me tomorrow, on your knees with my cock in your mouth." I say as I trace a finger down her arm. Her body relaxes underneath my touch. "Sweetheart?"

"Mm?"

"When were you going to tell me that cockless fuck was still contacting you?" I ask, and I feel her body stiffen.

"He's harmless," she finally says after a few moments.

"Hmm." I breathe in her scent. "I don't give a fuck, he doesn't get to speak with you." I turn her around, her front now firmly pressed against mine. "He doesn't even get to *breathe* in your direction, do you understand?" My hand slithers down and grips her ass, tightly enough that I know it'll probably bruise.

She winces. "Ezra."

"I mean it," I say through gritted teeth. "You're mine." I kiss her with everything I have whirling inside me—hate, greed, power, lust, love—and I hope to a god I don't believe in that she somewhat feels the same for me.

After she falls asleep, I grab her phone and walk to the large en suite. Turning the shower on, I wait for the hot water to run as I take out her SIM card and flush it down the toilet. Walking back out, I dial Henry's number from my phone.

"Yes, boss?" he answers on the first ring.

"Get Ray here and tie him up in the basement," I say before I hang up, throwing my phone on the bed and jumping into the now warm shower.

He will learn what it means to dance with the devil. I smile as I think about my plan. I watch as the dried blood slowly washes off my face in the floor-length mirror across from the shower, revealing the evil hidden underneath. A normal man might feel shame or guilt after what I had just done, but all it does is spur me on further. I want everyone to know she is mine, that I will never let her go.

CHAPTER FIFTEEN
Ezra

I t's been a couple of weeks since I've been back in London, and so far, we haven't made much progress with the Brayfords. Things like this always take time, but my patience isn't my strongest quality.

Tonight, we are holding a fundraiser, the same event we host every year in honour of the founding families. The Brayfords, The Dixons, The Guerras, and us. The fundraiser night should be a night where I get to relax, talk to the men who have stood by me my entire life and get to know what really makes them stay. Instead, all I can do is watch her, the way her hips sway as she walks in her stunning bloodred dress that falls effortlessly against her perfect curves. There has never been another time when a woman has affected me this much.

"Mr Casella, it is so nice to see you tonight." A woman speaks in front of me, my eyes remaining on my wife on the opposite side of the room. "This is such a beautiful event," she continues talking, but I ignore her as I watch Aries being approached by someone.

"Excuse me." I slip past her, weaving through the crowd as I make my way to Aries when I'm interrupted by Jackson. His large hand lands on my shoulder, his body stepping in front of mine.

"Ezra…" He smiles, a whiskey glass in his hand. "It's been a whilst, brother." Whilst he's not blood, I do consider him as such.

I smirk, remembering all the terrible shit we used to get up to in our teen years. Our families are allies and have been since the beginning. Our blood ties run true, and I consider his family as my own. If he were to come to me tomorrow and ask for my help to bury someone, I'd grab two shovels and ask no questions. Our loyalty is blind to each other.

"Jackson." I pull him into a quick hug. "I've been busy," I say as my eyes flee to Aries and back to him. His eyes follow mine, and he nods.

"Of course, the great Ezra Casella is now a married man." He laughs. "She is…*something*."

My hands curl into fists, and he removes his hand from my shoulder.

"Now, now, don't get all territorial." He looks at her again, and I want to rip the smirk from his mouth. "She's got fire. The way she's been talking with the women, I don't think I've ever heard someone who isn't part of this world be able to stand up for themselves like that."

My jaw clenches at his words, at the thought of people not making her feel welcome, but I knew that would be part of it. A part of me is proud, but I also knew she could manage the mafia princesses with no effort.

"She's a force, and she doesn't even know it yet," I say.

"Listen, there's been some talk." His face turns serious as he returns his focus to me. "People are saying the Brayfords are working with the police."

"They have nothing and no leg to stand on," I reassure him. "Don't forget how many men I have on my payroll."

He shifts his weight onto his other leg. "Just be careful.

I think they're up to something," he warns. "If you need me, you know where I'll be."

Jackson Guerra is a couple years older than me, so naturally, I looked up to him when I was a young. He taught me all there is to know about how to please our fathers. When to talk back and when to shut the fuck up. I trust him like I trust Nico.

With my life.

"Thanks, Jackson." I pat him on the shoulder, my eyes now searching for Aries. "Now if you'll excuse me, I need to find my wife."

I search for her in the last place I saw her, but she isn't there. My eyes sweep the crowd as they land on Nico, chatting up some girl at the bar. Then I catch sight of a gold sparkle, the bracelet she's wearing glinting in the light as she slips out of the large doors. I follow her out, keeping my distance, watching as she heads outside, into the garden, which is now dark, barring the moonlight that shines through it. She stops in the middle of the garden and looks up to the sky, and I wonder what she is thinking, as she stands there with a drink in her hand. I stalk up to her, careful not to make a sound, and when my hand lands on her shoulder, she shrieks, turning around and dropping her glass on the ground.

I chuckle. "Did I scare you?"

Her hand rushes to her now heaving chest. "Yes, you scared me...every other *normal* person announces themselves."

My eyes skate over her chest as she looks up at me, her doe eyes sparkling in the moonlight.

"You shouldn't be alone."

"Why?" she asks. "I thought this was *your* event."

"It is, but you don't know who else may want access to

this event." I snake my arm around her waist, pulling her body into mine. "…to me."

She rolls her eyes. "You mean those needy women who clung to you earlier?"

I smirk. "Is that jealousy I sense in your voice, sweetheart?"

She pushes me away, but I keep her exactly where I want her. Against me.

"No." Her voice changes as her eyebrows pull in.

"You don't have to hide it from me…" I lower my lips to hers. "…I like it when you're jealous," I whisper onto her perfect lips.

"I'm not jealous," she says as she wraps her arms around my neck.

"Hmmm…" My tongue darts out to lick her lips, tasting her, and instantly sends my cock straining against my pants. "You have nothing to worry about," I reassure her.

"Because here's the truth…" My hands travel down to her ass as my fingers press deep into her. "My skin burns when you are not near, and my eyes search only for you in a sea of people. You drive me so fucking crazy that there is no room for me to *think* about anything else. You occupy every inch inside my brain, like a migraine rattling my mind until I give in, except I welcome it. I *crave* it…" I push my erection into her. "…I crave *you.*"

My mouth crashes into hers, her hands travelling down my neck, to my chest.

Someone clears their throat behind me, and I clench my jaw at the interruption.

"Sir…" Henry pauses, my eyes still on Aries.

"Spit it out, Henry," I say through gritted teeth.

"Apologies for the interruption, sir, but…we need you."

"Give me a minute with my wife."

I hear his footsteps retreat as Aries begins to pull away from me. "You're needed. You should go."

I pull her back. "Nico will be here. If you need anything, go to him."

She nods, and it kills me to leave her. I would do anything to stay with her right now and fuck her in the middle of this garden, but duty calls.

"I told you they were up to something," Jackson says as we stare at the cop now tied to the chair, our men surrounding us on the yacht.

I sigh, running my hand over my face.

"Speak, before my patience wears out, and I take out my anger on you," I direct at the cop.

He looks up, like a wounded puppy, begging me with his eyes. "Please, I swear, we didn't agree to it. We warned him, but he didn't listen." I look over at the other cop who is now face down on the floor, blood continuing to pool around his head.

"What did they promise you?" I ask.

"More money..." His breathing accelerates. "But I promise, we didn't accept it. Our loyalty is to the Casella family."

I lightly slap his cheek. "I believe you."

Here's the difference between us and the Brayfords... they might have a lot of money, but we have the fear. Thanks to Dominic, the fear he instilled in our men and the cops on our payroll still runs deep.

Jackson kneels in front of him, his thick legs stretching the material of his pants. "What else did they say?"

"N-Nothing. I swear," he splutters. "We would never be disloyal to you, Mr Casella," he tries to reassure me.

I nod, my mind churning with a thought.

"I have a way you can prove that sentiment, Lieutenant." A smirk pulls against my lips. "But it will be at the expense of your badge and your so-called honour."

"No, please, this is all I have." He pulls at the chains restraining him in the chair. "I gave up my life to be a cop."

"And you're doing a really lousy job at it." My boot meets the middle of his chest as he falls back onto the deck with a smack. Jackson's laugh fills the dark night, the sound of water splashing against the yacht.

I drag the chair with him in it across the yacht to the back, where the water drifts onto the flat surface. It's usually used for diving, but not tonight. I stare at his terrified face as I speak.

"If you don't tell me what you know, it'll be death by drowning," I promise him.

"Please, I beg you, please. I don't know anything!" he sobs, tears streaming from his eyes.

I grunt as I lower his head off the boat, the bottom of the chair now tipping up, the water grazing his head.

"Last chance, Lieutenant."

He goes to speak, but I don't wait as I submerge his head entirely into the water. He's lucky the boat is idle, otherwise he'd have a harder time with the propellers. I bring the chair back up so all four legs rest on the boat, his body now drenched as he coughs and tries to regain his breath.

"I'm getting bored, Lieutenant." I pace the deck. "You're forgetting I don't *need* you. I have thousands of cops on my payroll who would drop to their knees at my whim."

There is silence for a moment before either of us speaks.

"He's planning to overthrow you by undercutting you in all your exports in weaponry and overcompensating the cops on your payroll." He coughs again. "Some have no loyalty to you, sir, and some just thirst for the money."

I nod. The knowledge is nothing new to me, there will always be weasels amongst the den. It's something my father also knew.

"Give me their names," Jackson demands, and he does, giving him a list of names who plan to betray me. None of the names ring a bell, so they must be new. Either way, it doesn't matter because they will all die before the sun rises again.

Once the order is given, I'm free to take his life.

"I promise, I let everyone know, I warned them not to accept the bribe," he stutters.

I nod, walking towards his shivering body still seated in the chair. "You did great." I smile as he visibly relaxes. The engine of the boat roars as the propellers churn the water. "Now your death will be the perfect example." The yacht begins to move as my boot meets the middle of his chest once again, sending him whirling into the water, streaks of crimson now turning the water red.

CHAPTER SIXTEEN
Aries

The past few days have been insane, as I've been trying to keep up with this lifestyle. The blood, the tears, the power, the show, all of it. Some things don't faze me as much now, like Ezra being covered in blood almost every night after he comes back from wherever he has gone. I miss my sister. I used to see her every day, and now I barely get to see her or speak to her. Not either of our faults, though. She's been consumed by motherhood, and I've been trying to navigate this whole mafia-queen lifestyle.

Today, I'm glad to have a little time to myself. I've spent the majority of my morning in the office Ezra has created for me, going through my emails, and preparing for my upcoming events. Realising I haven't touched my phone in so long, I walk into our bedroom to find it. I found it odd that I didn't receive a single text or call from Giselle.

That's weird, the reception bar is empty, and it's telling me to insert a SIM card.

What the fuck?

I fiddle with my phone, trying to figure out what in the world is happening, and when I open the SIM card slot to check the sim is in there, disbelief washes over me.

Empty.

Running down the stairs, I open the front door and see Henry standing out front, leaning on the black Beemer.

"Call Ezra right now," I demand, and without hesitation, he does exactly as I ask, then hands me the phone.

"Henry." His beautiful deep voice fills my ear, making my blood boil.

"What did you do to my phone, Ezra?" My voice comes out harsh.

"What needed to be done, sweetheart," he says.

"How the fuck am I supposed to call my sister, or run my business?" I question.

"Henry was supposed to slip out this morning to get you a new one today," he says as Henry slips his hand inside his jacket pocket, and hands me a new sim card with a smirk playing on his lips.

I snatch it off him and grumble.

"I had all my contacts saved on there!" I yell.

"I told you, that cockless fuck cannot be in contact with you ever again."

Did he really just get rid of my old SIM card because of Ray? Who am I kidding? Of course he fucking did.

"I'll be home soon." He chuckles. "I have a surprise for you."

I hang up without saying a word, not giving him the satisfaction of a goodbye. I throw the phone at Henry, and he catches it as I stomp inside, slamming the front door.

I spend the afternoon trying to get all my contacts back. Luckily, I have them saved on my cloud. I hear the front door open and close as Ezra walks up the stairs. I look around the room for something to launch at his head.

I'm still fuming that he had the audacity to get rid of my SIM card.

I see him enter the office, the entire room's energy shifts as his formidable aura obliterates everything else. His eyes penetrate mine, glimmering with pure animal dominance that's hard not to look away, and my heart pounds beneath my chest as he slowly paces toward me, leaning on my oak desk with both hands, his face an inch from mine. His large frame towers over me.

"Hang up on me again, and I will remind you who the fuck I am." His voice sends a quiver down between my legs, and I press my thighs together.

I purse my lips, dropping my eyes, refusing to give him the satisfaction of answering back. He lifts my chin with a finger.

"Eyes on me, sweetheart," he demands, and like a car crash, I can't look away. His dark eyes are hungry, no, thirsty, but I don't know what for.

I swallow. "What's the surprise?" I ask, and he smirks, his eyes hinting at danger.

"I'm so glad you asked."

He walks around to me, grabbing my hand, guiding me downstairs. We stop in front of the basement door, where I have never been before. The hairs on the back of my neck stand up, and I get the feeling I am not going to enjoy this. I feel his breath on the back of my neck.

"I don't share, Aries, and those who challenge my power will meet the monster I attempt to hide with the mask of the King."

I swallow down my nerves as he opens the basement door.

The stench of rotting fills my nostrils as I walk down the creaky steps, following Ezra. The closer I get to the bottom, the stronger the smell gets, and I cover my nose with the crook of my elbow as my heart thumps beneath my chest, threatening to explode or escape my rib cage and run for its life.

The lights flicker on, illuminating the entire room, and the breath escapes from my lungs as I barrel over, tripping backwards over my feet as I stare at Ray hung from the ceiling, hooks digging into his back, blood spilling from the wounds. Dried blood is pooled on the floor beneath him, his head slumped over like he's dead. I feel my stomach contract as bile rises beneath my throat. Bending over, I empty the entire contents of my stomach onto the floor, struggling to catch my breath between the retching. Ezra rubs my back, pulling my hair away from my face, as I wipe my mouth with the back of my hand.

"He's very much alive." He steadies my swaying body, turning my face with one hand, making me stare at Ray. I swallow the bile threatening to come up my throat again.

He did this because Ray tried to contact me?

Slow realisation creeps in that the killing is not always of "bad" guys, and it stabs me in the chest that the man who can be so sweet to me could be so different to others, regardless if they are bad or good people.

Finally, I find some words. "Are you going to kill him?" I ask, my voice small.

"Eventually," he says, pushing my vomit-covered hair away from my face. "I warned him, at our wedding, and he didn't listen." He kisses my cheek softly, like he hasn't just mangled my ex and showed him to me like a cat would leave a mouse at your doorstep.

Even though I don't particularly care what Ray does, I don't want him to die. He hasn't done anything to deserve it, but I don't think this matters to Ezra because evidently, the criteria for killing someone is you either have to be part of the enemy, speak to me, or be my ex.

He turns me to face him. "My place does not reside in the confines of societal norm, Aries, nor is it a place where dim light shines through the shadows. My home is in the darkness where the only thing you can hear is the laughter of my demons, and the only stench you can smell is the rotting of my enemies' corpses." My breathing accelerates at his words, a shiver travelling down my spine. "I am very well acquainted with the darkness that lives within me, but you, sweetheart, could use a lesson to see that the abyss which claws at you from within could be your liberation."

I don't know what to say, so I don't say anything, and instead, I think about how I can escape, and I'm not sure if I want to escape from Ezra or from the darkness he ignites within me.

I feel stupid.

What did I think was going to happen when I accepted Ezra's offer?

Ray lifts his head slightly, revealing blood trailing out from his nose, down his face, and to his chest. Staining his crisp white dress shirt.

"I want you to show him." Ezra's voice fills my ear.

"Show him what?"

"How my darkness calls out to yours, like a lighthouse during a storm." I feel his body behind mine, his hands resting on my hips. "You don't have to lie to me, sweetheart. I know he did more than leave you at the altar."

I hold my breath at his words, unsure of how he knows this. My eyes find Ray's as he looks up at me, defeat written all over his face.

"I know you want revenge," he whispers in my ear. "I know you want to hurt him, just like he hurt you."

I shake my head, feeling like the devil himself has perched himself on my shoulder, snaking his way through my thoughts. A wave rushes over my body, and in that moment, I feel what can only be described as power. Watching Ray hanging in front of me gives me a sense of the fire that I knew I had buried within me so long ago. When I met Ray, we were only starting our journey into adulthood, so it makes sense that he would be able to manipulate me when I didn't know who I was. I was so scared he would leave that I never once spoke out of turn, never once said I didn't want to do something he did. I feel fury poke around in my chest, and without thought, my hand curls into a fist and pain radiates through my knuckles and my wrist as Ray's scream thunders through the basement.

I hear Ezra's deep chuckle behind me as Ray spits blood onto the floor.

"You know, you've always been a bitch, but even this is a bit low for you, don't you think?" Ray croaks.

Ezra steps around me and comes to stand in front of Ray. "I want to know, Ray, what does it feel like having your power stripped away from you?"

"You'll never get away with this."

Ezra laughs. "That's where you're sorely mistaken." He walks over to the other side of the basement and unlocks a padlock on the wall, revealing a cupboard filled with weaponry. "You see..." He pauses, removing what looks like an old knife. "Whilst you spent your years studying to become a respectable part of society, I spent them learning how to dismember a human body."

Ray grits his teeth as I watch, my body frozen in time.

"Have you ever heard of *Ling Chi?*" he asks, and Ray doesn't respond. "*Ling Chi* is an ancient form of torture known as *death by a thousand cuts*."

Ray swallows, and I watch as Ezra walks over to us with a knife in his hand. His body and aura oozes power just in the way he walks alone.

Ray's screams crack through the tense air as I watch Ezra slice away a small piece of skin on his arm and bile bubbles beneath my throat as I watch the blood dripping from his wound onto the floor.

"There are countless ways to kill a man, but this is one of my favourites," he says as the piece of flesh drops to the floor with a squelching sound. "I get to watch as the pain slowly creeps its way to the top, choking you, leaving you gasping for an ounce of relief." He begins cutting another piece from Ray's leg as he thrashes about. "But that relief never comes and the only thing you will feel before you take your last pathetic breath will be the edge of my knife, cutting into you, over and over again."

I swallow as I watch Ezra slowly cut pieces of Ray's skin and throws it on the floor like a lolly wrapper. As if this person hanging in front of him didn't have a life, a mother, a father, and in this moment, I realise who he truly is.

I realise why I'm drawn to him, and the terror is back, churning in my gut.

The effortless way in which he takes what he wants, without a single thought about consequence, the way he inflicts pain without a single twitch, like he was truly the devil himself. It makes me realise how much I want that, and it frightens me.

It's one in the morning, and I've been sitting in the front room, watching Henry like a hawk. He eventually will need to use the restroom, and when he does, I will use that chance to run. Run like fucking hell and never look back. I packed a small suitcase and stashed it away so Ezra wouldn't see it, and when he left after dinner, I used that opportunity to come up with a plan. A plan that would get me the fuck out of here. I considered helping Ray, but I will only have a small window, and I can't chance that.

After what seems like a fucking eternity, I watch as Henry walks up to the house, and opens the front door. Quickly shuffling into my seat, I open my book and pretend to read.

"It's a bit late, Mrs Casella, but do you mind if I use the restroom?" he asks, and I nod.

As soon as the bathroom door clicks, my muscles fire, and I move the fastest I've ever moved before. Grabbing my suitcase from the storage room, I fly out the door, flinging the bag into the back seat of the Beemer, jumping into the driver's seat, and turning the car on. The car revs under me as I watch Henry bolt out the door, shouting, but I can't hear him over the thumping of my heart in my ears.

I don't wait for him to get closer and floor the gas, almost losing control of the car as I drive out of the driveway and speed down the road. I have absolutely no idea where I am going, but I know where I am not. I can't go to my sister's because he fucking owns that place too. All I know is that I have to ditch this fucking car.

I drive for a whilst until I'm out of the city and find an old dingy car park to park the car and walk myself over to the nearest service station. I ask the person behind the counter to call me a cab, and he kindly obliges.

"Miss, are you okay?" he asks, and I notice him staring at my pyjamas.

"Fine, can I stay inside until the cab arrives?" I ask.

"Of course." He gives me a warm smile.

I gasp as I realise the new sim card Henry had got for me is still in my phone, I quickly take it out and break it in half, placing it in the bin and praying to God that he hasn't traced my location already.

What are you going to do, Aries?

I think hard about what my next move is going to be, knowing well that I cannot possibly take on the Mafia King. Tears of terror threaten to surge through as realisation sets in that there is no out.

There is no returning to who I was before I fucked him covered in blood, before the thrill and rush of taking the King's power.

What was an innocent marriage of convenience has turned into something I could never have imagined, and the most fucked up part is a part of me didn't want to leave.

Not for the loss of the lifestyle, or the power, or everything else that comes with being the queen, but the distance I have created between us.

I feel exposed.

Unprotected.

Naked, without him.

I push the feelings down deep into my chest as I watch the cab roll up. I slide into the back. "Drive to the next motel, please," I say and sink deeper into the seat and let a tear slip through the cracks. Getting into the motel, I lock the door and place a chair underneath the handle as I rest my back on the wall, and my legs give out, the adrenaline dissipating out of my system as I drop to the floor, sobs racking through my body.

Uncertainty taints my thoughts as I obsess about what is going to happen, and I know for a fact Henry has already let Ezra know, and it's only a matter of time before he finds me. Sliding my knees up to my chest, I wrap my arms around them, barely holding myself together as I face the feelings I've tried to suppress bubbling to the surface and sizzling in my chest.

You can't.

I tell myself the lie which I don't believe because I know I do.

I love his power, I love his lust, his greed.

I love everything about his darkness.

I don't know if I'm running because I'm scared of him or scared of *me.*

What if he's right?

What if there is a certain darkness inside me, just begging to be released?

It wasn't just fear that I felt when I saw Ray, it was fury, and it was all-consuming.

CHAPTER SEVENTEEN
Ezra

My blood boils, curdles and sets in stone like lava spilling out of a volcano. I clench my jaw so hard I'm surprised I haven't cracked my teeth in two.

"Where is she?" I growl at Henry at the sight of our empty bed.

He bows his head. "I tried to stop her, but she was too quick," he says.

I inhale a long breath, trying to quiet my demons and crack my neck from side to side, closing my eyes, focusing on anything but the red-hot rage filling my vision.

"We found her. She's at a motel just outside the city, sir." He flinches as I turn, storming out to my Porsche.

I take the steps of the porch three at a time, watching Nico lean against my car, with a cigarette between his lips. His face drops as he takes one look at me. "Whoa, brother." He raises his hands in front of me. "Just remember, she's not from our world." He tries to stop me, and I pull away from his hold. "She's probably overwhelmed or scared."

I knew the moment I met her, there was a different side to her, a fiery side, which she conceals, in fear of it overcoming her. She's more like me than she knows, and

I'd be fucking damned if I wasn't going to show her. Even if she never acknowledges her darkness, I will swallow her up in mine because she is the only one who can make me feel something other than emptiness.

"I'm bringing my wife home, Nico," I breathe, feeling my breath burn my lungs. "Get the fuck out of my way." I slip into the driver's seat and floor it, the tail of the car swirling as I pull out onto the road, watching Nico get smaller and smaller in my rearview mirror.

I reach the motel and ask the receptionist which room Aries had reserved. It doesn't take much convincing on my part for the receptionist to comply, telling me her room number.

Reaching her room, I see her curtains are drawn. Placing my hand on the doorknob, I twist.

Locked.

To a regular person, there are two ways this could go.

To me, there is only one.

I lean against the door. "I know you're in there, sweetheart," I say, and I hear shuffling behind the door. "You have two choices—you can either let me in, or I can break this fucking door down." I wait a few moments before watching her shadow move closer to the door.

"Leave me alone." Her small voice floats through the door.

"Not a chance, baby." I take a few steps back, preparing to fly into the door with my shoulder when it creaks open, revealing her bloodshot eyes. I stalk through the door, and she moves back as I close the door behind me. I watch her wrap her arms around herself and notice an ocean of uncertainty in her eyes.

"Why did you run?" I ask, not making a move toward her.

"Are you kidding me?" She huffs, her hands flying out, running through her hair. "You're really standing there, asking me that?"

I knew she wouldn't take kindly to me torturing her perfect ex-fiancé, but I didn't foresee her bolting because of it. The darkness is buried so deep inside her that she doesn't see it herself. Or maybe she does, and she wants to keep it buried.

"Let me make this easy for you to understand." I take a step toward her. "I am not the good guy." I watch as her eyes land on mine. "I am not your Prince Charming, and I can never be." I reach her, our bodies now an inch apart, and I feel her release a breath. "What I am is powerful, loyal, and fucking crazy about you." My hand reaches up to caress her cheek. "I see darkness in you baby, the same darkness that ignites me from within. I watch how you choose when to let it roam free and when to snuff it out." My lips brush hers gently. "That night you fucked me, covered in blood, I saw it in your eyes, and I felt it everywhere within you, drawing me in like a beacon."

She closes her eyes, taking a shaky breath. "No—I…"

"You liked it," I whisper onto her lips. "You liked the way it made you feel. You liked the fact that the man who could kill in cold blood could fuck you like you mean the world to him. You love when my world overthrows yours, and most of all, you love just how much you can make me weak at the knees, when nothing or no one else can." My tongue flies out to lick her bottom lip, and she looks up at me. "You love the power, sweetheart, just like me." I step toward her again, our bodies now flush, her eyes staring at my lips, practically begging me to kiss her, but I won't.

It's her turn.

Her turn to admit to herself who she truly is.

Who she *wants* to be.

"You love the rush you get, knowing you are the only person who can take my power." I wait, watching her internal debate through her decadent chocolate-brown eyes. My eyes graze down to her near-to-nothing pyjamas, and my cock immediately hardens beneath my jeans. "I want you to admit it."

"I'm not admitting shit." She finally speaks, that familiar fire sparking in her eyes.

I feel the corner of my mouth curl at her words.

"If you think I'm leaving, think again." I press her against the wall behind her, my hands on either side of her head. "The more you resist, the more it turns me on, so be careful with this little game you're playing, sweetheart."

"Or what?" There her mouth goes again, making my dick jerk, straining against my jeans.

"Or I might just have to *make* you see what I see." I growl in warning and her breath hitches as she feels me press my cock against her stomach.

"H-how?" she stutters, biting her bottom lip.

A smirk plays on my lips as her eyes fill with lust. "By breaking you," I whisper in her ear. "Now, you either get in the car, and we go home with your dignity intact, or I throw you over my shoulder, spank you, and take you home regardless."

Her nose tips up in defiance, and without wasting another second, I throw her over my shoulder, and my hand lands on her ass hard, her scream bellowing through the room.

"Put me down!" she yells as I open the motel door and walk through, straight to my Porsche, not giving a fuck who's watching this commotion. My hand lands down on her ass again, and she whacks her hands on my back, squeezing her thighs together.

I chuckle. "Is this turning you on, baby?"

She wriggles in my hold, and I put her down beside the passenger door. My fingers dig into her hips as I press her into the car. Her hand flies up between us, and a sting arises where her hand had landed on the side of my face. Excitement surfaces under my skin, a smile creeping onto my lips as I taste the familiar metallic taste of blood in my mouth.

"You're fucking crazy!" she yells.

I pull out the switchblade I have hidden inside my belt loop. Flicking it open, I hold the blade on the flushed skin of her neck and her eyes grow wide, tears brimming on at their edges. I lick from her chin, slowly up the side of her face, now tasting her salty tears running freely from her eyes. I lean in close and inhale her scent.

"Do you want me to show you how alike we are?" I whisper into her ear.

Her body feels warm against mine, her pretty pink lips slightly apart. My eyes meet hers, her chest rising and falling beneath my arm.

"I want you to let me go." Her lips move, but her body betrays her as her hips buck into me.

"I'll give you a head start, but make no mistake, sweetheart, *when* I catch you, you will belong to me." I press my erection into her, and a breathy sound leaves her mouth. "I will pay no mind to your pleas...*nothing* will save you from me." I step away from her, my eyes raking over her delicious body.

She hesitates for a moment, staring at me, panting. Then she takes off in a flash, running toward the highway, and I watch as she crosses the highway, heading into the empty field.

Nothing in view for miles. My cock strains as I watch her running, and I feel my heart thumping faster beneath my chest as her thin camisole blows in the breeze. I begin chasing after her, quickly gaining on her. I know I'll catch her, and I know she will be mine, but I can't help wanting to have a bit of fun with her.

She looks back at me and almost takes a stumble as I chuckle.

"Run, baby, I'm getting closer!" I torment her as the wind howls in my ears.

The grass rustles as I take each stride, eating up the distance between us. As I get closer and closer, I can almost taste her lips on mine, and my hand connects with her arm as I swing her around, her body slamming into me.

"I told you you'd never escape me." I speak the words through gritted teeth as she fights me. I force her to her knees in the middle of the field, one hand firmly gripping the hair at the top of her head. "Take off my belt," I demand.

She licks her lips, her mouth parting slightly as she looks up at me, and this is when she looks the most beautiful, on her knees before me, ready to please.

"Do it, Aries." My voice now stern.

Her hands move hesitantly as she undoes my belt and slides it off.

ARIES

My hands tremble as I look up at him, placing his belt on the grass beside me. My legs quiver at the outline of his cock beneath his pants, and I can already feel my arousal on my panties soaking through.

"This is where I break you." His gravelly voice surrounds me, pulling me into his trance, and I see nothing else but him. "Pull them down," he orders, and I comply, my clit throbbing at the sight of his power. His cock juts out, thick, and long, and I swallow at the sight of it. "Open your mouth."

I grit my teeth, like I almost *want* him to be rough with me. I watch as his eyes darken at my defiance, and he pries my mouth open with one hand, the other still in my hair. He thrusts himself inside my mouth, filling it up quickly with his length. His eyes roll back and after a second, regain their focus on mine. The thrill that anyone could see us, in the middle of this field, spurs my arousal further, and my body begins to crave friction. I slide my hand down into my panties when he slaps me, and the moan that leaves my mouth takes me by surprise.

"No. You don't get to touch yourself." He continues to thrust into my mouth, hitting the back of my throat. "This is a punishment for thinking you could run from me." He forces himself farther down my throat. "That's it, baby, stick your tongue out..." he says, his eyebrows coming together as he pulls me forward by my hair, forcing himself deeper. "Fuck..." he groans.

I force myself to focus on breathing through my nose, then he pinches it shut, tears stinging my eyes as they flow down the side of my face. I feel my lungs seize, screaming for air as I gag again. He finally pulls himself out, and the sound of my choking echoes in my ears.

"Open your mouth," he commands again, and I comply. He spits into my mouth, the vulgar act which should disgust me only turns me on further. "Swallow." He yanks at my hair, and I obey. "That's a good girl."

He removes his hold on my hair for a moment, and I use this chance I have to run. I don't get very far, in fact, I don't get anywhere at all. I'm yanked to the ground, as his strong hands tear off my panties. I open my mouth to scream, only to feel the lacy material being shoved into my mouth. The more I fight, the more my body begs for his touch. I feel the heat encapsulate me, as his hand closes around my throat, pushing me into the ground. My hands fly up to meet his wrist, and I pull, trying desperately to get him off me, but it's no use. He's bigger, stronger, and more depraved than ever. He parts my legs with his knee, my skin scraping on the grass and gravel beneath us, and he forces himself inside me in one swift motion, filling me up. My eyes bulge as I stretch around him.

"I love it when you fight me," he groans as he slams into me, his hold on my throat tightening slowly. The air begins to thin, as I fight to breathe and fight against my body from reacting to his touch. He tears my camisole off completely with one hand, the breeze causing my nipples to harden.

"There's nowhere left to run, sweetheart," he grunts as he rams into me. "You are *mine*."

My vision begins to dim as euphoria continues to build inside me. Just as my eyes begin to close, he loosens his grip on my neck, and I inhale a sharp breath through my nose. He reaches for his belt with one hand, and in a flash, my wrists are secured together, in front of me, the leather of his belt cinching my skin.

"I promise to make it hurt when I break you."

He flips me over, my face now pressing into the ground. My shoulders scream at me in agony as my tied wrists rest underneath me, the metal of his belt pressing into my pubic bone. I hear his retreating footsteps, and my heart sinks, thinking he's about to leave me, bound, in the middle of a field. Then I hear him return, and a sting radiates through my skin as something makes contact with my ass.

"That's for leaving me."

Whack.

"That's for denying me."

Whack.

"And that's for lying to me."

My screams are muffled as tears run down my face, the pain morphing with the pleasure. I feel his fingers run over my pussy, gliding easily against me.

"You see, sweetheart…" He leans down and holds his fingers near my face, my arousal glimmering in the moonlight, coating his fingers. "We are more alike than you care to admit."

He pulls my hips up, the pressure now excruciating on my shoulders as I'm pressed farther into the ground. I feel him enter me slowly, a low rumble leaving his throat as he buries himself completely inside me.

The position is unforgiving as I feel every inch of him stretching me from within, and my core aches to let go around him, to let the ecstasy take me into its embrace.

"If you come on my cock, I will punish you," he rasps as his fingers dig into my hips, and the sensation from the pain in my shoulders to the pleasure between my legs rattles my brain. "You don't get to come tonight, sweetheart." I squeeze my eyes shut at his words, focusing on controlling my pleasure as he takes his.

"So fucking needy," he groans as I push my hips back, meeting his thrusts. His hand lands down on my ass hard, the loud slap echoing through the empty air, and I just know I'm going to be sore. I feel him remove my panties from my mouth, and I immediately take a huge gulp of air into my lungs. A loud moan escapes me as his thumb dances around my ass, then enters me.

He rams into me hard, jerking my body against the ground, the belt cinching the skin on my wrists further. I moan with pleasure as he uses me, taking what he wants.

"Now pray." He slips his thumb out of me and pulls my hair back, my body following, relieving the pressure off my shoulders. "Pray to me for your salvation." I feel his breath beneath my ear as my neck is craned backward.

"Please..." I manage to say through bated breath.

He thrusts in and out of me, as his other hand snakes between my breasts, and closes on my throat.

"...Forgive me," I whisper, and I don't recognise the sound of my own voice, so depraved and breathless.

"Some rise by sin, and some by virtue fall." He quotes Shakespeare as he tightens the hold on my neck. "I vow to show you that by sin, you and I will rule the world, combined and intertwined together in all our darkness."

I whimper as he pulls out of me, the loss of friction making my clit throb with need, and before I can blink, he's in front of me.

"Open your mouth," he says, and I moan as he forces himself inside me, and with a few thrusts, I feel his cock pulse, warm liquid pooling inside my mouth. "Swallow every last fucking drop," he growls as he looks down at me, his black eyes darker than the night sky.

I do exactly as he says, tasting him on my tongue, the warm, salty liquid travelling down my throat.

"That's my good girl." His lips curve into a twisted smile as his fingers grip my cheeks, forcing my lips to pout. "Now don't you ever disobey me or run from me again.

Unless you want me to put you on your knees and watch you beg me to fuck you, like the slut I know you want to be. For me."

EZRA

"Look at him." My voice is stern as I watch as Aries slowly lift her head, and stare at Ray. The blood is now dried on his skin as he sits in the middle of my basement, hands tied behind his back. "Now tell him what you couldn't." I push a stray hair away from her face, then cross my arms and lean against the wall, waiting and watching, hoping that even a sliver of the darkness within her will emerge.

She takes a deep breath in, closing her eyes.

"Aries, help me," he whispers, his head bowed, energy probably on the brink of running out from the amount of time he's been down here without food.

I push off the wall, stepping forward, I walk behind Ray, pulling his head up. "It's rude not to look at the person you're speaking with."

"He's a murderer, a killer, a psychopath." He swallows before continuing. "Aries, call the police, do something!" he yells, struggling in my hold.

She stands there, staring back at Ray, and a small flash of darkness glides into her eyes, slowly growing larger as the seconds pass.

"Shut up, Ray," she speaks, gritting her teeth.

There she is.

I grin, watching the darkness consume her vision as she clenches her fists at her sides, and I know what she's feeling because I'd been there.

Several years ago, when my father had me kill a man, I knew in that moment I'd never be the same again. In that split second it took for my finger to leave the trigger as the bullet flew between the fucker's eyes, something in me split open, and a thick cloud of black seeped into every crevice of my body, paving the way for the monster I am today.

"That's it, sweetheart, let it in." I walk out of the way and watch, intrigued by what she will say, what she might do.

"Aries," Ray whispers, sobbing softly.

"I said shut up." She steps closer to him, and before I know it, her arm swings out, slapping him across the face, his head whipping to the side. I feel my mouth twitch into a smile. She wipes her cheek with the back of her hand, sniffling, and it takes everything in me not to scoop her up in my arms and make her pain mine. "You're such a coward."

"Please just let me go."

"I need to say this. I've kept it hidden like some sort of embarrassing secret for too fucking long." Her breath shakes as she speaks. Ray looks up to her, his cheek red, her hand imprinted onto his skin. "That day you left me at the altar, a part of me died." She looks to the floor. "I loved you, I put my trust in you, and you broke me." My chest cracks so loud I fear she may have heard it.

"I gave you so many years of my life, I wasted so much of my youth, only for you to decide it wasn't enough." Tears roll down her cheeks as she speaks, and I grit my teeth, holding myself back.

"You never apologised, not once did you give me a reason, you simply decided it wasn't something you wanted to do anymore. Someone you didn't love anymore. I thought you brought out the best in me, the light in me, but you were just a stepping stone. You were something I needed, to show me how much I held myself back in fear of outshining you. How much I lived in the shadows because I feared your searing judgement on what I liked or didn't." My skin crawls with pins, itching to kick the teeth out of his head at her words.

"I'm sorry," he utters, sobbing with his head bowed.

"I'm not," she says, and I raise my eyebrows, her response taking me aback.

Ray looks up at her, and she stands tall.

"For too long I felt inferior, like I didn't deserve to have someone like you, but the truth was you couldn't handle someone like me."

"Someone like you?" He scoffs.

"Someone who is different from all those preppy women who clung onto you like you held their trust fund in your hands." She moves forward, her face an inch away from his, and my lips curl into a snarl. "Someone who wasn't given the opportunities you had in life, and who had to make her own. Someone who is stronger than you'll ever be, so you felt like you needed me to be a watered-down version of my true self because *you* wanted all the credit for everything *I* had endured. Like some wounded puppy you had rescued off the streets." Her hand lands on his cheek again, whipping his head in the opposite direction.

"You fucking disgust me," she says, leaning back and watching him whimper. Her breathing accelerates as her chest rises and falls quicker than I've ever seen. Her hands clench at her sides, and I watch, my chest swelling with pride.

Her screams fill the basement as she claws at him, her nails digging into his face, blood seeping from the deep cuts.

She turns to walk away from him, heading to me.

Leaning into me, she whispers, her head resting on my chest, "Take me upstairs."

You don't have to ask me again, sweetheart.

I scoop her up in my arms and take her to our bedroom, laying her on the crisp white sheets. I turn to head back down to the basement to finish what I started, but she grabs my wrist, tears pooling in her eyes again. "Don't leave me right now, please," she pleads, and I nod, slipping into the bed beside her, pushing the thirst for blood back down into my stomach.

She comes first.

"How do you feel?" I ask her, hoping she will share herself with me.

"Like a weight has been lifted off me." She sighs, her body beginning to relax against mine. "Like I'm burning, and the only thing that can put me out is a river of Ray's tears." Her fingers weave into mine on her stomach. "Like something inside me has crawled out from the darkest depths and latched on to me, like a tumour, growing by the second, only I welcome it."

"I never said it would be easy, sweetheart." I kiss the back of her head. "But the more you learn to give in to the darkness, the easier it will be to see through it."

CHAPTER EIGHTEEN
Aries

I hear the shower running as I roll over, Ezra's side of the bed now empty. Walking into the en suite, steam bellows out as I open the door. Ezra's hands are placed on the wall, his head bowed, facing the faucet. I stop as I watch beads of water flow down his muscular back, all the way over his bare, toned ass, down to his hamstrings, and to the floor.

I swallow—the sight of him enough to cause a whirlwind inside me.

"I think I want to see Giselle today," I say, watching him turn, his chiselled chest coming into view, my eyes skimming down from his abs, down between his legs. He grins, watching me take him in.

The shower screams luxury, no glass, just completely open, the length of an entire wall.

"Are you still a flight risk?" He moves closer to me, my mouth going dry as the space closes between us.

"Am I a prisoner?" I ask, lifting my chin, my eyes meeting his swirls of black. His hand comes up and caresses my cheek, his eyes falling to my lips.

"The only prisoners between us are the things we leave unsaid." He steps in closer to me, our bodies now pressed together, my arms itching to wrap around him.

I think back to last night, all the things I said to Ray and the things I wanted to do to him, the sick, twisted things that had crossed my mind, but I held back. I feel the darkness sizzling, wanting to rise to the surface the more I'm around Ezra, and it scares me, just how much of me is revealed through him.

"Is there something you wish to tell me?" I ask, licking my lips, leaning into him, feeling his cock growing between us, pressing into my stomach.

He chuckles, the low vibrations sending a tingle between my legs.

"I could." He leans into me, his lips hovering over mine. "I think you might enjoy it more if I *showed* you." He places his lips lightly on mine. "But after what you pulled last night, I'm not sure how much you deserve it."

My eyes go wide.

"Believe it or not, sweetheart, even the monster has a heart, and when you walked out willingly, it left a mark." His eyes skim down my body, sending a shiver down my spine.

"I'm sorry," I whisper.

"Sorry is not good enough." His eyes darken as they land on mine.

"What will you have me do?" My mouth salivates watching the water run down his body. "I'll do anything." I sound desperate, but that's because I am. I want him to touch me, to make me feel good. I want to come undone around him.

He turns and resumes standing under the showerhead, the water flowing down to his now fully erect cock, and I can't tear my eyes away. "I'm sure you'll think of something." He smirks, winking.

"He's what?!" Giselle's eyes are almost popping out of her head after I explained everything to her from what Ezra does to who he has tied up in his basement. I can feel her judgement oozing from her pores as she stares at me in disbelief. "And you're still with him?" She glances at the baby monitor, then back at me. "Jesus, Aries, what have you gotten yourself into?"

I sigh, not knowing how to respond because that's exactly how I felt at the start, but now I desperately want to show him how much I meant my apology.

"I think I have feelings for him, G." I bite the inside of my lip, knowing what her response will be.

"He's a killer, part of the Mafia," she whispers, looking around as if someone will hear, when that's impossible because I came to visit her at her new place.

"I know!" My hands come up, and I run my fingers through my hair. "Sometimes we just can't help the way we feel, G, and right now, the things I feel for this man scares me more than anything else in this world."

She gives me a look of sympathy, no doubt thinking about Ray.

"I can't pretend to approve, Aries. I know he helped with this house, and I knew there was something deeper going on, and now that I know what it is, I don't think you have an escape."

"I don't want an escape." I purse my lips. "I thought I did, but I don't. I want to be with him. I want to be his wife."

"You hardly know this man."

I disagree, I think I know him better than I knew Ray. I

191

know he won't hurt me. I know he would protect me even if it meant giving his life for mine, and although his moral compass not only doesn't point north, it is non-existent, and I really don't care.

"I don't think there is anything you can say that will deter me," I admit, and she throws her hands in the air in defeat.

I didn't expect her to understand because Giselle has always been someone who relies heavily on her moral compass to know right from wrong. She genuinely doesn't have a bad bone in her body. Meanwhilst, here I stand, feeling the darkness within me fester, growing with every passing second, now awakened from its slumber.

"How's Dad?" I ask.

"You know him, sticks to himself mostly. I haven't heard from him since we moved out. Only when he needs money."

This isn't new. He's always been this way, ever since I could remember. He'd gamble away all his money or drink it. There is no in-between for him. Even though I don't want to, I feel a strange nagging feeling in the pit of my stomach, urging me to check up on him. He hasn't ever been on his own—he's always had Giselle or me living in the same house, doing the groceries and everything else.

"Should I check on him?" I ask.

Giselle shrugs. "If you want to." She begins preparing a bottle. "I know things haven't been smooth between you two, especially since Mum died, but he's still your father."

I hate that.

That phrase is the most harmful phrase to ever exist in this century. Considering someone as family just because they're blood, no matter their wrong-doings or their toxic behaviour towards you, disgusts me, and I never agreed with the notion.

"He may be blood, G, but that doesn't change the fact that he's still a piece of shit." I remark.

She purses her lips and sighs, clearly not agreeing with me.

We spend the rest of the afternoon together with my nephew as I silently think about how I can prove my feelings to Ezra.

My breath stalls as I reach for the familiar rusty doorknob on my childhood home. I still have the key, so I help myself inside. As soon as I step foot inside, I regret my decision of coming back here because the memories I've tried so hard to subdue come crawling back again.

"What do you want?" My father's deep voice comes from the lounge room, and I walk in to see him sprawled on the sofa. Beer cans litter the coffee table which looks like it hasn't been wiped down since Giselle and I left.

"Just checking in on you." I look around the room. Not much has changed since I've been here, beside the floor now being littered with pizza boxes.

"I don't need you to check in."

Why did I bother to come here? I knew how he would be. Why would he change in the short amount of time since I left? I guess part of me hoped that he could change for such a long time that I still wanted to believe it. It's hard to give up on people you love, even if they may have not helped you much in life. Especially if they are related to you.

"Why is there a man in my home?" he grumbles as he

stands up from the sofa, looking over my shoulder, and I notice Henry had followed me in.

"He's my bodyguard." I admit.

"Why would *you* need a bodyguard?"

I sigh, not wanting to tell him about my marriage to the city's most notorious gangster. I don't have to tell him anything. I can just walk out of this fucking house and be done with it, but like an idiot, I stay.

"I'm married to someone who needs bodyguards," I say and watch his eyes practically light up.

"Who?"

"Ezra Casella."

His demeanour immediately changes from hope to disgust.

"A fucking mobster?" he questions, the beer still in his hand. "You married the city's most dangerous mobster?"

My brows pull in, wondering if I was the only one who didn't know who Ezra was before I met him. Was I truly that naïve?

"Tell me you're in it for the money at least." His words send a sting to my chest. Technically I did marry Ezra initially because he agreed to pay me, but now, all I want is to prove to him that I belong in his world.

"No, I love him," I say the words to convince him, but it's the truth.

He scoffs, "What do you know of love?"

I clench my jaw at his response. Is he truly that blind to not see how much his absence affected both mine and Giselle's lives?

"More than you," I counter, and he steps toward me.

Henry immediately steps in front of me, his tall, jacked build hovering over my father, and he backs off.

"Miss, we should leave now," Henry says, and without another word, I'm out the door.

Fuck him.

The amount of time I spent trying to mend the relationship between us throughout my teenage years will forever be wasted on him. I will never get that time back, and nothing he ever does will be enough for me to ever forgive him. I can't pretend like it doesn't hurt me because it does. Every girl deserves a father who sets a bar so high that no other male in their life could ever possibly reach it, but the bar is set so stupidly low for me that it's no wonder I fell for Ray. The sad reality of life is the fact that we accept the love we think we deserve, even if we deserve so much more.

I ask Henry to take me home, and as I walk through the door, the only thing I have on my mind is Ezra. Walking up the stairs, I search for him, only to find each room empty.

"Where's Ezra?" I ask Henry.

"He's out, Mrs Casella. He will be back shortly."

I pick up my phone and dial Nicholas's number.

"Aries!" he yells my name into the phone with a tone that makes me sense he has a smile on his face.

"Can you talk?"

"What did he do now?" His tone turns serious.

"No, nothing, I just...I need help with something, and I think you'd be the best person to help me with it. Can you come over?"

"Yeah, of course, just give me about twenty minutes."

I hang up and pace back and forth, plotting. An uneasy feeling settles in my stomach as I realise what I am about to ask of Nico, but it's my only option. It's the only way I can think of earning my place as a Casella.

I stare at the empty wall as the sun starts to set outside, waiting for Nico, thinking of every possible option I have, and my jaw clenches. My mind is made up. There's a knock on my door, and I open it, letting Nico inside.

"What's going on?" His eyes skate over me. "Are you hurt?"

"No, nothing like that." I breathe, my heart thumping beneath my rib cage.

He pauses. "Why do you look like you're about to ask me to do something I most likely will not agree with?" He leans his head to one side.

I bite my lip as I reconsider, watching him watch me, his eyes never leaving mine.

"Tell me everything, about your father's death, about your enemies, everything." I swallow, watching as he raises his eyebrows.

"Has Ezra not shared anything with you?" he asks.

"He has, but I know he's keeping details from me, and I need to know."

"Why?" He crosses his arms, and like I guessed, he isn't going to make this easy for me.

I don't dare tell him about my plan because like he said, he would not agree to it and would put me on house arrest, probably tell Ezra, and I'll end up chained to the bed. No, I keep the finer details to myself, but I tell him about me gaining Ezra's trust back, and how I want to earn my place as a Casella. He seems to buy it and begins explaining the history between the Casella family and the Brayford family, the way their father passed, and how they've been committing crimes since they were teenagers.

"Promise me that I didn't just sign my death warrant."

He smiles, an uneasy smile as he looks for an answer in my eyes.

"Don't worry, it'll be our secret." I force a smile as he nods and begins heading for the door.

"I know Ezra can seem like a lot, but the entire empire rests on his shoulders." He looks back to me as he opens the front door. "Just don't mistake his silence for absence." He smiles, a warm smile now. "You two are quite similar, you know. I see so much of him in you."

"So I've heard." I let out a soft chuckle.

"We're family now, Aries. If you need anything, we've got your back." He nods and leaves, closing the door behind him, leaving me with a decision to make.

I need to start with Ray.

Hesitantly, I make my way into the basement, the stairs creaking beneath me. I knew for a while what I felt that day in the church when Ray never showed up, but I pushed it so deep within that I thought I had snuffed it out completely.

Until I met Ezra.

I hear Ray cough as he enters my vision. He's been moved and now sits, bound to an iron chair. His head lifts, and his eyes make contact with mine. I thought I wanted to marry him all those years ago, and now I realise how much of a huge mistake that would have been…how much of a setback that would have been for me.

"Aries." His voice croaks as he pleads. "Let me go."

"I need to know, Ray." I step closer to him, kneeling in front of him. "Did you ever love me?"

A smile creeps onto his face, and it has my stomach sinking. "Not as much as you loved me."

I nod, expecting that answer from him, but what comes out of his mouth next takes me off guard.

"It was your father." I grit my teeth at his words. "The reason why I never married you."

"What?" I feel a sharp cut slice through my chest at his confession.

"He is a piece of shit." He chuckles. "A pathetic one too." The chains on his wrists rattle behind his back as he tries to move. "His weak attempt at forcing my hand to marry you was the last straw."

"Forcing your hand?"

"He threatened me and my family that if I didn't marry you, he would personally make me suffer." He shrugs. "It was easier to leave you at the altar than become chained to you and your father forever."

The flames alight within me, burning like a fucking inferno with no sign of slowing down. I close my eyes to focus on keeping my cool, but this time, the control I feel I had before is slowly slipping through my fingers. I feel a fury overcome me as I stomp over to the lockbox on the wall, prying it open with the key already in the lock and grabbing the butcher knife resting on the bottom shelf.

Ray's eyes widen as I make my way over to him. "Aries, wait."

"I wasted my fucking youth on a goddamn coward like you," I grip the knife tighter in my hand. "And all it took for you to decide I wasn't worth it was my drunk father?" The rage builds and climbs within my chest, until I'm back there, in my wedding dress, crying in the middle of a field.

That isn't love. I may not know exactly what love is, but that's not it. Someone who loves you should be someone who would never leave you, even if they had to take on the world to have you. It wouldn't matter who you're related to or what type of person they are.

"If you didn't want to marry me, why did you object when I was about to marry Ezra?" I question.

"That's complicated."

I grip the knife in my hand and move it to rest the blade on his neck. "Does this make it less complicated?"

He swallows, the knife bobbing against his Adam's apple.

"Okay, okay," he pants, his eyes moving from my hand that grips the knife, up to my eyes. "I knew of Ezra long before you were about to be married to him."

My brows pull in. "How long?"

"Years," he sighs, looking away from me. "I may have worked with his enemies to attempt to get him locked up."

I pause, standing up and removing the knife from his throat.

"I can't believe I wasted so many years on you."

"That's on you."

Tears sting the back of my eyes, but I don't relent. Clenching my jaw, I take a deep breath. "You never knew me." I wait for a response, but he stays silent.

There's a long pause before either of us speaks.

"Your father owed money to them. He gambled away his fucking life savings down to a box of beer." He snickers. "Pathetic."

"I couldn't taint my name by being associated with you anymore," he admits. "That's why I slept with Heather."

My eyes snap shut at his confession, and although I had a feeling he had slept with my best friend, I always squashed it down and pretended like everything was okay because I thought I loved him so much that losing him would be the end of my happiness.

How wrong I was.

"Heather comes from a respectable family, Aries. You and I both know that's who I should be married to."

I shouldn't feel this angry, this upset, but I do. My hand begins to shake as I open my eyes to find him smirking at me. After all he's said to me, he thinks I'm just going to let him go, but like I said, he doesn't know me.

"You don't belong in this world, Aries, look at you." He tries to get under my skin. "Just a pathetic little girl in search of the love her father never gave her."

That was my last straw, my last inch of kindness being stripped away by a few words. My blood boils in my veins as my hand lashes out, bringing the knife to slash across his throat. I stand there, chest heaving, as I watch the blood squirt from the open wound, running like a fountain down his neck.

The reality of what I've just done hasn't sunk in yet, as I stand here, staring at Ray's lifeless body. I felt another piece of my soul crack and leave my body as soon as Ray took his last breath. I wish I could say I felt guilt. I wish I could say I'm remorseful, but all I feel is an overwhelming sense of power.

CHAPTER NINETEEN
Ezra

I wipe the vomit off my hand and throw Nico's arm over my shoulder. It's late, and I'd much rather be in bed with my wife than cleaning up after my brother. The breeze hits us both as I walk him to the car.

"Why do you do this to yourself?" I ask, not thinking I would get a reply with him being so heavily intoxicated.

"You know why." He slurs his words, barely being able to move one foot in front of the other. "If the King hates picking up after his brother, why not get Henry to do it?"

"You're *my* brother." I squeeze his wrist tighter as we round the corner, the Porsche shining in the distance, parked on the side of the street. "You need to talk about it, Nico."

"Talking is for pussies." He burps. "I'd rather drown myself in alcohol and endless pussy."

"Suit yourself." There's only so much I can say, so much I can do, at some point he'll learn. Whether it's the easy way or the hard way, he will learn.

"I'm not like you, brother. I'm not fuelled by darkness," he admits.

"I know."

"You have no idea what goes through my sick, twisted

mind." I grit my teeth at my brother's words. I try to understand him, and it hurts that I can't be the one to help him. The things we saw as children, the things we did, will always be with us, no matter how hard we try to change it. I've learnt to bask in the pain, the dark, the nothingness, but Nico was too young to have witnessed everything he did.

I was sixteen and Nico was thirteen when our father forced us to kill for the very first time. I wish I could say I didn't revel in the power that came with it, but I know Nico didn't. I know it affected him more than it did me, and I can't pretend to know what it must have felt like for him.

"She's alright you know." He smiles a half smile through the drunkenness. "Aries."

I feel a tug in my chest at her name.

"She's more than alright, she's the bullet in my guns, the blood in my veins, but mostly, she's the reason I think I'm starting to believe we can be loved." I grit my teeth as I watch a tear roll down my brother's face.

"Whatever you do, don't lose her," he whispers to me as I help him into the car and shut the door.

You have no idea how much the thought of losing her terrifies me, brother.

After dropping Nico off at his house, I head to the one place I know I can find solace. Putting the key into the lock, I turn it and walk into our home and straight upstairs to the master bedroom in search of my wife. It's been one hell of a day, and the only thing I want to do is slide right up inside my beautiful wife and make her scream my name, then watch as she drifts off to sleep, tucked safely beside me. The door creaks as I push it open, revealing an untouched bed, perfectly made with crisp white sheets.

"Sweetheart?" I call out, my eyes landing on the door to the en suite bathroom. The light is off, and my mind begins to race. "Are you in there?" I turn the knob and walk through.

Empty.

My heartbeat picks up, thrashing against my chest as I race into the other rooms in search of her, but I come up empty each time.

"Boss, you better come see this." I hear Henry from downstairs, my footsteps banging on the staircase as I reach him. The door to the basement is wide open, the stench of blood and sweat seeping into the hallway. My jaw clenches as I walk down the stairs, into the basement, the light still on. Not many things can shock me given the circumstances I grew up in and continue to live in, but the sight of dead Ray with a note pinned to his chest is a first. I rip the paper off his body, the pin staying in place.

I know what I must do now. I know how to prove to you that I belong in your world. Don't come after me. Let me do this for you, Ezra.

My stomach flips, bile rising to the surface as I rack my brain for what she could possibly be up to. Heat surfaces within me until the flames lick at my edges, fury bubbling to the surface.

"Find her," I say through gritted teeth to Henry standing beside me.

The door flies open, banging on the wall behind. I scan the room, my eyes falling to my brother lying on his couch, still asleep, dead to the entire world. I kick one of his feet that is dangling off the edge, and he murmurs something inaudible.

"Get the fuck up!" I yell, rage lacing my voice. His eyes shoot open, his hands immediately finding his gun and aiming it at me.

"Ezra?" He turns the safety back on and places the gun on the table, sitting up to face me. He's still very much drunk given I only dropped him off an hour ago.

"What did you say to Aries?" I force myself to stay calm, wanting to hear what Nico has to say.

"What?" He looks up at me confused, and my mouth turns into a snarl as I lunge forward, grabbing the front of his shirt with both hands, lifting him up, our faces now just inches apart.

"If she's hurt Nico, I swear on our dead father's grave that I will bury you next to him. Alive." My veins pulse as I watch something change inside his eyes, as if realisation had set in. He grabs my wrists and pries my hands off his shirt, his eyes never leaving mine, and it reminds me of our childhood when we used to fight. I'd always win because I was older, stronger and faster, but somewhere along the line, Nico caught up.

"I know it's not your thing, but you need to stay calm for what I am about to tell you, because if she's done what I think she has done, I have a plan." His voice is calm and calculated, making me think about the feeling I have in my gut, the feeling I've never had before. The ugly, swirling, awful sensation that I may never be okay again until I have Aries in my arms. As Nico explains, the anxiety grows inside me, thrashing like waves in a storm when I realise what she has done.

I grip my brother's forearms, my knuckles going white. "She's gone to the Brayfords," I whisper, the fear inside me growing at an unfamiliar rate.

"She's smart. She will be okay," Nico tries to reassure me, but it's no use. I want to storm their home, kill everyone in sight, and take my wife home, no matter how many people must die for it.

"I should have seen through her questions, I should have picked it up, but I didn't." His hand lands on my shoulder, squeezing. "She wants to prove herself to you."

She doesn't fucking need to.

All the shit I said to her was to make her sweat, to make her realise that she's not the good girl she thinks she is, not for her to waltz right into the enemy's home to prove a point, and least of all to me. Regret slices through me like a sharp knife cutting into fresh meat.

"What's your plan?" I ask, my eyes finding his, desperate to know what he's thinking because at this very moment, all I can think about is her and for her to be okay.

Nico smiles, the familiar psychopathic smile I see three seconds before he kills. "I think we finally have a way in, brother." His teeth white against the shine of the moon through the large bay windows. My hands fly out, pushing him backwards, his body only moving in the slightest.

"If you think for one second that I will be leaving my wife in the viper's den, you are devastatingly mistaken." I reach for my guns, pulling them out, I head to the door, ready to wreak havoc on the entire world if I have to, ready to burn every motherfucker in my way, when Nico stops me.

"Think about it, Ezra," his grip tightens on my arm, and everything in me wants to ignore him, but I know he's the one with the calculated plans, and if I want things to go smoothly, I should listen. "She's in their home," he whispers, cunning malice dripping from his voice.

CHAPTER TWENTY
Aries

I feel the hairs on my arms stand as the cool night breeze brushes against my bare skin. Staring up at the large black fence, a trickle of hesitation rushes through me. I could easily walk away, and they would be none the wiser. I could easily just turn around and go back to Ezra, to our warm bed, but I won't.

Not after what I had already done.

Not after promising him I would prove it to him, how much I am meant to be in his world.

I glance down at myself, my jeans and my shirt splattered in blood, *Ray's blood*. A part of me died when he did. The nicest version of me, the pushover version of me, no longer exists. I am Aries Casella, and I will prove that I deserve the name, even if I might die trying. Gathering all the courage I have, I press the buzzer on the wall of the fence, and after a few rings, a deep voice answers.

"You shouldn't be here, Miss."

"I have something the Brayfords want." I steel my spine, standing up straight, noting that they are probably watching me because the house is without a doubt littered with security cameras.

"We're not interested in what you're selling."

"I'm not selling shit," I look up into the camera on the

brick wall of the fence, steeling my nerves. "I'm Aries Casella." A moment later, the fence buzzes, opening slowly.

It wasn't easy sneaking out of the house, thanks to the previous delusional escape plan I had. I needed to come up with another way out. Thankfully, Henry is always on a schedule and never steps out of line, even for a minute. As soon as his shift was over, and someone else was to replace him, I took the opportunity to trick the poor guy into 'helping' me rearrange furniture in the upstairs office. Using the excuse of having to use the restroom whilst he heaved the heavy bookcase from one room to another, I took that chance and ran, knowing that if I didn't, I'd have hesitated.

I stare up at the mansion-looking house sitting on acreage. It didn't take long for me to find out a few things about them. They're prestigious after all, their name plastered all over the city for their donations to various charities. I reach the large front doors, and one of them creaks open revealing an older woman, dressed in what I can only assume to be a maid uniform, with an apron around her waist. She waves me in and tells me to wait in the lounge room. Most older homes in this area are worn down over time, leaving them smelling dank, but not this one. This one smelled of fresh lavender, as if someone had just cleaned and lit a candle, expecting a guest.

"Mrs Casella." A deep voice cuts into my thoughts as I whirl around. "You shouldn't be here." I glance up to a tall grey-haired man in a fancy dark-blue robe with striped pyjamas beneath it. His icy blue eyes cut through me like a dagger as he eyes me warily.

"I disagree." I try to control my breath from shaking as I speak.

"Let's not waste time with the games. Drop the act, and tell me why you're *really* here."

"I'm here for revenge." I hold my breath, afraid that if I breathe, he will somehow see through my lies.

"And how does that benefit me?" He cocks his head to the right, eyeing me up and down.

"I have something you want."

"The only thing I want is for the Casella family to suffer." His jaw tics. "And *you* are a Casella. Are you sure you've thought this through?"

"What if I told you I know where your stolen goods are?" His eyes flash at my words as my heart thumps rapidly beneath my chest, climbing up into my throat.

"If you are bluffing, I will make your death so painfully slow that you will beg me to kill you."

I reach into my pocket and hand him the folded piece of paper I had written on earlier in the night, knowing that it was my ticket in, my only salvation in this mission.

His eyes glimmer when he reads the location on the paper, and he takes a step toward me, the floorboards creaking under his weight. "Why should I believe you?" he asks as he tucks the piece of paper in the pocket of his robe.

"Because if you truly want them to suffer, I am your only hope." I clench my jaw and remind myself to stand up straight. I can't show weakness at this time, I just can't. I need him to believe me, and I need him to trust me.

"And why would his *wife* want revenge?" He leans in closer, his face inches away from mine.

I take a deep breath before I speak, steadying my legs, cementing them into the ground.

"Because I am his prisoner." I grit my teeth and hope he believes me and takes the bait.

His eyes narrow as I hold my breath, my heart threatening to shatter my ribcage. "You're telling me the *wife* he paraded around in front of the multiple mafia families of London, is a *prisoner?*" He crosses his arms.

"Be my guest. Send your men to the location I just gave you." I wave at nothing. "I can guarantee your stock will be there." The thing is, I can't guarantee it because I know Ezra will know where I am right now, and Nico would have told him all he told me, so there's a chance it could be empty, but I'm hoping otherwise.

He eyes me up and down and nods. "If I send my men, and they come back empty-handed, I will have your head." His voice is like ice, sending beads of sweat trickling down my back. "For the meantime, I'm sure we can make you *uncomfortable* through the duration of your stay." He smiles a sick, twisted smile, making my stomach churn as he steps aside and motions for me to walk.

We walk through a dark hallway, toward the back of the house, the walls beginning to close in until we stop at an old wooden door. He opens the door and gestures for me to enter. I begin descending the steps into the darkness with only the small amount of light filtering through the hallway into the room. I reach the ground and look up the stairs as the door locks behind him. I slump down into the cold corner of the basement, wrapping my arms around myself and hoping I made the right decision. Even if I didn't, it's too late now.

I spent the entire night awake, my eyes feel heavily strained, my skin cool against the wall of the basement. A shiver rolls down my spine at the thought of what Ezra might be thinking or feeling right now. He hasn't come for me, and that's what I wanted. I smile.

He trusts me.

I have absolutely no idea what I'm doing, and I realise I'm in way over my head, but it's too late to back out now. I want to prove to him that I can do this. That I belong in his twisted world. I don't care what it takes for me to make this right. I want him to see the side of me I've been hiding for so long, afraid of judgement. It's easy to say I love you, it's easy to give people promises you don't intend to keep, but it's harder to prove love. To prove you truly want someone because of who they are instead of what they have to give.

I look around the room, taking it all in, trying to formulate a plan, but the room is bare. Four walls with a table on one side, an old, dusty bookcase next to it, and a small bed on the opposite side. I couldn't sleep. I couldn't move from the spot I am in right now. Not until I know for certain that the Brayfords have fallen for it. Not until I know I have them right where I want them. I hear faint footsteps from above me, the voice of two men, and I strain my ears to hear, but it's no use—they're too far away, and the floor is too thick. I lick my lips, my mouth dryer than ever, and all I want is a glass of cold water. The door to the basement creaks open, and all thoughts of my discomforts vanish, my body stiffening, and my eyes darting to the door as I stand from my spot.

I watch as a figure moves slowly down the stairs, and as soon as their face comes into view, my eyebrows shoot up.

A woman.

She's petite, probably the same height as me. Her long auburn hair curls down her front, bouncing as she takes the stairs. She's pretty and looks somewhat familiar. I clench my jaw as she begins to inch closer to me. Her moss-green eyes shine in the moonlight creeping in from the small window of the basement. She looks me up and down and smiles, lifting a brow.

"Mrs Casella." She singsongs, placing a hand on her hip and shifting her body weight to one leg. "You don't look too bad."

I lift my chin, not wanting to engage.

"Look, I get it, the whole 'proving yourself to fit in' and all that bullshit because you suddenly feel like you belong in this world." My heart catches in my throat at her words.

Fuck.

"But you know what, Aries? You don't." Her tone is stern, the smile dropping from her face, replaced with a scowl. "The world you want to be part of is fucked up, morally unjust, and unethical in every way."

"I don't know what you're talking about." I clench my fists, preparing myself for a fight.

"Spare me, honey." She drops her eyes to my fists and looks back up to me. "You don't stand a chance." She turns and begins walking up the steps before she stops and looks back at me, her eyes piercing into mine. "One word of advice. Don't let them see you sweat."

Her words confuse me. Was she warning me, or was she threatening me?

She disappears as quickly as she came, leaving me with a swirling mind and churning gut. I need to come up with a solution quickly if they return empty-handed. The fear sizzles inside my veins, coating every surface until it reaches my middle, but then something else happens, something I thought I had to work for, something that I believed would never happen to me. The deep-seated darkness I harbour inside me awakens, the thick black cloud rolling in waves, snuffing the fear, coating my insides with a velvety calm, and I let it take over me. A small smile creeps across my face, my heart thumping faster beneath my chest.

If I can't convince them, there's only one other way.

CHAPTER TWENTY-ONE

Ezra

My jaw aches from clenching as I pace back and forth in our warehouse, Nico and Henry beside me. It's been almost twenty-four hours since she's left, and I still have no word from anyone if she's okay. A sickening feeling rushes over me at the thought of her hurt, and I think I just might kill everyone in my path to get to her.

"Will you fucking quit it?" Nico lifts his cigarette to his lips and takes a puff, letting out a breath of smoke, clouding his face for a second. "Pacing isn't going to change anything. Sit down." I let out a low grumble, cursing him under my breath, cursing the moment I decided to listen to my brother and not go after Aries and storm the Brayford house. I don't care that we had plans to bring them to their knees. I don't care that we wanted them to surrender to us, giving us all they own, because right now all I can think about is ripping them from the fucking Earth.

"What do you suggest I do, huh?" I continue pacing, raising my voice. "This is *your* fault. She is there because of *you*, because *you* couldn't keep your fat mouth shut!"

Nico shakes his head, and my blood boils, gripping him

by his shirt and getting in his face. "I swear Nico, if your plan goes to shit, I will dig that grave myself."

Marco runs into the warehouse, out of breath, causing me to let go of Nico and face him. "Ezra, Nico, they've raided the base. The stock is gone." He puffs as he tries to catch his breath.

I turn my head to Nico who is smiling, the cigarette hanging between his teeth. "So, they took the bait." He chuckles, reaching into his pocket and sliding out his phone. He taps away on the screen with a smirk.

"Bait?" I watch as he slides the phone back into his pocket.

"Don't worry, brother. Now we know she's safe because now they have half of their product that *we* stole, and *she* was the one who delivered it to them." He slaps a hand on my shoulder. "Seems she knows what she's doing after all."

That was beside the point. I *knew* Aries was smart. I know she knows what she's doing, but that doesn't mean it's safe, that doesn't mean she should be with my lifelong nemesis. She should be here, under my protection, where I wouldn't let even a fly land on her shoulder. Even after Nico's words, nothing inside me has calmed, the storms still rage, and I grow impatient as each minute passes without her by my side.

"Do you have a contact inside the Brayfords that you're not telling me about?" I question him, knowing he wouldn't hide such information from me, but I have to be sure.

"If I did, we would be on our way to retrieve Aries right now." He takes another puff from his cigarette. "Unfortunately for you, brother, it's still a waiting game."

The problem with revenge is not the bloodshed or the

hate. I's when it becomes so deeply engraved into your soul that you see nothing else. You need to be cold and calculated to be able to stay true to a promise like revenge, and although I have always been true to my words, I'm not doing this for my father. I'm doing this for our family.

Dominic Casella doesn't deserve revenge, but his sons do.

I might play the King well, but what everyone doesn't see is how much I crave to feel something other than complete emptiness. That's what Aries gives me...feeling. I know the monster inside craves blood, craves violence, hate, and revenge, but when she's with me, all I see is her.

All I *want* is her.

It's been two days. Two whole days without a word from Aries or anyone for that matter, just static silence. I keep prodding my men for any information, if they've seen anyone or noticed anything suspicious around our bars, our clubs, our distilleries, and our warehouses, but each time, I get a sympathetic look and a shake of a head.

I'm fucking tired of waiting, of sitting on my hands and wishing I could be beside her. I know how much we need this. I know how much we have sacrificed over the years to have an in or even a little bit of knowledge on how to get the Brayfords to bend at the knee—so to speak—but after my father's death, we needed it even more.

No.

We *wanted* it.

I realise the courage it would've taken Aries to do something like this, and I can't help but notice my heart swelling with pride as a smile takes over my face. I feel the sweat slide down my face from my temple to my chin and onto the floor as I look up to my reflection in the mirror. The only thing I seem to be able to do is workout. Everything else I do, I end up thinking about Aries, wanting to storm the Brayford house and ruin all of Nico's plans.

If there is one thing I have learnt in the past, it's that I need to trust my brother a lot more when it comes to strategy because he has the mind for it.

I may be king, but what king doesn't listen to his advisers?

"You know, I think this is the most time we've spent together in years." Nico's voice snaps me back into the room.

I glance over at him sprawled out on the floor, looking at the ceiling, lost in whatever thoughts he has. It's true what he says. We rarely ever spend time together unless it has to do with work, and it's been that way for a long time, since we basically stopped being teenagers.

"Well maybe we would if you weren't drunk or high all the time." I stand and walk over to the squat rack, placing weights on either side.

"Dick."

"Ass," I retort, and he chuckles. "You don't need to babysit me."

"I disagree." He interlocks his hands, placing them behind his head on the floor. "Ezra Casella is dangerous, but the Casella King in love"—he blows out a breath—"could wreak havoc and fuck up Houdini's plans."

I don't say anything. Instead, I stand, the bar resting on my shoulders, behind my neck and begin squatting, revelling in the strain in my muscles, the pain in my legs.

"I never thought I would see you like this…" He pauses. "So worried about someone else." He continues talking, and I wish he would stop.

"She's not just *someone*." I huff, placing the bar on the rack and turning to face him. "She is my *wife.*" Nico grins, his eyes meeting mine.

"Whipped." He chuckles as he rises, his eyes become sombre as we stare at each other. "She's family now." He takes a few steps toward me, as he places his hands inside his pockets. "If I can promise you one thing, brother." I watch the sincerity in his eyes grow. "It's that I will have her back in your arms, no matter the cost."

I appreciate his sentiment, but I know I would kill him myself if he died in the process. He's smarter than that, and I know what he said meant something else.

I would rather die than have you live your life without the woman you love.

Because *that's* what Nico wants. Love. Even if he will never truly admit it, he wants a love that consumes him, someone who would walk to the ends of the Earth with him, who will love him more than they love themselves.

"I appreciate you, Nico." My voice is low, unsure. I rarely express my feelings and least of all to my family, but I refuse to repeat the same mistakes my father made. "I trust you with my life."

Nico smiles, and something inside me breaks because his smile isn't full like it used to be. It looks different, almost like it's *fractured*.

His phone rings, interrupting, and his face turns serious, answering the call.

"Speak." Even his voice is different. He takes one look at me and steps to turn away. I grab his shoulder with one hand and squeeze.

"If that's about my wife, I deserve to know," I say through gritted teeth, and he nods, placing the call on speaker.

"Repeat what you just told me. Ezra is here," he speaks into the phone.

"Sir, we're in," Marco's voice filters through the phone. "We have eyes and ears on Aries, and she's safe. From what we know, they're keeping her in the basement, but that's about as much information we have right now."

My heart does a little flip at the mention of her name.

"Who's the person responsible for giving us this information?" I question.

"We don't know, sir." His voice falters. "*They* called *us.*"

"What do you mean?" Confusion rattles my brain as he continues.

"They used a voice changer and hung up before we could trace the call," he pauses, waiting for me to respond, then adds, "They also sent us a photo of her, as proof." Nico's phone dings, and he opens the message. The photo looks like it's been screen captured from a security camera. Aries is sitting in the corner of the almost empty room, her head resting on the wall behind her.

I'm conflicted between feeling at ease at the sight of her unharmed, and furious that she has put herself in this situation.

"I guess we owe them a huge thanks." Nico speaks for me, my mind unable to come up with anything, or think of anyone inside the Brayford house who would be willing to help us at all.

For the first time in days, I feel a little less psychotic, a little less tense, and a lot more faithful that Nico's plan will work. He hangs up, a smirk playing on his lips.

"Don't." I walk away from him and pick up my duffel, slinging it over my shoulder. Nico raises his hands in surrender.

"I wasn't about to say anything." He chuckles as we both make our way out to my Porsche.

CHAPTER TWENTY-TWO
Aries

A shiver rolls down my spine, goose bumps forming on my arms as the cold settles into my bones. It's been three days since I've been here, waiting. They've fed me, given me soup with bread and water, which is more than I expected them to, but I can't help the nagging feeling taking over my mind. I can't exactly give them more information on the Casellas without compromising them too much, which leaves me in an even shittier position than when I came here. I wrack my brain for ideas, my arms wrapping around myself, trying to keep my body warm as I sit on the cold concrete floor. The basement door flies open, thudding when it hits the wall behind. Black boots descend the staircase, until the same man I saw the first night I came here stands before me, with three men standing tall behind him. I get to my feet immediately, putting some distance between us.

"Turns out your information checks out." He smiles, a sinister feeling swirling inside my stomach as his eyes narrow.

"So will you give me a proper reception?" I place my hand on my hips, and I'm shocked at how calm I am. "Since I practically helped you get back your product from your lifelong nemesis?"

He chuckles, the throaty sound filling the empty space in the basement. "You are brave, I'll give you that." He lunges forward, both hands clasping around my shirt, lifting me up off the floor. He bangs me against the wall behind, the back of my head stinging from the impact. "Do you think you're smarter than the rest of us, you bitch?" I grip his hands, trying to pry them off, his stale breath fans my face as he speaks. "Do you think I would just let you into my home, if I didn't already have a plan for you?" Terror clumps in my throat at his words.

Is he onto me?

"Don't think for one second that if I find out that your intentions aren't what they seem, that I will let you live. I will dismember you in front of Ezra and save his sweet death for last." His knuckles bruise my collarbone as he presses me into the wall. "And one more thing." He leans in, the stench of cigar mixed with whiskey engulfing my surroundings as he whispers into my ear. "It was only half the product." He drops me and steps away, cool air brushing my cheek as I steady myself against the wall.

My heart pounds in my ears as I think of what to say next.

"I needed to make sure you wouldn't kill me." I rub the sore spot on my collarbone. "I know where the rest of it is."

"Go on then, love. I don't have all fucking day." He lights up a cigar, waiting for my answer, and I search my mind for somewhere, anywhere I can lead them without them catching onto what I'm doing or what my plan is.

"They have a distillery." My voice comes out scratchy.

"They have many." His eyes are focused on me, the men behind him haven't moved a muscle. "What about them?"

I hesitate, hoping that what I am about to tell him next is correct, otherwise I might just be handing him my head on a silver platter. If I know Ezra, I know he wouldn't be stupid enough to hide the rest of the product in their warehouses There are too many cops searching illegal facilities. Instead, what better place to hide it than right under their noses?

"The rest of your product is in their Brixton distillery," I say through a clenched jaw.

He snaps his fingers, and all three men walk up the stairs and out of the basement. The air grows thick as he watches me, whilst he brings his cigar to his mouth, sucking then blowing out a puff of smoke.

"You know, I used to think the Casella boys were smart," he drawls. I don't dare speak, afraid of what I might say. "But now," his eyes graze from my face down my body to my feet and back up again. "I've realised they're dumb enough to trust a woman." He steps closer, causing me to back up against the wall. He steals the space, sucking it up like a black hole, as his eyes throw daggers into mine. The hatred rolls off his skin, cascading through the air and settling over me like hard pellets of rain. He leans in, his nose brushing the top of my ear, sending a shiver rolling down my spine. "I won't be making the same mistake," he whispers, as nausea bubbles inside my stomach and a searing pain lodges itself on my arm, my screams billowing through the emptiness as he retreats, walking back up the stairs without another word. I look at my arm, the burnt flesh angry and red, raised above the rest of my skin.

Fucker.

He fucking burnt me with the end of his cigar.

I just hope the information I gave them is correct and

that they do find what they're looking for, otherwise I'm dead, and this effort to prove something will have been in vain.

I blow on my fresh wound, hoping it'll ease the stinging somehow, and it doesn't. Tears well up in my eyes at the pain searing deep into my bones, and I wish I could just cut it off and be done with it, but life doesn't work that way. Life makes you work for it, live through it, and heal by the end of it, even if it leaves a hideous scar. I clench my teeth from the sting and just as I'm about to rip the end of my jeans to have something to wrap my wound with, I hear the door to the basement click, my eyes darting to it. The door opens slowly, as the pounding in my chest rapidly increases, revealing the same woman from before. Walking in, she gently closes the door and makes her way down the steps with a black box in her hand.

"Come to tell me how much I don't belong again?" My voice is cruel, but I don't care. The pain has overtaken my body, and all I want to do is hurt them right back.

She doesn't reply, just stares at me, and her eyes glance down to my wound. Hastily I place my arm behind me, her eyes finding mine again. She releases a heavy sigh and places the black box on the floor, opening it to rummage through the contents. I try to peek at what she's doing and what's in the box, but I can't see from this distance. I almost think she's about to pull a weapon or torturous device on me, but when her hand comes into view, she's holding gauze, a wrap, and ointment. My brows furrow with confusion as she walks over to me. Grabbing my arm, she begins to clean the wound with a cotton ball and antiseptic. I wince when I feel the sting, her hand grabbing onto my arm harder to stop me from moving.

"Why are you helping me?" I question, and she purses her lips, never once taking her eyes off my arm.

"Are you surprised?" She answers my question with a question, the one thing I absolutely despise.

"Are you incapable of answering a question with an answer?" I almost regret asking her when she presses the cotton ball into my wound harder, and I rip my arm out of her hold with a yelp. Her eyes meet mine, and she pauses as if she's trying to decipher something.

"Why did you come here?" Her voice is small, almost a whisper, catching me off guard as I expected her to hurt me further. I stay silent for a beat.

"For revenge," I finally say, feeling her eyes blaze a hole through me.

"Don't lie, Aries." Her brows draw in together, creating small lines between them. "I know you're here because you want to help the Casella brothers."

I swallow, hoping she didn't see that. "No—I..." I don't get to finish when she cuts in.

"Don't be that fucking stupid and blind to see that it's not working," her words are cutthroat, but maybe that's what I need, to stop living in delusion that my act is working because it's not. She points to the door. "They will fucking kill you and feed you to them for sport. This is not some game of chess, Aries. This is a war which has been going on for generations before us. Men, women, and children have died at the hands of these men because of a feud that started so many years ago." I feel a clump growing in my throat.

"You didn't answer my question." I divert the conversation, not wanting to give anything away just yet, not until I know I can trust her. She looks to the floor then back up at me.

"Let's just say you're not the first to be in this position."
She lifts her long sleeve shirt, revealing multiple scars, some that are burns, some that are deep gashes. My heart immediately sinks, realising the torture and torment she must have gone through.

"Who are you to them?" I ask. "Did they do this to you?" I whisper, my voice now lowers in case anyone might be spying on us.

"You're not asking the right questions." She shakes her head as if she's tired of the conversation. Grabbing my arm, she continues to dab the cotton on my wound. "You need to find a way out of here," her eyes meet mine. "Before they kill you."

Her hands slip into her back pocket, as she reveals a key, holding it up in front of me. "It's the key to the basement door. The guards on the grounds swap shifts at midnight, which will give you the perfect opportunity to slip through when they switch with the cover of darkness." I stare at her blankly, still shocked that she's helping me.

"But won't they know you helped me?" I ask, now worried about leaving her here.

"Don't worry about me. I can handle myself around them." She smiles, but it doesn't reach her eyes. "Take it." She shakes the key in my face as I reach up and take it from her, shoving it into my back pocket. She wraps my wound in silence and begins packing up the contents of the box when she's finished.

"When you reach the front gate, run and don't fucking look back." She heads for the stairs, and before I know it, she's gone, leaving me with a sickening feeling growing heavier in my belly.

CHAPTER TWENTY-THREE
Ezra

Silence fills the air as I stare at my laptop, my mind far from what I should be doing right now. It's been twenty-four hours since the last contact from the traitor inside the Brayford house, and all I can think about is my wife sitting on the cold concrete floor of their filthy basement. Who knows how many people they have killed or tortured there. I push the thoughts from my mind and try to regain my focus on the spreadsheet in front of me. Failing miserably when I check my phone for the hundredth time in the last ten minutes, only to see it blank, no text, no call, nothing. Growing impatient, I head outside and find Henry standing with his hands clasped in front of him. He tips his head to acknowledge my presence.

"Where's Nico?" I ask just as my phone buzzes.

Speaking of the fucker.

"You were supposed to be here an hour ago," I seethe into the phone.

"Relax, I'm leaving the warehouse now." I hear shuffling in the background as he speaks.

"Just meet me there, it'll take you too long in traffic to come here." I hang up the phone, and just as I slip into my

Porsche, I watch as Henry gets a call. His face contorts as he begins to walk around to me.

"Boss, you need to hear this." He clenches his jaw as he hands me the phone.

"What the fuck is it now?"

"Uh…" Marco hesitates.

"Spit it out, Marco."

"Sir, the distillery in Brixton has been raided." He pauses, waiting for me to reply, but all I can see is red.

"Motherfucker!" Rage coils through me as I take in a deep breath, attempting to steady my mind and keep myself from doing something I will regret. I hang up the phone and hand it to Henry.

"Go to my mother's place. I need you there in case shit gets fucked," I speak, as I turn the engine of the Porsche on, the roar of the exhaust filling my ears as I slam the door shut.

I have one goal and one goal only. That is to get to the distillery in record time.

Fumes burn my nostrils as I walk into the distillery with Nico standing on my left. My jaw clenches at the sight of the wreckage left behind. Barrels of alcohol have been stolen along with the rest of the stash we had from the Brayfords.

"Did she know about this too?" I question Nico, as I watch him take in the sight.

"She did," he confirms, but all it does is form a twist further inside my gut.

My mind betrays me as it questions her loyalty, and I quickly shut it down.

"Get everyone working on making this into a

respectable distillery again." I grab Nico by the collar with both hands, blind fury emanating from every pore of my body. "We're doing this *my* way now." I let him go and walk out the door as he follows. I gave Nico a chance to do things his way, the civil way, to see if it would work, but there is only one language these fuckers will understand.

The language of a deranged fucking psychopath.

I want my wife back, and I will set the world on fire for her, burning everyone and everything in my path until I have her in my arms. Leaving her to prove something to me was the wrong decision. I see that now even though it wasn't what I wanted, it's what *she* wanted.

Regardless of what she wants, I will show her exactly how fucked up our world can be. For her, I will go further into the darkness, until there isn't a shred of light left, even if I never reemerge.

My guns hang heavy in their holsters as I watch the boys gather their ammunition, armed with everything from guns down to knives and c4.

"What exactly is the plan, brother?" Nico questions as he cocks his gun after loading it.

"We tear through everything and everyone in sight under the cover of darkness." A smile grows on my lips at the promise of bloodshed. "I don't give a fuck who you kill, as long as I get my wife back."

"This will change everything, you know that, right?" Nico raises his eyebrows, and I hear the question in his tone, without him having to say anything.

Am I sure I want to do it this way and make it a public spectacle like we promised the family? The reality is I wouldn't have Aries in this position more than a minute longer than necessary. I would abandon all my beliefs, my prior plans, and absolutely everything else to ensure her safety in my arms again. I nod once and without another look, he gathers our weapons and heads to the three black vans waiting outside the warehouse, loading it up. I crack my neck, pressure settling into the base of my stomach, the pressure of her safety riding heavily on my shoulders.

The treaty our ancestors had signed hundreds of years ago should have been obeyed, but like any human, we got greedy. We wanted more. Eventually, the thirst for power overruled a silly little treaty between our ancestors. I wasn't planning to do this, to create another war between the mafia families of London. Not when I know for a fact how much we could all benefit by working together. There is enough money in the world to set up our future families for years to come, but no one is smart enough to put their pride aside and forget about revenge. It's no secret that when we do this, the other families will retaliate in response, making us their target.

Like I said, men haven't changed, and we will kill each other, until the earth dries up, and we are no longer.

"Listen up!" I project my voice so the guys at the back can hear. "Tonight will be the night we have all been waiting for." I watch all the faces gathered in front of me, some family, some friends of the Casella family for years. "We will storm the Brayford house and take back what's mine. I don't care that this is not how it was supposed to be done, and if you so much as *think* about questioning it, leave now." A few exchange glances around the table and avert their gazes to the floor. "I'm not asking you to go to war…" I pause, watching some of the men in the room, most of them old enough to be fathers, all of which are sons. "I am asking you to die." The silence is thick with tension, but my mind is made up. I will get my wife back tonight, no matter how many have to die. Nico walks through the doors, looks to me, and nods.

"We're with you until the end, boss," one of them calls out, and they all nod, gathering their weapons and heading to the vans.

CHAPTER TWENTY-FOUR
Aries

My stomach growls as the sun rises, shining through the small window of the basement, illuminating the small dust particles in the air.

I slowly approach the steps and begin ascending, trying to be as quiet as possible. Usually by this time the guards have switched over, and the 'nicer' one of the two should be on duty. I press my ear to the wooden door but have no luck with hearing anything beyond it. I rap my knuckles on it lightly, hoping for a reply from the nicer guard.

"What?" His tone is flat and almost bored.

"I need to pee," I say softly, hoping he'll accommodate me. I hear a low grumble followed by fumbling keys. Taking a few steps back, I wait for the door to open, revealing the nicer guard.

"Make it quick." He nods toward the bathroom which is directly opposite the basement, and I'm so thankful that I sprint up the steps.

I wash my hands and take a look at myself in the mirror. My hair is basically stuck to my scalp, black rings surround my eyes, and my gaze drops down to the mark that bastard left on my arm, I rip my gaze from it and shut off the faucet. The spot still aches and reminds me of the depth of my situation. I'm starting to get the sinking feeling that perhaps that woman was right. I might need to plan for an escape if he comes back, and my information hasn't checked out. My heart beats faster inside my chest, pounding and rattling my ribcage.

"Hurry up." The guard's voice filters through the door, and I open it, walking back inside the basement and down the steps.

It has to be tonight. I have to escape tonight, but not before I have something on them. Not before I can go back to Ezra with some sort of information. I ponder and plan my escape as I hear footsteps approaching the basement, and I tense, my eyes immediately finding the door as it opens. My heart picks up speed only to realise it's her, the same woman from before. She gently closes the door and walks down the steps, balancing a tray of food in her hands. Reaching me, she places it down on the floor and takes a seat in front of me. I glance at the tray, delicious scones, danishes, and pastries on a large plate with a glass of orange juice. My mouth practically salivates with the scent alone.

"Is this a bribe of some sort?" I nod to the woman, and she shakes her head.

"We over ordered." She smiles half a smile.

"How do I know it's not poisoned?" I lick my lips to stop from drooling.

"You think if I wanted to kill you that I wouldn't have done it sooner?" she raises an eyebrow, and she has a point. I begin with the cherry danish, taking a massive bite, bigger than I can fit in my mouth, and the first taste has me rolling my eyes back into my skull. It's fucking heavenly.

"What's your name anyway?" I ask through my mouthful. She hesitates for a moment, her eyes dropping to the tray of food, then back to mine. A moment passes, and I almost think she won't answer.

"Darcy." She says in a small voice.

"Well, you already know my name." I laugh as pastry flies out of my mouth and onto the floor. She stares at me a minute before she laughs, and I can't help but feel my trust growing for her a little more. "Who are you, Darcy? And why are you helping me?" I question, watching her reaction.

"You're still asking the wrong questions, Aries." She sighs. "Have you come up with a plan to get the fuck out of here?"

I shrug. "I'll figure it out."

Her brows pull in as she stands.

"Do you seriously have no urgency?" Her voice is raised, and my frustration begins to creep in.

"How the fuck am I supposed to get out of a heavily fortified stronghold with guards crawling in every nook and cranny?" I stand, frustrated with her switching emotions on me like a light switch. "I'm one person, and as you so eloquently put it, Darcy, I am not from this world, so I don't know hand to hand combat."

She sighs. "Look, I'll come back after Leo questions you again, and we will work something out together." She reaches out her hand. "Deal?"

I shake her hand and agree, "Fine."

Unless she wants to get out of here too?

The minutes and hours tick by as I wait, the sun now moved to the other side of the window, creating shadows in the already dark basement. I can't stop thinking about what Darcy said to me and the feeling I got when she asked me if I had a plan. I shake the thoughts of her out of my head and focus on something—*or someone*—that's going to make me feel better. I imagine the night after our wedding.

"By the time you go to sleep tonight, I'll know every curve of your body, every line and scar on your skin."

My body shivers with the memory, a reminder of just how much he affects me and just how much I want to succeed with what I came here to do. Determination floods my body, as I pick up the fork off the tray and stash it in my back pocket.

I'll be ready.

The basement door is unlocked as I watch Leo trudge down the steps with a shit-eating grin plastered on his face.

"There she is, boys!" His voice bellows through the basement as two men walk behind him. A whiff of cigar and whiskey hits my nose, and I breathe from my mouth, not wanting to puke up the contents of my breakfast. "Well, Mrs Casella, looks like you may be useful to us after all."

I swallow, the small feeling of relief rushing over me, but I keep my eyes firmly on his to anticipate his next move.

"You see." He walks around me, circling me like prey. "Now that I have had a *taste* of what it's like to win against the Casellas," he leans into my ear, his breath fanning my neck, sending a disgusting wave of tingles through my spine. "I want more," he whispers.

I consider reaching for my fork and stabbing him, but I'm no match for the other two guards who look like they're three times my size.

"I want to see their empire crumble before I make

them bleed." He grins, coming back around to face me. "Tell me how to get into their warehouse."

My heart sinks. "I-I don't know."

He scoffs, "You are his *wife*."

"He never really shared this part of his life with me." I tell the truth, although I doubt Leo will believe it.

He grips my chin, squeezing until my lips jut out and the burning sensation seeps into my skin from his hold. "Don't *fucking* lie to me." My heart thumps beneath my chest, so fast I almost pass out.

"I'm not lying, I truly don't know." My voice is desperate for him to let go.

He removes his hand, pushing me with force, and I land on my ass on the hard concrete floor, the fork digging into my jeans.

"Fucking pathetic." He spits at the ground, his eyes reaching mine with menace and hatred. Then something else flashes in them, like he had an idea, and a skin crawling smirk replaces his scowl. "If you won't give me the information willingly, then I will *take* it."

My stomach twists at his sinister smile, an uneasy feeling washing over me.

I should have taken the chance to stab him when he was close.

CHAPTER
TWENTY-FIVE
Aries

My screams thunder through the basement walls as both my arms are hung from the ceiling, my hands desperately grappling at the chains to hold my weight as my legs dangle under me. Fear is lodged firmly in my throat as I watch a man with a black mask gripping a large iron stick that looks like a cane walk towards me. My eyes swing to Leo on one side of the room, leaning against the wall, his expression almost bored at the sight of me.

"I told you I don't know." I breathe through the pain radiating through my wrist and into my arms.

"I'm sure you do," he nods to the man with the stick. "Somewhere in that little brain of yours, you have stored information. I'm just trying to help you access it, love." He grins, a sickening feeling planting itself in my chest. My heart thumps louder, threatening to break through my ribs as I watch the man lower the stick into burning coal, the tip of the stick now bright orange as he lifts it up to my face. I wrack my brain for any information I can muster, something, anything, that I can think of, but nothing comes to me.

"Does it make you feel good?" I seethe, my eyes firmly

locked on Leo's. His eyebrows pull together as he notices the shift in my voice.

"I don't think you're in the position to be asking questions." He pushes off the wall and walks over to me to stand directly in my line of sight.

"Does it feel good to hurt people who you believe are incapable of defending themselves?" I spit at his feet, hoping to draw some sort of reaction from him.

He clenches his jaw. "You know *nothing* about me."

"I know more than you think I do." I grin through the pain as he nods to the man in the corner who lowers me to the floor, the pressure finally releasing from my wrists.

"Do tell me what you think you know."

"You have a traitor amongst you," I whisper. "Someone who has been aiding me."

His face drops as he looks around the room. "No one would dare betray me."

My lips curve into a smile as I watch his eyes grow wide.

"How do I know you're telling the truth?" he questions.

"Check my pockets."

Sure enough, when he finds the key to the basement door, his eyes draw in as he paces the basement floor in front of me. "Tell me who it is," he demands, his voice dropping low.

I shake my head from side to side with a smirk firmly plastered on my lips. "It doesn't work that way." He stares at me, contemplating his next move, and I know I have him right where I want him. "First, I need you to let me out of these restraints."

He nods to the man in the corner, and the old rusty shackles are taken off, freeing my wrists.

"If you're not careful, this person will be the cause of

your foundation crumbling." I speak, biding my time, trying to come up with the best way to get what I want.

"Stop with the theatrics, and spit it out." His jaw tics as he raises his chin.

"Now why would I do that when my safety is not guaranteed?" I rub my wrists. "I have something *you* want, and you have something *I* want." I smile, making him even more mad. "I'm sure we can come to some sort of agreement."

"Get to the fucking point," he snaps.

"I want you to destroy everything you have on the Casella family and burn all the stock you own," I demand. "I want to see it with my own eyes."

He pauses for a moment, and then his laughter echoes through the emptiness of the basement. "Who the fuck do you think you are making a demand like that?"

I raise my chin. "I am a Casella."

He scowls as he takes a step toward me, my feet firmly planted on the ground. I don't dare make a move. "I should've killed you the moment you stepped foot on this property."

"That's one thing we can agree on, but you didn't." I grin. "Now, if you want to know who has been betraying you, I suggest you do what I want."

He hesitates for a minute, considering my words. "How will I know you're telling the truth?"

"I have proof." I lie.

I'm not ready to serve up Darcy to them on a silver platter, so I'm going to drag this out as much as I can until I know what I want has been done.

"I don't trust you," he whispers as he leans in.

I watch as multiple pages of paper burn and disintegrate in the fire. I personally read through each one, ensuring that they were related to the Casellas. Some files contained images of Nico and Ezra committing several felonies, others contained their father's past information.

The stars burn in the night sky as the flames crackle in the darkness, whilst I watch as Leo throws chunks of paper onto the burning pile.

"Wait." I stop him as his hand reaches for the documents which contain the Casella family's history. It could be useful information for Ezra to know what they had on him and his family, so I keep the documents under my arm and gesture for Leo to continue. "Keep going." My eyes quickly skim through the paperwork, searching, and my mouth drops open as I realise what it is I'm reading.

There's no way this is real.

I watch from the corner of my eye as Darcy stands a few feet behind Leo. Her eyes find mine, and she shoots me a warning glance, her eyes fleeting to the large gates behind me. I'm certain she doesn't know that I've told Leo he has a traitor in his team because if she knew, she'd probably gut me where I stand. My eyes follow hers to the gate, and I consider running, but I'm too deeply invested now to abandon what I came here to do.

There's a roar in the distance of a vehicle, the headlights shining through the gates as everyone's heads turn in confusion to watch the lights illuminate the yard.

"Sir?" One of the men looks to Leo as he reaches for his gun.

"Get to your fucking formations!" he yells, and my heart sinks into my stomach as I run. I run towards the trees surrounding the property as firm hands grab at me.

"Where the fuck do you think you're going?" One of Leo's men has his arms around me pulling me back to the house. My breathing is erratic as I launch my head back, making contact with his. Pain radiates through my skull at the impact as he rears back, giving me just enough time to sprint for cover.

"Aries!" I hear Darcy's voice and make the mistake of looking behind me, a huge brick of a man tackles me to the ground as the roar of engines get closer. Both our eyes whip to the large iron gate as two vans ram through them, bursting them open. They come to a stop, and countless men cascade out of the vans wearing all black, holding multiple weapons. My heart is in my throat as I watch guns being fired until I'm lifted up over this man's shoulders and taken into the vast forest behind the property. No matter how much I struggle, how hard I hit, he doesn't let go of me.

"Put me down!" I kick and scream, and he pushes me off his shoulder, the ground coming up to meet my back, hard and fast. Insurmountable pain bursts through my shoulder, as I hear a loud pop when I make contact with the ground. Tears sting my eyes as I scream, straining my throat, my hand coming up to cradle my dislocated shoulder.

I'm helpless as I lay on the ground, watching him tower over me.

He grins, causing my stomach to twist at his sickening smile. Swiftly I lift my foot, kicking him right between the legs as he topples forward, groaning, cradling his crotch with both hands. Swivelling backwards, I make myself get up, ignoring the shooting pain in my shoulder and the air now burning my lungs as I run through the trees, unsure of where I'm heading. For all I know, I could just be heading back to the house. I didn't recognise any of the vehicles or the men who came bursting into the yard, so I don't know if I can trust them.

What if they're law enforcement?

There goes my hope, making itself known again, although right now I need to stay sceptical.

My thighs burn as I continue through the trees, looking back to make sure he isn't following me. I stop, leaning against a trunk, sucking up as much air as I can, my lungs heaving.

I hear the crunch of leaves, and my head whips around, my eyes darting back and forth, searching through the darkness.

CHAPTER TWENTY-SIX

Ezra

Gunfire pierces through the quiet of the night as my men rush into the stronghold that is the Brayford family home.

"Aries!" I yell her name with some fucking hope that she's outside and not within those walls. The air lingers with revenge and violence as we rush the few men left on the field.

"We need to get Leo!" Nico shouts as he aims his gun and fires three shots into a man's chest. I survey the grounds, searching for Leo, my heart pumping in my chest, adrenaline surging through my veins.

I'm going for blood tonight.

"I'm going in there." I nod toward the house, and Nico shakes his head as if to say it's a bad idea. "Cover me, brother. I'm going to get my wife."

I shoot my way through the field as the smoke from the fire bellows up into the dark night sky. I take the porch steps three at a time and barge straight through the wooden door with my shoulder.

It's quiet.

Too quiet.

I begin to take slow steps into the large mansion,

scanning each room as I pass it, with only one thing on my mind.

Aries.

The floorboards squeak on my left, and I whip myself around, taking aim and shooting the fucker right between the eyes. The commotion continues outside as bullets fly through the windows at the front. I know my brother can handle himself, and I can trust my men to follow instructions, but what I don't trust is myself.

I'm not scared, no.

I'm fucking *terrified* that if I find Aries harmed in any way, there will be no end for my thirst for revenge. I push the thoughts from my mind as I sneak through toward the back of the mansion to the large kitchen overlooking the back garden.

It's empty, besides a few pieces of patio furniture. It's surrounded by thick shrubbery and tall trees. I squint as something glints in the moonlight behind the trees. This whole time I've been searching in here, but I never once considered she could be out there.

My heart drops low into my stomach at the thought of her in the dark, in the woods, unprotected. I exit through the back door, scanning the area with my gun raised as I head into the thick forest, beginning my search. I walk for a whilst and come across nothing.

My jaw clenches at the thought that I've wasted all this precious time.

Aries, where are you?

I turn back to head toward the house when I notice the gunfire has stopped. This could mean two things, and I sure as fuck hope it's the outcome that's in my favour.

I make my way around the side of the mansion toward the front, and when I reach the fire, my heart sinks and fury ignites within me. I watch as Nico is being forced to his knees, some of my men alongside him.

Still no fucking sign of Aries or Leo.

"Let them go," I demand, walking toward the men pointing their guns at Nico.

"Fucking took you long enough, brother." Nico smirks, the crazy in his eyes swirling.

"Lower your weapons," I say as I drop my gun on the grass. "It's me you want, so let them go."

"I would've expected so much more from you Casella brothers," a voice says from behind me, and I turn to watch as Leo and another man stacked like a fucking tree walk toward us. As they get closer, I notice he's carrying a woman on his shoulder. My blood curdles at the familiar brunette hair swaying with each step he takes.

Please be alive.

Please be alive.

She groans, and relief rushes over me.

He will die first.

The pressure in my temples rises as I clench my jaw, forcing myself to stay where I am, when every part of me screams to be next to her. Leo nods to the man, and he places Aries on the ground, then moves to where Nico and the rest of my men kneel.

"So, this is it, Ezra?" Leo asks as he walks to me, a smirk playing on his lips. I don't give him the satisfaction of a reply. I just stare back at him. "You know what I'm going to enjoy the most?" He leans in, and it takes everything in me not to pummel him to the floor and gouge out his eyes. "Killing her right in front of you." All my muscles tense at his words.

"If you lay a single finger on her, I will have your head on a fucking pike." My voice is laced with venom with every intention of poisoning him with it. He laughs at my words, leaning back, his laughter grows louder and eventually stops.

"I'm not going to stop at her. I will kill your brother, and then I will kill you." He nods to the man standing behind Nico, and in a flash, a bullet flies through the air as Nico's screams pierce my ears, and my heart lodges in my throat.

Nico.

I watch as he falls to his side, groaning in pain. I can't see from here where he is shot but if I don't do something now, I might not get another chance.

"Why don't you stop with the spectacle and get to the fucking point." I take my jacket off. "You want to kill me?" I shrug, my arms wide. "I'm right here, Leo. Just like my father was."

He aims his gun at me, and in this moment, it isn't the promise of death that scares me, it's the fear of losing the people I love.

"No!" Nico shouts, and I watch as Leo's finger dances with the trigger.

"You don't know how many times I dreamt of this very moment." His face lights up with a sinister grin. "How many times I've killed you in my dreams."

"The world is too small for the both of us, Leo." I take a step toward him. "So fucking do it."

"Indeed, it is." He aims the gun between my eyes. "But before you die, I will do you a kindness."

I raise my eyebrows, surprised by his words.

"I will tell you a secret that the Brayford family has held on to for almost thirty years. A secret that your pretty wife no doubt figured out tonight," he smirks. "You are not the eldest Casella."

My brows draw in, chest rising and falling as my fists clench beside me.

What the fuck?

"Your mother was a fucking whore," he spits.

"Keep my mother out of your fucking mouth before I feed you your fucking entrails, you cocksucker." I move forward, the barrel of his gun now firmly pressed on my forehead.

"She had a son before she wed Dominic." He laughs. "A bastard son, condemned to a life outside of ours."

My mind swirls, reeling with the thought of another brother roaming the earth, until my eyes catch sight of movement from the ground where Aries is. I watch as she curls her hand around my gun, aiming it straight for Leo.

My heart is in my throat as Leo turns, and within a flash, the sound of gunfire ricochets throughout the air.

No, no, no.

I watch in horror as the bullet sinks into Aries's chest, her shirt slowly pooling with blood. My muscles work on their own accord, and just before Leo can turn to me, I grab him from behind, snapping his neck. There are muffled sounds of struggle and gunfire as I drop to my knees, cradling her limp body against mine.

"No!" I roar, my voice piercing through the sky.

Removing my jacket and my shirt, I crumple the shirt in my hands and press it on her bullet wound, the material soaking up the thick red blood.

"Open your eyes, sweetheart," I beg and plead. "Don't you fucking dare leave me."

My eyes find Nico's as he limps over to us. He looks to her, then to me, visible sadness in his eyes.

"What the fuck are you just standing there for!?" I yell. "Go get the fucking car!"

He nods to Henry who disappears.

I look down to her, the blood now soaking the shirt completely, pooling at her neck.

"You don't get to die," I whisper. "Do you fucking hear me!?" I caress her cheek. "If you die, I will knock down the gates of heaven to find you because you belong in the darkness…with *me*."

"Ezra." Her voice is barely a whisper, but it's enough to illuminate the darkest parts of me.

"It's…all my fault…" Her eyes are heavy as she looks up at me, tears sliding down the sides of her face.

"No, sweetheart. It's mine." I remove the soaked shirt and throw it to the ground, pressing my hand directly on her wound, trying desperately to stop the bleeding. "Don't talk, okay? Save your strength."

Someone emerges from the shadows, her hand covering her mouth as she watches me cradling Aries.

"I'm so sorry," she says as Nico raises his gun to her head.

"Please, don't hurt me." She stops walking as she carefully eyes Nico.

"Darcy." Aries chokes as she tries to speak.

Henry pulls up in the van, swinging the door open, helping me carry Aries into the back.

"Henry, take that woman to the house, and don't let her fucking leave. Nico will drive." I say, and he nods. Nico gets in the driver's seat and takes off.

My hands are slick with blood, the sensation which would usually give me pleasure is now making me sick to my stomach. If this is what heartache feels like, I now understand why people say, 'the human heart is the only thing in this world that weighs more when it's broken'.

CHAPTER TWENTY-SEVEN
Ezra

Her body is limp against mine as I carry her through the large doors. Ethan waits, dressed in his operating gown, motioning me to the operating theatre where multiple others wait.

I place her down on the metal table, and he gets to work immediately, cutting off her top. One of the assistant's ushers me out of the room and closes the door behind him. I run my hands through my hair as reality comes crashing into me. There's a fifty-fifty chance I could lose her, and my blood runs cold at the thought as I pace the hall—nothing else on my mind besides my wife. The years I have spent, feeling nothing…complete emptiness… and in a few weeks, she has made me feel things I never thought possible.

Not for me, anyway.

But I stand here, wishing, hoping that by some miracle she will live, that the universe wouldn't be that cruel as to dangle something like love in my face and just as I'm ready to grasp it with two hands, rip it away.

I hear footsteps approaching, and as I look up, I see Nico, one of his pant legs are cut, a bandage now secured on his thigh.

"No major arteries," he says, giving me a sympathetic smile. "I got lucky."

I nod, unable to find words, the silence hanging heavy in the air, sticking to the walls.

"She will be okay." Nico tries to comfort me, and I grit my teeth.

My eyes find his. "If she dies, I will burn this fucking city to the ground." My hands curl into fists. "I will unleash my wrath on those who think they can take her from me. Kingdom be damned."

The quiet beeping of the machines is the only sound that echoes throughout the room. My hands clasp hers as I sit beside the bed, still covered in her blood. It took Ethan and his team five hours to remove the bullet from her chest, and by some fucking miracle, it missed her heart.

"There's no guarantee she will make it through this."

I remember his words, my heart taking another hit as I watch her lay there connected to multiple machines. It's been eight hours since the operation, and I haven't left her side once. Nico lies on the lounge in the corner of the room, blood seeping into the white bandage as he sleeps.

Ethan has been in our lives since I can remember, tending to our wounds. It's vital to have someone like him on your team because in our line of work, tomorrow is not guaranteed, and since I don't believe in God, Ethan is the next best thing. He has mended both Nico and I since we were teens, and as someone who wants to avoid law enforcement sticking their noses in my fucking business, it works better.

There's a knock at the door, then Ethan walks in and

begins checking her vitals. He's an older man, probably the same age my father was when he died. Thick grey hair and piercing blue eyes.

"When will she wake?" I ask.

He looks to me, sympathy in his eyes. "We're keeping her as comfortable as we can. It's up to her now."

My chest caves at his words as Nico stands, walking to the other side of her bed.

Ethan's words echo through my mind as he leaves.

"It's my fault, brother," Nico says, pain etched in his voice.

Then I feel her hand twitch under mine, and I stand, my eyes searching her face for movement.

"She just moved," I whisper, still watching her and waiting.

"Come back to me, sweetheart." I squeeze her hand in mine as her eyes slowly flicker open.

CHAPTER TWENTY-EIGHT

Aries

The pain in my chest radiates throughout my entire body as I fight to open my eyes. Everything feels heavy. I try to move my legs, but they feel like lead.

My eyes flicker open, the bright light almost blinding me. I see Ezra's face first, and all my emotions crash into me like a tidal wave.

I was shot.

Tears begin to stream from my eyes as I look up at him. Not so much from the pain I feel, but from the relief that I'm still alive.

"I'm sorry." My voice comes out all croaky, as he gazes down into my eyes.

"I fucked it up." I breathe, trying my best to squeeze his hand in mine. "I wanted to prove that I belonged in your world, and I fucked it up."

He cups my cheek, wiping away my tears with his thumb.

"You don't need to prove *anything* to me," he explains as he leans down, his lips brushing mine. "I'm sorry for waiting as long as I did to come for you."

"You have no idea what I felt when I watched you bleeding out." His breath shakes as his eyebrows draw together. "I thought I lost you, and in that moment, I was ready to set fire to the fucking world."

Tears sting behind my eyes as I try to blink away the sensation.

"And the worst part was, I never told you how much I fucking needed you." My heart flutters at his words. "So I'm saying it now, and I'll say it until I die. I need you so fucking much." He leans down, placing his lips on my forehead, planting a small kiss against my skin. "I will never let you go again," he whispers against my skin. "I'm not scared of death, sweetheart, but the one thing that instils fear deep inside me, is the thought of not being with you."

The organ beneath my chest beats harder at his confession. "I was wrong," I whisper, his brows pull in, his beautiful dark eyes never leaving mine. "I thought I shouldn't love you because you scared me, but I was just scared to love you because you brought life to a darkness within me. A darkness I had buried deep so long ago," I confess, as a smirk plays at the corner of his lips.

"You never have to hide from me," he whispers as he stares deep into my soul, his thumb wiping away another tear. "Ever."

I watch from afar as Ezra and Nico question Darcy. I explained to them how much she helped me and how willing she was to get me out of there even if she didn't know me.

I spent two whole weeks in that awful underground hospital, bored out of my brain, focusing on my recovery. Ezra only ever left my side to shower and change, but he was always there. Feeding me, listening to me whine about the pain every time I moved.

"Do you want to explain to us how you're involved with the Brayford family?" Nico questions as she stares up at him with a smirk.

"Look, I know you think you know everything about the Brayfords, but you don't," she seethes.

"Then tell us," Nico says, his voice calm. Ezra stands in the corner, hands in his pockets, letting his brother lead the questioning. I can't help but feel like I need to step in, like I have some sort of kinship with Darcy because she tried to aid me.

"What's in it for me?" she asks as Ezra looks at Nico. A moment passes, and neither of them answer. "As soon as I tell you both *anything*, I'm dead, right?"

"We can't have someone who knows too much," Ezra explains.

"Can't, or won't?" She looks to me, and I avert my gaze, looking to the floor. I rack my brain for a possible solution to all of this where she doesn't have to lose her life, and I struggle to come up with one. *I'm sorry* I mouth to her as she rips her gaze from mine.

"If there's one thing you should know, it's that Leo wasn't lying about your brother," she confesses, and all eyes are on her. "He's out there. I have seen him and spoken to him myself."

"Does he know about us?" Nico asks.

"He knows *of* you."

"Where is he now?" Ezra questions in a hard tone.

"If I tell you, will you let me live?"

"If you tell us, and we can corroborate your story, we will spare your life," Ezra confirms as he steps closer to

Darcy. "But not because I pity you, only because you helped my wife."

"He's in Italy," she confesses, and Ezra looks to Nico. The room falls silent as both brothers exchange a look that even *I* cannot recognise.

"Wait." Nico looks to Darcy as his face changes. "You're Darcy Brayford, aren't you?" He asks, and her face falls at his realisation. "The Mafia princess."

My mouth falls open as I work to make sense of the fact that she helped me, when she could've killed me.

It's been a week of planning and preparing to visit Italy in search of Ezra's estranged brother. Every single action taken has been in secret, in hiding from Ezra's mother as he and Nico gathered all of their information before confronting her about it. It's not my place, so I've stayed out of it. I've been focusing on getting to know Darcy a little more. Even though she acts like a closed book, I can sense that she wants the same thing. She wants a friend she can confide in. I lay on our large king-size bed that takes up almost the entire room, texting with Giselle and apologising for being MIA over the past few weeks. It's late into the night, and she's up with Ryan, texting me about how much he's changed in such a short time, when I hear the door to the bedroom open. My eyes find Ezra's as I watch him walk in, his white shirt covered in blood and spread across his face as he grins at me. My heart stutters as I take him in, black distressed jeans, a white shirt now stained in thick red blood, his dark hair dishevelled. It should scare anyone, but it excites me.

I swallow at the sight of him, his eyes pulling me in like

a beacon. "I thought we had killed our enemies," I say as I prop myself up on my elbows.

"Turns out the little guys want a taste." His lips pull at the corner, his eyes growing darker by the second. "If I'm not mistaken, sweetheart, you owe me something." He takes a step closer to the bed, slipping off his shirt. My mouth almost hangs open at the bruises covering his skin, his muscles glistening with sweat under the moonlight.

"I—"

"You owe me the promise of your lips around my cock," he growls as he makes his way around the bed, staring down at me. I swivel myself so my legs are dangling off the edge of the bed as he unbuttons his jeans and pulls the zipper down.

"Get on your knees, baby, and open that pretty little mouth," he mutters.

I do exactly as he says, feeling the heat pooling between my legs at his words. He releases his cock, and it juts out, large and thick. My mouth waters at the sight of the veins, and I reach up, but before I can wrap my hands around him, his hand grips my wrist.

"Mouth only," he warns.

I open my mouth as he grips the base of his cock and slides the tip inside. The salty taste of him engulfs my tongue as I take him deeper, watching as his brows draw in.

"Fuck, baby," he groans as he forces himself deeper.

I watch him crane his neck backward as I take him further down my throat. I force myself to focus on not gagging as he pulls back, giving me the opportunity to take a breath then forces himself deeper down my throat.

"Oh fuck," he rasps as he grips the hair on the top of

my head, moving his hips backward and forward. "You look so fucking pretty with my cock deep in your throat."

He lets go of my wrist and pinches my nose, cutting off my air as he forces himself deeper and deeper with each thrust, tears beginning to run down my face as I fight for air. I heave in a gulp of air as he pulls back, the string of saliva still connecting us. His hand pumps his cock with a few strokes, then gathers the saliva remaining on my chin and smears it over my face.

"Such a good girl," he grunts, and my thighs quiver with the need to press them together, to alleviate the growing pressure between my legs.

"Ezra," I whisper as my chest rises and falls, my heart pattering beneath my chest.

"Remove your clothes, and get on the bed," he commands as he removes his own, and I obey. In a flash, I'm on the bed.

"Turn around and show me what's mine." He smirks, the pupils in his eyes dilated making his eyes look black in the moonlight. I do as he says, facing away from him on all fours.

He lowers himself, and I feel him all along my back. My pussy aches with the need for him, and I close my eyes as his tongue licks from my shoulder to my neck.

"I need to feel you wrapped around my dick," he moans as he thrusts into me. My gasp is audible as I feel the entire length of him deeply buried inside me. His hand grips my hip as he thrusts into me hard, and I feel his hot breath on my ear. "Your pussy feels so fucking good," he groans, and it takes everything in me not to come undone around him at the sound of his ragged breathing. My moans fill the air as the sound of our bodies slapping echoes through the room.

"Ezra," I moan.

"Fuck, baby, hearing my name ooze from your mouth whilst my dick is inside you drives me fucking crazy." He thrusts harder, his fingers digging into my hip. "How much of me are you willing to take, sweetheart?" he questions as he slides out of me.

I groan at the empty feeling, peeking around my shoulder, and my brows pull in as I watch him pour something over his cock. Within a second, he's back behind me, grabbing my arms and holding them behind me with one hand. I feel something tightening around my wrists as he ties them together. The material is rough, causing friction on my skin.

"Wha—" My eyes almost pop out of my head. "Ezra?" I feel the head of his dick right near my ass, and my heart pounds harder, threatening to shatter my ribs.

"I asked you a question." He grips the top of my head and yanks it up, craning my neck, and I feel my pussy throb with the way he handles me.

"All of you." My chest heaves as I hear him reach for his belt, fastening it around my neck like a collar.

"That night in the field was just the beginning of your submission, sweetheart." His thumb begins to caress my ass as his other hand remains in my hair. His hand comes down on my ass hard, and I revel in the sting it leaves behind, a buzz now forming between my legs. I moan into the sheets as I push my hips out further, my body practically begging him to use me just as he desires.

"I love watching your body react to me," he says, his thumb entering my ass. I moan again as he removes his thumb and inserts two fingers instead. He stretches me, pushing into me further. He releases my hair, and I fall back onto the bed.

"Oh my god." My breathless voice is muffled beneath the sheets. I feel something cold, like metal, at my pussy and before I can peek a look, I feel it being slid inside me. It's thick, and long, and the sensation that builds at my core is unlike any other that I had experienced before.

"It's only going to get *so* much better." He chuckles as he removes his fingers from my ass, and I feel something else enter me, it's similar to what he's put inside my pussy, but it doesn't feel cold.

He slides it into my ass, stretching it slowly. "Look at the way your body responds to me, sweetheart." He pushes further, and my eyes close, the foreign object sliding deeper into me. "You're fucking dripping all over yourself...so fucking pretty." He slips it in farther, and I whimper, feeling full and desperately craving friction. He stands and pulls on the belt around my neck, forcing me up.

"Get on the floor, on your knees," he says, as he holds the end of the belt in his hand. I struggle, but I make it to the floor and drop to my knees, spreading them wide as I look up at him. My mouth falls open at the sight of him staring down at me. His tattoos on display, covering his chest and arms, as he steps out of his jeans and briefs, now completely naked in front of me.

"I'm going to take what I want from you, Aries." He steps closer, gathering the belt and looping it around his hand. "I'm going to show you that inside our darkness, there is no room for anything else but the selfish desire and need for each other." I open my mouth wide as he forces himself inside me, pulling on the belt around my neck. "Open your eyes, sweetheart, the darkness is where you and I belong...where you and I prosper." He thrusts deep into my throat, and I stick out my tongue, inviting him further.

"You're such a good fucking girl." He begins to fuck my mouth, tears sliding down the side of my face. "By the time the night is over, you will feel me echo in every single part of you."

He pulls out of my mouth, and I pant, trying to catch my breath. He forces me to stand and turn around so I'm facing the bed, then pushes me onto it so my hips are at the edge of the bed.

I whimper as I rock my hips, desperate for a release.

"I know sweetheart," I feel him begin to remove the object in my ass, and I take a deep breath through my nose as the pleasure within me surges. A moan slips from my mouth when he removes it completely.

My heart pumps nervously as I feel the tip of his cock forcing its way inside my ass, stretching me. I squeeze my eyes shut as my face presses into the mattress. It feels so fucking good to be filled in every hole...to be taken by Ezra with no remorse.

"Ezra, I..." I gasp as he pushes in further, my eyes widening as he pulls on the belt wrapped around my neck.

"Be a good girl and open up for me." He grunts as he buries himself completely inside me. "Let me in until it fucking hurts," he rasps, and my lips quiver as he takes me, the pain melting with the pleasure. "I promise to make it feel good," he whispers in my ear as he pulls out and slams into me, my cries filling the room. "Only after I make it hurt so fucking much that you beg me for more."

CHAPTER TWENTY-NINE
Ezra

"I told you one day you'd have more than my finger in your ass," I rasp as my hand lands on the silky-smooth skin of her ass. She squeezes her eyes shut, clenching her jaw. "How does it feel to be full of me?"

"It hurts," she moans as I slide in and out of her.

"I know, baby," I slide my tongue from her shoulder to the base of her ear. "But it's about to feel so fucking good," I whisper as I slide one arm around her waist, pulling her onto me as I lay on the bed with her back to my front. My hand grabs her breast and slides down to her pussy. She bucks against my hand and moans as I remove the metal dildo from her pussy and slip two fingers inside her, my cock still filling her ass.

"Holy fuck!" she yells as she rests her head back next to mine. My fingers move inside her, massaging the exact place I know drives her insane, as my cock moves in and out of her. She feels so fucking tight, her ass suffocating my cock. Her arousal coating my fingers, dripping down to my balls, and it makes me harder as I listen to her losing her mind because of me.

If there's one thing I love more than shedding blood, it's watching Aries come undone by my doing. "It feels s-so good," she moans, her chest heaving. "Please, don't s-stop," she pants.

"Tell me how much you love it," I whisper into her ear as my fingers and my cock pump into her relentlessly. "Tell me how much you love being filled in every hole by me."

"I-I..." she stutters as I feel her pussy clenching, pushing my fingers out of her, her loud moans rip through the air as my fingers rub her clit. "Fuck!" she yells as I feel her squirt all over my hand. I don't give her any time to recover from her orgasm as I flip her over, kneeling behind her again. My fist clenches the hair on her crown as I pull up, bringing her ear to my mouth.

"I want to fill every inch of you with me." I bite down on the side of her cheek. "I want you to know that I own every single part of you," I whisper as I thrust into her ass harder, chasing my release.

Her mouth hangs open, and I force my fingers inside as I thrust into her, causing her breasts to bounce with each plunge. She pants as her hands grip the sheets. My hand snakes around her throat as I pull her up to me, both of us on our knees, her back plastered to my front.

"I don't want to fucking *breathe* without you," I whisper as I thrust into her once more, an animalistic growl ripping through my throat as I release inside of her.

"Do you have it?" I question as I step out of my Porsche, walking over to Nico. We've spent the last couple of weeks searching for the birth certificate, and I can tell you right now it wasn't the easiest thing to find. It was buried deep by those who wanted to hide this information to use it against us in the future, but no amount of power or money could hide it from me. Nico hands me an envelope, and I slide the paper out of it, reading the birth certificate in my hands. There is now no denying the confirmation that Nico and I have a brother.

"When do we tell her?" he asks as he lifts a cigarette up to his lips, lighting it.

"Right now." I hold up the envelope. "This is concrete proof, but I need to hear it from her."

The car drive is tense as my brother and I come to terms with the reality we're about to face. Neither of us wants to bring this up, especially with our mother, but there's no other choice because we don't exclude family.

I step into the kitchen, watching as she slowly brings the wooden spoon to her mouth, tasting what she's just cooked.

"Mama," I say as I cross my arms whilst Nico leans against the bench. Her eyes find mine, and she smiles.

"Ezra, Nico, come taste." She holds out the wooden spoon to Nico as he takes a slurp, nodding his head.

"Mama, we need to talk." I say, watching as her eyes meet mine. I can't tell if its realisation setting in, but her face immediately changes.

"Let's all take a seat." She turns the stove off and gestures to the lounge room, filled with a large plush leather couch. Nico takes a seat beside her, and I take my place on the other side. A silence fills the room as she looks from me to Nico. "Well?"

I sigh. "Is it true, Mama?"

"Is what true?" she questions.

"Do you have another son?" I feel her tense at my question as she purses her lips. I feel my jaw clench at her hesitation, and I just know in this moment that she's confirmed it.

"It was a very long time ago." Her brows pull in as her eyes focus on something in the distance. "I never meant for anyone to find out."

Standing, I walk over to the other side of the room, running a hand through my hair. "Do you know what this means?" I ask.

I watch her glance at Nico and back to me. "What?"

"We have to find him, mama. We have to know if he knows anything about our world, about anything that can put a target on our backs," I explain. "What if he was trained and groomed by the Brayfords or the Dixons?"

Her face goes white like she's seen a ghost. "F-find him?"

"We have confirmation that he's been living in Italy this entire time." I watch as she swallows.

"They told me he died," she whispers, tears beginning to well in her eyes. My eyes snap to Nico's as he shakes his head.

"He's alive, Mama," he says as he comforts her.

"They told me my baby was born dead and took him away before I got a chance to hold him." Tears fall over her cheeks as Nico brushes them away. My blood boils at the scene unfolding before me. They lied to her. Took her firstborn son to use in a game of chess like a fucking pawn.

"We will find him," I assure her as Nico's eyes meet with mine, a fury swirling inside them as he nods.

"What about Darcy?" she asks. "What are you going to do with her?"

I grit my teeth. As much as I want to kill her, I promised Aries I would try to find another way to resolve the issue of Darcy, but right now, I don't see another way out. There's still more we need to find out about her, and I'm losing my patience the more she decides not to share.

"We're not sure yet," I admit.

"I might have a solution," she says. My brows draw in, intrigued. "But you're not going to like it." She looks to Nico and purses her lips.

"No." Nico stands and walks over to me. "There is no fucking way, you hear me!?" he yells as he glances back at our mother. It takes me a little to catch on, and when I do, I can't believe I didn't think about it myself.

"It may be our only choice," I confess as Nico shakes his head.

"How can you agree with her, after everything you've done, going against her wishes to marry Aries?" he pushes me, anger and tension settling in the air. I feel his frustration—marrying someone you don't know, let alone marrying someone who was the enemy, is never at the top of the list.

"It's your turn to do something for this family," I say through gritted teeth.

"This is fucking bullshit!" he spits as his hands fly up into his hair, reality dawning on him that he doesn't get a choice.

"It's the only way to stop further unnecessary bloodshed," Mother says as Nico fumes.

"I won't do it." He shoulders past me as I turn and grab him by the arm.

"Yes, you fucking will," I say as he rips away from my hold.

"The day I marry that bitch will be the day you'd have to put a fucking bullet in my head, brother." His jaw tenses as he looks at me, and I feel a pang of guilt in my chest for forcing this on him. He doesn't get a choice. It's what we must do for the Casella family. I've done my bit, practically given up my entire life to ensure the success and fruition of our empire, now it's Nico's turn to take some weight onto his shoulders.

I grip him firmly behind his neck. "Listen to me, if you don't do this, they will be after her. She's a liability if she's not tethered to a Casella."

He takes a deep breath, his eyes closing for a mere second before he speaks. "I'm not like you, brother. I can't."

"You can, and you will. You will show her that without us, she will suffer under the hands of those who want to be on top." I pause, sighing. "I know this is not how you imagined it, brother, and I can't promise that it'll ever be something you want, but you *will* do this, for our family."

He squeezes the bridge of his nose with his fingers as he sighs.

"I'll handle the preparations," Mother says from behind us as she slips back into the kitchen.

"I need a fucking drink," Nico says as he walks out slamming the door behind him, leaving me to wonder if this is the right choice. Our whole lives we've been groomed to do anything and everything that benefited our family. It's been ingrained in us, etched into our skin, that we don't have choices, and now as the King, it makes me see the truth behind it.

No matter what we do, the importance of the future generation weighs heavily on my conscience.

I have a chance to do things differently, but if it were Dominic in charge, he would have easily killed her and been done with it, and although my logic is telling me the exact same thing, I promised my wife I would give her a chance.

The rest is up to Nico.

CHAPTER THIRTY
Aries

Giselle and I sit at the café with Ryan in her lap as we catch up. She tells me that motherhood is no easy feat, which I did not assume it was, but that it's better now that they have space for all his things.

"I can't thank Ezra enough." She takes a sip of her coffee. "Ever since we moved into the new place, it's been such a breath of fresh air. We've even started Ryan on a sleep schedule, and last night, I had my first night of six hours of uninterrupted sleep," she says in disbelief.

I smile. "You must have felt so refreshed."

"I forgot how much I used to take my sleep for granted." She chuckles and checks the time on her watch. "Oh, I'm so late. I'm meeting Arthur, and we're going to his parents' place for dinner tonight." She stands, as do I, walking to the door of the café.

I notice a familiar face standing outside the café, leaning against the large window. I could have sworn I knew her, but I'm having trouble placing her face to a name. Giselle wheels the pram out of the café, and I give her a kiss on the cheek.

"I guess I'll see you soon?" I ask, and she nods. "Maybe we should walk you to your car…" I glance over at Henry behind me, and he steps forward.

"No, don't be ridiculous. I've parked around the corner. It'll be fine," she reassures.

"Alright, message me when you meet Arthur, so I know you've got there safely?" I ask, and she nods.

She begins to walk off into the distance, waving as she turns a corner, and Henry and I walk the opposite direction to the car parked on the other side of the street. I look back over to the woman who looked familiar, but she is no longer there. It isn't until I slide into the back seat of the car that I remember who she was.

The woman from the club, the night Ezra and I made our appearance as a couple, the one who cornered me in the women's restroom.

Opening my laptop, I sift through the countless emails I had received throughout my time away from the world of weddings. A few of my clients had been furious with me with my lack of support and cancelled, requesting a refund, which is completely justified. Earlier in the week I had contacted my assistant to ask her to take over, but I know it's a lot of work to handle for just one person. I know I don't have to work, being the wife of a Casella, but my work brings me pleasure and gives me some sort of purpose. I don't think I could just sit by Ezra and not do anything.

I'm interrupted by Ezra's delicious dark eyes peering at me from the archway of the door to my study. "Still working at this hour?" A smile plays on his lips, and I think to myself how lucky I am that I have a man who looks like he does. I drink him in, watching as the shadows play in the perfect spots on his skin, accentuating every divot of his muscles.

"I'm almost done." I smile back at him as he walks towards me, his bottom half covered in a towel, his skin still sparkling with water droplets.

"All work and no play," he whispers as he stands behind me, massaging my shoulders. I feel the tension in them release as he lowers his lips near my ear. "I want to play." His gravelly voice glides over my skin, goose bumps forming in its wake. I stand, throwing my arms around his neck as he lifts me on top of the oak desk. Heat bellows deep within my belly as I feel his hands glide over my skin and his mouth crash into mine. My core aches for him as my mind reels with the memories of what he did to me a few nights ago, filling every inch of me with him.

"Wait," I pant, remembering I'm all out of my contraception. "We can't. We have to wait." My hands push him away, but he doesn't budge.

"Wait for what?" he says, kissing my neck, sending tingles all the way through to my toes.

"I-I don't have any more contraception," I explain, and his eyes find mine. A flash passes through those dark irises as he drops his towel, his hand coming between us to stroke his cock.

"I love it when you talk dirty." He groans as he enters me, my mouth opening as his hand quickly covers my gasp. I wrap my legs around him, feeling him move his hips sensually, taking his time. "You have no idea how much I want to see you pregnant with my child." He thrusts deep inside me, his hand coming down and wrapping around my neck. My mind swirls with the possibility of pregnancy, but the only thing I can seem to focus on is how he makes me feel, buried so deep inside me. He grips my throat tighter as I moan with each thrust, moving my hips to meet his.

"You look like a fucking goddess," he whispers as he bites my jaw, the sting mixing with the swell of pleasure. "A deity I'd thirst to worship on my knees, for the rest of my life."

"Do you love me?" I ask as my eyes meet his—hunger, lust, and love mixed all in one big ball of fury inside his eyes.

"Love is nothing but a notion to me. What I feel for you cannot be measured. It cannot be seen." He brings his forehead to mine. "What I feel for you is dark, it's ugly and messy." His hand fists my hair and pulls back, the sting pulsing through my skull. "I would burn the entire fucking world to ashes if it meant you'd be mine in all lifetimes beyond this one."

My eyes roll back as he thrusts into me, his words ringing in my ears like an echo of a caress. "I don't know who I am without you anymore," I say, and he growls at my confession, his hand gripping my hip. It feels so fucking good to be taken by Ezra, to be swallowed up whole by his darkness.

"It's a good thing you will *never* be without me again," he whispers as his hips meet mine with force.

"Ezra." I moan as I feel the pressure building inside me, swirling like a whirlpool just waiting to suck me into its rush. "Harder," I pant.

His hands grip onto my hips as he thrusts harder and faster into me, my arms wrapping around his neck.

"Fuck, you drive me fucking insane," he pants between thrusts. I feel the release hit me like a tidal wave as I ride out the pleasure, rolling my hips on his cock as my loud moans fill the room. "That's it, baby, cover me in your cum." I feel my arousal all over him as he pounds into me. The wetness coating my inner thighs as he chases his own release.

"Let's make a prince." I whisper in his ear, and he growls as he jerks inside me, his forehead landing on my shoulder as his chest heaves for air.

"She won't listen to me," I plead as Ezra and I walk towards Darcy's room. It's been about a week since the choice had been made for Nico to marry Darcy. Somehow, I got roped into talking to her and making her see that this is the lesser of the two evils. Ezra gives me a kiss on my shoulder and leaves as I stand in front of her door. Raising my hand, I knock and wait.

"Do we suddenly have boundaries now?" she calls out from behind the door, and I open it, walking into the room and shutting it behind me. She watches me as I walk over to the couch and take a seat. "What? They couldn't convince me, and now they send you in here to try?" She scoffs.

"Look, I know it's not an ideal situation,"

"Ideal situation? You can't fucking *force* me to marry him," she says bluntly.

"Trust me, I tried to reason with them, but they don't want you to become a liability," I explain.

"I swear to you, I will do whatever it takes. I will change my fucking name, or live in a different country. Please, I can't marry my enemy," she pleads as she stands and paces throughout the room.

"I'm sorry, Darcy, I really wish there was something I

could do or say, but…" I trail off, unsure of how to finish that sentence.

"My whole life I spent fighting them. My entire life was dedicated to bringing down the Casella brothers. That's all my uncle talked about," she explains as she continues pacing. "And now you want me to marry into that family."

I stand and make my way over to her, holding her hands. "I will forever be indebted to you for helping me, but this is me helping you, Darcy. If you don't marry Nico, they will kill you."

"Maybe death wouldn't be as bad as marrying a Casella." Her brows pull in as she considers her choices.

"I know you don't mean that," I whisper. There's a pause in the air as she considers my words, and a solemn look overcomes her feature. "What is it?" I ask.

"For so long I wanted to be free of them. My family. For so long I prayed that this moment would come, but now that it's here, I can't help but feel I'll be a slave to another set of hands." Her voice cracks, and it's the first time I've seen Darcy be vulnerable. The first time she's ever shared anything so innately private that it has me stunned.

"What did they do to you?" My voice is low, scared that if I talk at full volume that she will pull away from me, and that's the last thing I want. She bows her head and turns to walk towards the bed.

"I don't speak of it. Not to anyone." She sighs. "They're gone now, so it doesn't matter."

"You can trust me." I want to reach out to her, to comfort her, but I don't want to overstep. Nothing I say or do can make her past vanish, but I can be an ear to listen if she'll let me.

"That's the problem, Aries. I don't know that I can."

Her voice shakes as she sits on the bed, her head in her hands. "I don't have a choice, do I?" She peers up at me, her watery eyes holding on to a small bit of hope that I'll say she does. I bite my lip and shake my head, words evading me. I want her to trust me. I want her to have someone she can confide in, knowing that she won't be exposed no matter what she shares with me. Unfortunately, that doesn't change the situation we're in.

I make my way out the door, past the guards and into the large lounge area. I find Ezra and Nico huddled around the coffee table in what looks like a serious conversation. Nico's eyes find mine as I step into the room.

"So?" he asks, and I know he's hoping for the answer he wants.

"She didn't say much, but I don't think she will fight it," I explain as I glance at Ezra who nods. I wish I had more information to give, but until I can earn her trust, I'm keeping it to myself.

CHAPTER THIRTY-ONE
Ezra

Placing my guns in my holsters, I head downstairs as Henry places my suitcase in the van. I wait outside as Nico brings his luggage and throws it in the back of the van.

"Jesus. I know you're pissed off, but there is no need to take it out on the suitcase." I watch as he grunts, leaning against the van, lighting up a cigarette.

"What's our plan anyway?" he asks, blowing out a puff of smoke into the air.

"Well, we have to find out if he knows anything about us first," I explain.

"Surely he would, if the Brayfords had anything to do with it," he spits, the disdain oozing from his voice.

"We can't assume that," I explain as I watch my beautiful wife emerge from the front door of our house dressed in a floral dress, accentuating her delicious curves. "We need to be sure."

Aries walks down the steps and throws her arms around me. "I'll miss you," she whispers as I wrap my arms around her waist, pulling her into me.

Nico makes a gagging sound and walks into the house. "Let me know when we're ready to go, I'd rather not watch you two tongue fuck each other," he calls out, and Aries giggles.

"You have no idea how much I'd rather stay in bed and fuck you until the sun rises and sets." I place my lips on hers, lowering my hands to her ass.

"Promise me you'll be careful," she pleads.

A smirk curls in the corner of my mouth. "When have I ever given you the impression that I am careful?" I ask.

Her brows pull in. "Ezra."

"You have nothing to worry about, sweetheart." I kiss the top of her head, inhaling her scent before I call out to Nico, "We're leaving!"

Henry loads the car as Nico appears walking down the steps. He kisses Aries on the cheek then slides into the seat next to mine.

The trip to the tarmac is silent. I know my brother hates me right now, and I can't do much to fix it, so I stay quiet. There's about ten minutes left into the car trip when he finally speaks.

"You're so fucking lucky, you know that?" He grits his teeth with hate swirling in his stare. Being the youngest, Nico never truly understood the sacrifices I had to make, to take on the role I have, and I'm so fucking tired of him assuming it's been a smooth ride.

"Grow the fuck up. You really think this is the life I dreamt about when I was ten years old?" I seethe, sick with the blaming and self-loathing. "You have no fucking idea the shit I had to do so Dominic wouldn't make you do it. I'm fucking fed up with you drinking yourself into oblivion." I grit my teeth. "It's about time you came to the realisation that we don't always get what we want, brother." The air is dense as a silence takes over the space in the van, leaving my words hanging in the air. I don't care if I'm harsh with him anymore, he needs to hear the truth.

"What did he make you do?" Nico asks, his voice now calmer than before.

The memories flash before me as I remember the vile things I did for my father. They used to bother me, back when I was just a boy, but now they have become a part of me.

A part of me I embrace.

"It doesn't matter, Nico, because it's made me stronger. All I want is for you to embrace all that you try to bury within yourself. The further you push it down, the more it will break you until you can no longer piece yourself back together," I speak, watching as he looks out the window. "I don't want my brother to become a broken shell of a human. I want to see you thrive like I know you can. You're smart, you have so much talent in strategy, and yet you choose to be numb instead of homing in on your skills." He looks to me, visible hurt in his eyes. "I'm not saying this to hurt you. I want to see you at your full potential—" I'm interrupted by ringing. I slide the phone out of my pocket and see an unknown number on the screen.

Putting the phone to my ear, I answer. "Who is this?"

"Your worst fucking nightmare, Casella." My eyes fly to Nico's as I put the phone on speaker.

"I have no time for games."

"Oh, but you will. You will once you hear what I have to say." His voice sounds gravelly, almost like he's smoked a few too many cigarettes.

"Spit it out then."

"I have your nephew." He snickers.

I don't—

Ah fuck!

Nico's eyes flare as he realises what I do.

"If you want him back, alive, I suggest you hand over the Brayford bitch," he demands.

My jaw clenches as my mind reels to come up with a solution.

"I hope you know what you're doing." My voice is calm, in stark contrast to the fury bellowing inside me.

"Shut the fuck up. You will wait for my instruction." The phone beeps as he hangs up.

Nico buries his face in his hands, sighing. "An innocent baby, Ezra."

I crack my neck, loosening the stiff muscles. "Nothing's going to happen to him. They don't have the balls to cross me like that."

"How are you going to tell Aries?" My heart sinks at his question, and the answer is I don't fucking know. Just as Henry turns the car around, my phone vibrates in my hands, and I swallow at the name that appears on my phone.

Aries.

"They have him, Ezra!" Her voice filters through the phone, and I can feel her panic from here.

"I know baby, I know—"

"You can't let them get away with it! You have to find them!" she pleads, her voice shaking. "I will never forgive myself if something happens to him."

"It's not your fault." I hear her sob through the phone, and I feel the fractures forming in my chest.

"It is my fault! If I never agreed to be your wife, none of this would have happened!" she cries, and the cracks deepen as I grit my teeth. The helplessness I feel right now sends lightning strikes throughout my body. I clench my fists at the thought of an innocent baby being harmed because of me.

How could I let this happen?

"I'm coming home, baby. I will fix this," I promise her.

I exit the van swiftly, seeing Aries sprint down the steps and slam into me, her shoulders wracked with sobs as she cries into my shoulder. I instruct Henry to investigate the situation and gather our men immediately.

"It's alright, sweetheart, I will get him back." I hold her to me, feeling her panic seeping through her skin and into mine. Nico exits the van and immediately picks up his ringing phone.

"You!" I raise my eyes to Giselle, now pounding down the steps as Aries stands beside me. Her fist meets my jaw, snapping my head to the side, tasting blood on my tongue. "You did this! This is all your fault!" she yells as Aries tries to calm her.

"G, he's trying to help, please—"

"No!" She pushes Aries, the tears flowing down her face as she looks at me. "He's the reason this happened. If you never came into my sister's life, I wouldn't be living this hell." Her eyes throw daggers at mine. I clench my jaw, unsure of what to say because she's absolutely right. None of this would have happened if I hadn't fallen for Aries, but I don't give a fuck because I can't breathe without her.

"I promise you I will get him back." I keep my voice calm and low, doing my best not to provoke her further.

"If you don't, I'll walk right into the police station and tell them everything I know," she threatens, looking to me then to Aries. "I will do anything to have my baby back."

Aries looks to me, her eyes red and swollen as she

gently puts her arm around Giselle and guides her back inside. My blood boils as I realise the stakes of the circumstances.

I see Henry emerge from the side of the house, the phone to his ear. "Done, meet us there," he speaks into the phone as he nods to me, sliding into the driver's seat of the McLaren. "We have fifteen minutes to get to them before they vacate the premises." Nico nods at Henry and is already starting up the Bugatti. There's no question that I will be going to hell for the number of lives I've taken, but I'm going to thoroughly enjoy hurting these motherfuckers who would use an innocent baby as a pawn in their vile games.

Tick-tock, fuckers, your time's almost up.

CHAPTER THIRTY-TWO
Ezra

My foot meets the double door as they barrel over, hitting the floor with a thud. Both my guns are raised, as Nico and I walk through the old, dank office of a warehouse. My eyes cut to the basket sitting on the desk in the middle of the room. Immediate relief rushes over me as I walk up to the desk, peering into the shallow basket, Ryan's steel-blue eyes staring back into mine.

"It's empty." Nico says in a low voice. "Why would they leave the baby and go?" My mind doesn't register his words as I holster my guns and cradle Ryan in my arms. I watch as Nico pulls out a piece of folded-up paper from the bottom of the wicker basket, his eyes meeting mine as he unfolds it. "Even the King can be commanded like a dog on a leash." He reads the words off the page, and the dormant fire within me roars to life. "It doesn't make sense for them to leave the baby here." His voice barely a whisper, as if he's talking to himself, and that's when it hits us both, our eyes clashing.

"Get everyone out of the building right now!" I yell to Nico as I hold Ryan tight into my chest. My legs fire as I sprint toward the entrance, the innocent child in my arms my main priority. I have a few metres until I reach the open entrance, and all I can hear is the pounding of my heart beneath my chest and hurried feet hitting the ground behind me.

Explosions ring in my ears as I escape through the doors of the warehouse, leaping onto the tall grass. Pain radiates through my shoulder and back as I land on the hard ground, cradling Ryan into my chest. Fire bellows into the air as the entire building slowly collapses into itself. My eyes search for Nico, and panic ensues when I don't immediately find him. Ryan's cries fill my ears as I stand, ignoring the pain, desperately in search of my little brother.

A sting spreads across my cheek as I look up at my father. His dark eyes unimpressed with my efforts. Nothing I do ever seems to be good enough for him.

"Fucking disappointment." He spits at my feet as he walks back towards the punching bags. My knuckles feel raw, the skin scaling off in layers as blood seeps through the wounds. "I'm not raising a fucking pussy! Now hit like you fucking mean it!" he yells as Nico sits in the corner of the gym with wide eyes, his knees clutched to his chest. My fist flies into the bag once again, the flesh on my knuckles ripping further. I pick up speed as my fists ram the bag harder and faster with each punch. Tears brim behind my eyes, but I fight them back. There is no room for weakness in front of Dominic. He would feel no remorse. Instead, he would make you lick your own tears off the floor. He doesn't relent until my blood coats the punching bag, dripping onto the floor.

"Nico!" His voice is hard as he demands my brother's presence. "Take your brother's place." My brother's eyes flare as he stands and walks over to us.

"No. I want to keep going," I state, watching as Nico releases a sigh, his shoulders relaxing.

"Nico!" I yell through the ringing in my ears. "Nico!"

My heart constricts as I see his still body on the gravel just outside the warehouse. I kneel with Ryan in one arm, shaking my brother with the other.

"I swear to Lucifer, you better not be dead." I lean over him, my ear to his mouth, listening for his breathing as I place two fingers on his pulse. A low groan rumbles from his throat as he turns over onto his back. A sigh of relief escapes me as I sit back on my heels, clutching Ryan to my chest. "Oh, thank fuck."

Nico coughs, clutching his arm as he smiles up at me. "You won't be rid of me *that* easily, brother."

CHAPTER THIRTY-THREE
Aries

I pick at the skin surrounding my nails, my heart sinking further with each minute that passes. My eyes skate over to Giselle, head in her hands, seated on the couch across from me. A lump forms in my throat as I imagine all that she's going through.

It's all my fault.

Guilt rushes over me, suffocating me , and all I want to do is apologise to her. Her little sobs seep through the silence, and my heart breaks even further.

"I didn't mean for this to happen." My voice is small, afraid if I speak loudly, that I may set her off again.

She looks up at me, her hands clasping, falling between her knees. "You thought that marrying into the city's most notorious mafia family wouldn't come with consequences?"

Her words send a spear to my chest, but she's right. The space between us grows even more at the silence that falls in the air. Arthur steps into the lounge room from the kitchen holding a cup of tea. He hands it to her as he settles into the couch beside her.

"It's not her fault, G," he whispers to her, an arm over her shoulder. "Remember when we met, how infatuated we were with each other?" He tries to make light of the situation, and I admire him for it. Always the rock in their relationship. I've never seen my sister lose her temper in the slightest, and the way she looks at me now as if I'm a stranger that purposely caused her harm makes me curl into myself.

"I think I'll give you guys some space." I stand and take the stairs up to the second floor. I hold my phone in my hand hoping, praying that Ezra will call with good news. I stare at it, trying to will it to call as I walk into my study. I slump into my chair, tears stinging the back of my eyes.

She will never forgive you.

Is it wrong to want this life?

Is it wrong that I feel the power within myself continue to grow, the longer I am with Ezra?

I love my sister, but I don't know if I could ever be without Ezra. He's brought to life something within me that had frightened me since that very first day I felt it. The first time I ever wanted to hurt someone was the day my mother died. I wanted to scream at the top of my lungs as I hacked into my father's chest for hurting her. She never knew happiness, although she tried to hide it from us, I know she didn't. He was a pig, a drunk and an abuser, and she never should have stayed with him, but she did.

For us.

Although the darkness incites fear at first, it's only when we journey into it where we are able to find some sort of comfort in the silence and peace. No matter what, that darkness will always be a part of us. Some people may only have shadows within them, and others, like Ezra, have a chasm, swallowing up everything in its path like a black hole. The day I met Ezra, I didn't know what was going to happen. I thought we'd be married for a few months and divorce, just like he said, but somewhere along the line, I didn't want him to let me go.

I never knew a love like this could exist.

An all-consuming love.

It's something I've only read about in books or seen in movies, but never in the real world.

All-consuming to others may mean sunshine and a happily ever after, but to me, an all-consuming love is the way Ezra shows love.

With dominance, possessiveness, greed, power, and lust. He is everything they say he is but so much more. He is the person who would follow me into hell willingly, then proceed to kill Lucifer himself to give me the throne.

I hear the roar of the engines enter the large driveway and almost take a tumble as I run down the stairs. My heart pounds in my chest as I watch Nico exit the car, clutching his arm, his clothes all dirty. Then my stomach flips, my hands flying to cover my mouth as I watch Ezra step out of his car, clutching Ryan into his chest. Giselle barges past me, sprinting to Ezra, reaching out for Ryan, she scoops him into her arms and drops to her knees, tears running down her face. I feel hot tears wash over my face as I watch her relief unfold. My arms fly across Ezra's neck as our bodies slam into each other, and I breathe him in, holding him tight.

"You're okay." I breathe through my sobs. "You're okay." I try to convince myself more than anything.

"I'm okay, sweetheart." He kisses me. "I promised you I'd get him back."

Giselle walks into the house, and within minutes she's gathered her things, placing them into her car.

"Wait, please don't leave yet," I plead as I watch Ryan cooing from her arms.

She turns to me, her lips forming a line. "I'm vacating the house as soon as I can." She looks to Ezra. "I want no part in whatever you do. I will not put my family in danger, being associated with you."

"G, please. Don't do this." My voice is desperate as she looks at me, her brows furrowed.

"Don't contact me again, Aries." She walks over to her car, buckling in Ryan.

I plead and plead, but it's no use, she has made up her mind. I watch as they drive out of the driveway, my sister not sparing me another glance as they drive off into the distance. My heart cracks as I realise the two people I love most in life cannot be in my life at the same time. I feel Ezra's arms wrap around me, and my sobs come out muffled as I bury my face in his chest.

"She's my only sister," I whisper through the tears.

He kisses the top of my head, cradling me close into him. "I know, baby." He clasps my face in his hands, his eyes boring into mine. "I'm your family now."

"I'm sorry, Aries." I hear Nico say, still clutching his arm, bringing me back to reality. I love my sister, but I can't force her to be a part of a life I know will always be filled with murder. I help Nico up the stairs as he puts his arm over my shoulder for balance.

"Let's get you inside." I say as I look over my shoulder, waiting for Ezra to follow.

"You two head inside, I need to speak with Henry." Ezra motions for us to go ahead.

I settle Nico on the lounge as he slips his phone out, dialling a number. "Yeah, we need you here at Ezra's place." He hangs up and watches me as I sit across from him, considering all the ways I might be able to win my sister over again. "Do you think she'll come around?" he asks.

I shake my head. "I wouldn't." I look up to him. "If I was her, I wouldn't either."

I grip the tray in my hands as I walk over to the table, setting it down. The smell of freshly cooked bacon lingering in the air. It's been a few days since the incident with Ryan, and everyone has just been trying to recover. The trip to Italy had been cancelled for the foreseeable future as Ezra decides what action would be best to take. Meanwhile, although I'm not forced to, I chose to spend some more time with Darcy. We've been talking every day, and since that first time she had shared something *real* about herself with me, she's been a closed book.

"The chef made you an eggs benny this morning," I state, showing her the plate on the tray. Her eyes glance towards the tray, and I can hear her stomach rumble.

"I'm not really that hungry." She turns her nose up at me.

Sighing, I take a seat beside her. "Is there anything I can get you?"

Her green eyes look to me, as she raises her eyebrows. "Out of here would be nice."

"Come on, you know I can't do that. Is there anything you want? Like a book or something?" I ask again, feeling the guilt creep in. The time I spent stuck in the basement of the Brayford house was not fun, and I just know she's feeling trapped, but as much as I want her to have her freedom, I know the rival families would feast on her the moment she was out of Ezra and Nico's protection.

When she doesn't speak, I let the silence linger. My thoughts escaping to my sister's words.

"You thought that marrying into the city's most notorious mafia family wouldn't come with consequences?"

I feel a stab in the chest again as my heart cracks further the more I think about it.

"Hello?" Darcy waves her hand in my face, snapping me back into the room.

"What?" I run my palms along my jeans.

"I said what has gotten into you?" She looks at me expectantly, and I look away from her, remembering her words at the Brayford house.

"The world you want to be part of is fucked up, morally unjust and unethical in every way."

"My sister." I begin to explain to her, and just as I finish, she lets out a sigh, and I could've sworn I heard her voice in her sigh say '*I told you so*'.

"I'm sorry." Her voice is almost a whisper as she places her hand on mine.

"I don't blame her. It is my fault." I shrug, the sadness overcoming me at a loss so big I never thought I would endure.

"You don't have to stay strong for everyone all the time, Aries." She squeezes my hand. "It's okay to let go." I feel the tears sting my eyes at her words, and I can't control the pace at which they fall.

"Oh god, look at me crying to a woman who's being held captive." I reach for the tissues on the stand near the couch and wipe away my tears.

Darcy chuckles as she watches me. "It's not something that's foreign to me," she admits, causing me to pause. I know she's hiding something very dark beneath her icy exterior, and I think I'm afraid when I find out, I'm going to wish I never knew.

"You know I'm here for you, right? I know the Casella brothers are your enemies, but I can't help but feel we have some sort of a friendship or kinship since the Brayford house," I confess.

She smiles. "I like you, Aries. You seem genuine and caring. But please, don't ever ask me to relive what I have been through." Her eyebrows pull together as she stands, walking over to the window, and I know it hurts her to even think about it.

"I'm sorry. Whatever happened, I'm sorry." I clasp my hands in my lap as I think of what to say. "I just want you to know I never intended your captivity."

She smiles a half smile. "I know. Somehow, I know I can trust you."

"Tell me something about you, Darcy."

"What's there to tell?" she asks, looking out the window into nothing. "To everyone who sees me, I'm the mafia princess, the one who had everything given to her on a silver platter." Her hands brush the skin on her arms, over the ridges of her scars, and it makes me wonder if her family had done that to her. I don't ask because I don't want to pry. As much as I want to know, it's really not my place.

She takes a deep breath before speaking again. "Leo was my uncle." She looks back to me, her eyes brimming with tears, and I think to myself how hard it would have been for her to watch her uncle die.

CHAPTER THIRTY-FOUR

Ezra

The past couple of days have been tough on Aries. She won't admit it to me, but I see it. In everything she does. I hate that I'm the reason for the fallout between her and Giselle, but my need for Aries outweighs everything else in this universe. If it meant that I'd keep her, I wouldn't change a thing.

If that makes me selfish, so be it.

My life without Aries was filled with darkness, not to say it still isn't, but now, it's filled with her. Her laugh, her smile, her pretty little lips. I would do anything she asked in the blink of an eye. If she commanded it, I would watch as the world burnt beneath the throne she sat on with me bent at the knee, awaiting my next order. I've come to realise love is just a word. Sure, it's the reason behind why we do things, but the word holds no meaning without her. My love is different from hers. My love is dark, all-encompassing, and hers is light…authentic, and anyone who tries to disturb that peace will have their own personal Azrael to answer to.

Me.

"What are you going to do with them?" Nico asks from beside me as Henry watches from across the dank room.

My nostrils burn with the smell of the dead in the

corner of the space. "Whatever I want." My lips curl as I watch the horror solidify on the man's face knelt beneath me. I revel in his pain, in his terror. I love watching them take their last breath, and I almost feel the power seep into my bones as they leave the earth.

"P-please, n-no." He sniffs, the snot running down his chin. "D-don't kill me, I swear I can be of use to you. Please!" he begs, but it doesn't bother me. In fact, I enjoy it.

"Say that again for me." My voice gravelly, echoing throughout the emptiness of the shadowy room.

"P-please!" His breathing increases as I pull out my switchblade, unfolding the knife.

"Tell me again how you thought you could use an innocent child in your war games against us." My jaw clenches at the memory. The memory of my brother on the floor and Ryan cradled in my arms.

"It wasn't me! I swear! I didn't know anything! I was just the driver. It was them." He nods over to those who have made their peace with me moments ago before I sent them off to meet their maker.

"Come now, John," Nico says, crossing his arms and leaning on the chair behind him.

"It wasn't." He sobs. "It wasn't."

The tip of my blade makes contact with the soft flesh beneath his ear. "Do you know how many ways there are to kill a man?"

His panicked eyes dart from me to Nico. "W-what?"

"Too many to count, but I think I've probably done most of them." I press the blade into the soft spongy skin and watch as blood trickles down his neck.

He hisses in a breath of air, his muscles tensing.

"I'll let you in on a little secret, John," I whisper,

moving closer to his ear. "I don't plan on letting you live." My knife rips through his ear as I slice it clean off, throwing it across the room. Pained screams echo through the nothingness as blood gushes out of the wound. I hold the back of his neck, focusing my eyes on his as he comes down from the pain. His eyes meet mine, tears flowing freely down his cheeks. "I plan to enjoy every minute with you, until you tell me something of use because here's the thing, John. You may not have been the one giving the orders, but I know you know who does." I grab the top of his head, bringing it down hard on my knee, blood now rushing out of his nose like a faucet. The cartilage of his nose bent, indicating I've definitely broken it. Without giving him a moment to breathe, I swing my knife down into his thigh, spit flying from his mouth as he heaves for air between screams.

"Fuuuuuuck!" he exclaims as he squeezes his eyes shut.

I pry them open with my fingers. "Look at me, John. I want you to take a look at the man who has decided your fate."

He stares at me, eyes wild as adrenaline peaks throughout his body. I'm surprised he hasn't passed out yet.

"Speak up at any time, otherwise I'll just keep going. The more I continue, the fewer organs you'll have," I warn as I grab two pliers from the table behind Nico. "Now open your mouth." He shakes his head, and I sigh. Nico walks around behind him, forcing his mouth open. The pliers grasp his tongue as I raise the other pliers. "Last chance, John." He falls silent, his rattled eyes daring me to do it. I smile, placing the pliers on one of his molars and pulling with force. Blood squirts out of the wound, filling his mouth as Nico holds his head back, making him choke on his own blood. The gurgled sounds of him choking are like music to my ears.

Here's the thing about torture if you do it right. You destroy their identity, their soul. Some say it's worse than the gift of death.

"Ready to talk?" My patience is wearing thin.

Nico drops his head as John spits out the blood that had pooled inside his mouth along with his tooth I left in there.

"You can break me all you want, you'll get nothing out of me." He sneers up at me, and my insides boil with rage. I can almost feel my pupils dilate as I close the distance between us, gripping onto his face.

"You might need your tongue to talk." I slide my thumbs to his eyes, feeling the soft resistance beneath them. "But you sure as fuck don't need your eyes." I press my thumbs into his sockets as his agonised screams vibrate through me. I feel a chuckle leave my lips as it grows into laughter, slick, wet blood coating my hands and arms. His screams fade, replaced by heavy breathing, his head slumped forward. "Deny me again, and I'll make it hurt beyond your ability to comprehend."

His breathing is hoarse as he mumbles.

"I didn't quite catch that." I pick up the knife from the table and walk back over to him, toying with it between my fingers.

"James," he breathes, blood still flowing from his mouth. "James Dixon."

I pat his cheek with my hand. "There, was that so hard? Now explain to me exactly who this James Dixon is."

"The Dixon family is related closely to the Brayford family." He groans. "They've been allies since before your father and his father's generation." Nico looks to me, fire billowing beneath the surface of his eyes. "They had plans that if either of them went down, they would take action against you." I pet the side of his face as he speaks. "I swear that's all I know."

"Well done, John, well done." I nod to Henry who's beside me within a second. "Find out every single thing we can about this James Dixon. I want to know everything about him, who he's paying, who he's fucking, everything." Henry nods his head in understanding and is out the door.

"Please don't kill me," he pleads between sobs. "I don't want to die."

I sigh, standing in front of him. "You know what, John…" I pause, looking him over. "I don't want you to die either."

He jerks his head up in surprise, blood soaking through his clothes.

I lean close to his ear. "I want to own every single fucking scream that is left within your pathetic chest cavity before I pry it open with my bare hands." I grab my switchblade and begin carving into his chest. His sobs echo throughout the emptiness, and when I'm done, I stand back to admire my handiwork.

"Fuck, I almost forgot how sick you are." Nico stands beside me, watching John whimper in the chair.

"Casella" is carved into the skin on his chest, the blood seeping down to his pants.

My phone feels slippery in my hands as I place it on the counter before entering the bathroom, steam already filling the entire space, flowing out of the doorway. I remove every item of clothing now stained with blood, tossing them on the floor. Slipping into the shower, I watch as the water runs down my wife's delicious curves. There's just something about it. The way she stands underneath the water, letting it slide down her bare chest. Her eyes find mine, and instead of finding desire in them, I see sadness. It kills me that I can't be the one to take it away, to wipe it clean. She wraps her arms around me, the blood on my hands smearing across her back as I pull her into me, not a care in the world that I'm covered in someone else's blood. She sighs, melting into my skin, and I take comfort knowing she finds her solace in me.

"Do you think Nico will come around?" she asks, the water now running red.

"He doesn't have a choice." I gently brush the wet hair from her face, tucking it behind her ear as she looks up at me. "He will be married to Darcy."

"Sometimes I feel sorry for them." Her voice breaking, reminding me of how gentle her heart can be. In stark contrast to mine.

"It's the way of our world, sweetheart."

Her hands rest on my chest as I lower my lips to hers. Breaking the kiss, her eyes still closed, she whispers, "Make love to me, Ezra. Show me that I don't need anyone else in this life, besides you."

Before now, I don't think I ever knew what that meant. To make love to someone, and now, all I want to do is show her that I am her world, and she is mine. Nothing could take me away from her, and if they tried, I'd burn them alive with the inferno that runs hot inside me, for her.

Grabbing her behind her thighs, I lift her up, her legs immediately finding their way around my waist. Her back against the wall, I slide into her, deep, filling her with my cock as she gasps. Her breasts press into my chest, as I bury my head into her neck, kissing her delicate skin. It's not enough. I want to be closer to her, I want to fuse into her and be one. I thrust into her, the delicious sound of her breathy moans filling my ears as she tightens her hold around my neck.

"Fuck, sweetheart, you feel so good." I groan as I feel her pussy drip with arousal around me. I feel her teeth clamp the skin on my shoulder as she bucks her hips into mine, her moans growing louder the harder I thrust.

Her eyes find me, as she rests her forehead on mine. "I don't want a world without you in it," she whispers, and my cock grows harder inside her.

"You *are* my world." I thrust into her as I hold her up behind her knees, pushing her farther into the wall. I watch my cock enter her pink cunt, moving in and out slowly, her arousal coating every fucking inch of me. My hands are still red, the blood staining my skin.

"You could be on the other side of the world, and I'd fucking find you." I slam into her. "Do you understand me?"

She nods, her eyes trailing my chest.

"I would kill everyone on this forsaken planet if it meant it would be me and you forever." I bite her bottom lip as her moans vibrate through me. I build a rhythm with my cock and pound into her as I grunt, the warmth of her pussy sending my mind reeling into a whole new dimension—somewhere I thought I would never get a chance to experience.

I know I am condemned as a heartless monster, a killer, but if that means that she is condemned with me, I would die as the happiest man alive, knowing that even in another realm, I get to have her.

"Oh, Ezra, just like that," she pants through her moans as her tits bounce before me at the force of my thrusts.

"I vow to make you feel like this every fucking day of our blood-filled lives." I groan as she lets go, her eyes rolling back into her head as her pussy clamps down on me. "I vow to swallow you up in my darkness, where you will be free to be yourself." I thrust once more, and my own release follows hers as I come undone inside her.

CHAPTER THIRTY-FIVE
Aries

"You're fucking kidding, right?" Nico exclaims as he paces the room. "Tomorrow?" He scoffs, not believing a word that Ezra is saying.

"It must be done. Before anyone else can try anything, we need to look united." Ezra explains as I sit here across the room, watching them. It's become a regular thing now, for me to sit in on business meetings and most anything to do with the Casella family.

"One day." He breathes out the words like he's trying to convince himself. "You're giving me one fucking day to say goodbye to my single life."

"It has to be this way, Nico. Mama will arrange the wedding with Aries." Ezra leaves the room, done with the conversation as Nico takes a seat next to me, his head falling into his hands. I place a hand on his shoulder, wanting to comfort him but not knowing what to say at the same time.

"Maybe this could be good for you." I wince as soon as I say the words.

His chocolate eyes glance up at me, his hand dropping into his lap. "I am not husband material, Aries. I won't be good for anyone." I can almost feel the disdain for himself in his words as he speaks them, and my heart breaks for him. Ezra hasn't told me why Nico is the way he is, but just by looking at him, you can tell he's troubled. He has this aura that he carries into the room, and everything feels muted.

"You might surprise yourself. Don't be so harsh when you haven't tried." I squeeze his shoulder, hoping to offer comfort. "And I never apologised for what I did when I went to the Brayford house, so I'm sorry. I didn't mean to put you in the middle."

He shrugs. "Doesn't matter, it's done and now, you're here." He gives me half a smile. "But don't you ever try that shit again. I swear to God I cannot deal with Ezra like that again." He chuckles, and a more sincere smile covers his face. A comfortable silence falls between us as we sit together, neither of us wanting to be alone.

"Have you spoken to Darcy much?" he asks, breaking the silence, now sitting comfortably beside me.

"I have. She's quite an interesting person, although a closed book," I admit. "I think she may have had something happen to her in her past, which she won't talk about."

His eyebrows pull in at my words, considering them. "Do you trust her?"

"Honestly? I don't know, but I feel like I want to," I confess. "I'm sorry it has to be this way."

"I wasn't meant to be happy, Aries." He looks to me, and the pain in his eyes breaks my heart. "Dominic made sure of that."

I purse my lips, unsure of how to respond.

"Ezra got lucky with you," he continues. "He would have never been happy with some mafia princess."

I admire the intricate stained glass of the church as I watch the preparations for the ceremony take place. Although I asked Darcy what she would have wanted, had this been her dream wedding, she didn't give me much of an answer. So, I took it upon myself to make it spectacular, nonetheless. The pews are adorned with garlands of flowers, reaching the front of the church. Different height glass vases with fairy lights filled with peonies sit just before the steps, accentuating the beauty of the marble floors.

"You're actually quite good at this," my mother-in-law says from beside me, watching the altar being decorated with fresh flowers. I can't help but feel a small sense of pride at the compliment I have just received from her.

"Thank you." I smile.

"I never meant for any of this to happen," she sighs. "I thought my boys would have a secure life with who I had chosen for them. Someone who fit the description of what a Casella wife should be." I feel a twinge in my chest. "But I think you're better than any of those women I had on my list," she admits as she places her hand on mine. I feel my chest swell with appreciation at her words. I never thought I would have her approval, but hearing it from her now, I realise how much I wanted it. "My only hope is that I didn't make the wrong choice by suggesting Nico marry Darcy."

Darcy stands in front of me in her white dress, the small train

.   .   .

behind her. The lace clings onto her curvy figure, her auburn hair accentuated as it falls in loose curls down her back. She is absolutely breathtaking. Her porcelain skin is covered in the long lace sleeves of the dress, the front dropping down to her cleavage.

"Are you okay?" is all I can manage to ask her, with everything that's going on outside, the hustle of preparations taking place.

She turns to me, her moss-green eyes finding mine. "Are you really asking me that right now?"

"Look, I know you don't want this, and to be honest with you, neither does Nico, but you need to find a way past it because it's happening whether you like it or not." I give her the truth, and I don't care if it hurts because she needs to realise the gravity of the situation. "If you don't do this, you could be on the receiving end of some terrible acts by people who want to hurt you as well as us."

"What? So, you're doing me a favour?" She cocks one eyebrow.

"You know what? I've tried to be kind to you, I've tried to be your friend, but every time I think we make headway, you turn around and do this." I motion at the air. "I wanted to be here for you today because I know you don't want to go through with this, but if you are just going to be ungrateful, I'm going to leave."

I stand, ready to take my leave, waiting to see if she will stop me, and she doesn't. I walk out of the small room inside the church and close the door behind me. The church is almost full of all the invited guests as they mingle with each other before finding their seats. I feel a strong arm slide around my waist, Ezra's perfume engulfing my surroundings.

"I think there's something you need to see," he

whispers into my ear, guiding us out the back of the church.

The clouds grow closer as the sky darkens, the shadows falling over Ezra's beautifully carved face. He presses me into the thick bricked wall of the church as his finger grazes the exposed skin on my chest above the dress. I drink him in, dressed in his black tux, his dark hair slicked back, the harshness of his jaw accentuating his masculinity. I love everything about this man. From the danger he oozes to the raw, blackened soul beneath his hard exterior.

His hands gather my dress up as he slowly slips them beneath, placing his palms directly onto my skin. Heat courses through me as they slide up my thighs and come around behind me, squeezing my ass.

"Ezra," I breathe into him, his face just inches from mine, hunger growing in his darkening gaze. "People might see."

He takes my bottom lip between his teeth as he bites down, sucking it straight after. "Let them." He lifts one leg above his shoulder as he slides my G-string to the side. Unzipping his pants, I feel the tip of his cock at my opening. "Let them see how you scream for me." In one swift motion, he thrusts inside me, grunting as he enters me to the hilt. "Let them see that you are mine, and I am yours." He fucks me against the church hard as my moans fill the air around us. "I want you dripping with my cum for the rest of the night."

"Give it to me," I whisper as my hands wrap around the back of his neck, pulling his forehead to mine. "Smother me with your darkness."

EPILOGUE
Ezra

"Are you ready?" I ask as I stand here watching my wife bent over a bench, bound in the rope I knotted. Such a beautiful fucking sight, seeing her at my mercy, all her holes available for me to use for my pleasure.

She nods as a stray tear flows down her cheek, saliva drooling from the ball gag in her mouth. I know she wants it removed, and I know she hates it, but she's being punished.

"Do you know why you're bound and ready to be used like my personal slut?" I ask, whipping her face with a leather band. My belt is secured tightly around her neck, and it's my favourite thing to do to her. Collar her because she belongs to me.

She nods, softly whimpering and rocking her hips.

"I told you that only *I* can make you come." I grip her cheeks in my hand, forcing her face up to look at me. "And what did you do? You couldn't wait for me to get home, so you touched yourself." I slap her cheek lightly with my other hand. "Do you know how fucking crazy it makes me, watching you pleasure yourself?" I grip her hair at the top of her head and pull the ball gag and she sucks in air through her mouth.

"Now I'm going to take my time with you, fucking you in every single hole I want."

She whimpers.

"And if you come, I will make it hurt, sweetheart." I smile, watching the excitement grow in her eyes at the promise of pain with pleasure. "And I won't stop until I pull every single tear you have to give me."

I force my cock into her mouth, tugging her head with the grip I have on her hair. "Suck," I order, and she obeys.

I thrust into her throat, her tongue sliding out to accommodate me, and I can't help but smile at how much she's learnt.

"Good girl, just like that." I pull her head down onto me, shoving my cock deeper into her throat until she gags. I pull out, and she gasps for air. I bend down to her eye level, watching as the mascara runs freely down her face along with her tears.

"Ezra, please," she begs, and my cock twitches at the sound of her pleas.

I smear the mascara, tears, and saliva over her face, painting my own Mona Lisa. "I fucking love it when you beg."

I shift behind her, both her legs bound to either leg of the bench, her arms bound behind her back, and her chest bound to the table. The butt plug I had inserted earlier shines as she rocks her hips, her body begging for something more.

"I love watching you like this." I press the tip of my cock to her warm pussy and she whimpers. "So fucking needy for my cock." I chuckle.

My hand lands down on her creamy skin, and her body jerks at the sting. I rub the tip of my cock on her pussy, feeling how aroused I make her, and I groan as her arousal coats me. Sliding into her slowly, I feel her stretching to accommodate me and it feels so fucking good to be inside her. I grip her hips on either side and thrust myself into her.

Leaning forward, I grab the end of my belt, pulling it, and her head jerks back as the belt tightens around her neck. I ram into her harder, pounding as the skin on her ass ripples in response to my thrusts.

"Tell me, Aries." I tug at the belt again. "Do you enjoy being broken by me?" I ask.

Her breathy moans return as I release the belt slightly, allowing her some air.

"Y-yes," she breathes. "I crave it."

I lower myself over her, my lips almost touching her ear. "I crave you like an addict craves recovery, like the darkness seeks the light...like a secret craves release." I press into her to the hilt. "I need you like the moon needs the sun."

My knees hit the floor of the plane as I look up at my gorgeous wife. We've only been in the air for ten minutes, and I just know this is going to be one of my favourite moments with her.

"Are you sure?" I ask as she looks down at me, her smile wide and bright.

She nods, tears beginning to pool in her eyes. "I'm positive." She laughs as I grip her thighs, resting my head in her lap, my heart thumping like I've just jumped out of a plane without a parachute.

It's real, and it's happening.

Sometime within the next nine months, I will be a

father. Something I never thought I'd be this ecstatic about. I always knew it would happen, didn't matter who I was married to, but I'm so fucking lucky it's with Aries.

"I've taken like twenty of them." She begins to pull the pregnancy tests out of her bag. All double lines. "You know, just to be sure." She grins from ear to ear.

No one, and nothing, could wipe the smile from my face if they tried. I promise myself one thing in this moment, and that is to do better.

Better than the generations before me.

She places her hands on my face as my mind reels with thoughts of what the future will hold. Anxiety takes its place in the centre of my stomach as I come to the realisation of what this means.

Targets.

My family will be targets.

Although it comes with the territory in this world we are in, it makes my skin crawl thinking about anyone wanting to harm my family, and the protective husband and father inside me wants to wrap them up in a shield to stop any harm coming to them.

She places her lips softly on mine as I come up to meet her, and now the only thing I can think about is to eliminate the remaining threats to our family in this world.

Starting with my half brother and ending with the Dixons.

ARIES

I take a deep breath and knock on the door to Giselle's house. I convinced her to keep the house Ezra had purchased for her, and I'm glad she listened to me, given the rockiness between us. I know I can never expect her to forgive me, especially since I'm still with Ezra, but I don't want that to stop me from trying to mend things between us. She's my only sibling, and I refuse to let her go.

The door opens, and she takes a step back, inviting me in. I can almost feel the ice coming off her, and I wonder if I did the right thing by coming here.

We sit at the dining table, Ryan in his highchair, babbling away as he nibbles on his lunch.

"Why are you here, Aries?" Her tone is sharp, and I get it, she doesn't want me here.

I shift in my seat, unsure of how to tell her. "I want to try and mend things between us."

"I don't think so." She takes a sip of her tea, offering Ryan some water with her other hand.

I take a deep breath, and it comes out like word vomit. "I'm pregnant."

Her eyes widen as she looks to me, then down at the table. Neither of us speak for a short time, and it's the most awkward it's ever been between us. I could always tell Giselle anything and know she wouldn't judge me for it, but things have changed. I desperately want it to be what it was before, but I know it won't ever go back to that. The most I can hope for is for her to just simply talk to me.

"I don't know what to say." She grits her teeth as she clasps her cup with both hands.

"Say you'll at least talk to me," I plead with her, and she considers my words. "I can't do this without you by my side, G."

Her brows pull in, and I see her icy exterior crack a little.

"I'm happy for you, Aries, but…" She sighs. "I just need more time."

I frown, understanding what she means is that she's not

ready to move past it, and although I don't blame her for it, I wish I could do something about it.

I watch Ryan smile and coo at Giselle, and I can't help the smile that spreads across my face. I can't wait to have this, such a treasured and beautiful thing it is to be blessed with a life growing inside you, but it *kills* me that I won't have my sister's support.

I didn't expect for things to turn out the way they did, but I also don't regret them. I think everyone deserves a second chance, and I will show Giselle how much we need each other. Even if she doesn't see it now, I know she will in the future.

Thank You!

Thank you so much for reading!

The second book in this series is currently underway. Nico and Darcy's story will be an enemies-to-lovers with arranged marriage trope.

There will be tonnes of wild behaviour from both main characters as they try to tolerate one another. The second book in the series will be a slow burn, focusing on Nico and Darcy's character arcs. Although it is the second book in the series, it will be an interconnected stand-alone in the Casella brothers series.

If you love the enemies-to-lovers trope, hold on to your hats, folks. It's going to be a bumpy ride.

Are you ready for Darcy and Nicholas' story?
Their book **'The Casella Ruin'** will be releasing
July 2024!

DARCY

I've spent my life bound to a life I've hated for as long as I can remember...deep in the ugliness of the underworld, serving one of London's most ruthless mobsters. I wish I could say my life is filled with riches, from blood money, but it isn't, and it only gets worse when the Casella brothers find me and tether my life to his.
Nicholas Casella, the arrogant, self-righteous playboy.
Now I must fight with all I have for any chance at freedom before it's too late.
Before he kills me.

NICHOLAS

Secrets.
We live with so many damn secrets.
I wish I were one of them. I wish I could crawl into the abyss and never emerge again. The promise of a future with someone I don't love, let alone an enemy, is enough to claw me back into insatiable habits and into the resounding pain I've tried so hard to muffle over the many years.
I despise everything about her and as long as her life is tied to mine, I will make her suffer for the things her family has done. I won't stop, until she's begging on her knees for my mercy. Even then, I don't plan to give it to her.

About The Author

Welcome to my corner of heaven, where the villains and heroes drop to their knees before strong women. My books will have you clenching your thighs and reaching for the bedside table for your best friend.

If I'm not writing, you can find me chasing my favourite bands in concert, or curled up with a glass of red, reading a filthy book.

To be the first to find out about upcoming titles, you can sign up for my newsletter at
https://www.cbfreyauthor.com/subscribe

Thank you for supporting independently published authors.

Join C.B. Frey's Morally Grey's reader group:
https://www.facebook.com/groups/1501524207371036/

Find C.B. Frey on social media:

Facebook: https://www.facebook.com/profile.php?id=100094454168503

Instagram: https://www.instagram.com/c.b.freyauthor/

TikTok: https://www.tiktok.com/@c.b.freyauthor

Acknowledgments

To those who listened to me talk about becoming an author exhaustively for so long before it became a reality.

My husband, who puts up with my reading and writing habits on a daily basis. The nights I spent in the front room, away from him and our two dogs whilst our baby slept, and I wrote. I appreciate you beyond words for encouraging me to always live my dreams, to follow my passions, no matter what they may be at the time. Words cannot explain how much I love you for that.

My best friend who recently came back into my life. I adore your friendship so much, no one will understand the cosmic connection between us, which we have shared most of our lives. I'm so glad we reconnected and resolved our issues. Like we used to talk about in high school, even in death you'll haunt me, and I wouldn't have it any other way.

To my friend, I'm so thankful to have you on my team, always cheering me on, happy to lend a helping hand whenever I need it, and always listening to me talk about my smutty books. Your support doesn't go unnoticed.

To my cover designer Lee, from Coffin Print Designs, thank you for spending so much time on this cover and making it look like everything I wanted. I appreciate the work you do and the time you take to make everything look professional.

To my editor, I truly appreciate your work on this piece, and thank you for not judging the dark content in this book. My imagination can run wild, and when I let it, I let it take me places I usually wouldn't allow myself to go.

I am beyond grateful to have such a supportive team around me, always cheering me on to follow my dreams and desires no matter what they may be. I feel so very grateful to have had the opportunity to tell this story and look forward to where my author dreams will take me in the future.